Copyright © 2024 by Abby Millsaps

All rights reserved.

paperback ISBN: 9798990077058

No portion of this book may be reproduced, distributed, or transmitted in any form without written permission from the author, except by a reviewer who may quote brief passages in a book review.

This book is a work of fiction. Any resemblance to any person, living or dead, or any events or occurrences, is purely coincidental. The characters and story lines are created by the author's imagination and are used fictitiously.

Line Editing, Copyediting, and Proofreading by VB Edits
Cover Design © Silver at Bitter Sage Designs

Contents

Blurb	VI
Sincerest Gratitude	VIII
Dedication	IX
Content Warning	1
1. Levi	2
2. Greedy	7
3. Kabir	10
4. Levi	14
5. Hunter	20
6. Hunter	23
7. Kabir	31
8. Kabir	34
9. Greedy	37
10. Greedy	40
11. Greedy	43
12. Levi	49

13.	Levi	64
14.	Hunter	70
15.	Kabir	73
16.	Kabir	79
17.	Levi	84
18.	Kabir	88
19.	Hunter	92
20.	Hunter	101
21.	Kabir	107
22.	Greedy	111
23.	Greedy	116
24.	Hunter	121
25.	Hunter	124
26.	Hunter	131
27.	Levi	135
28.	Kabir	139
29.	Hunter	143
30.	Sione	147
31.	Hunter	154
32.	Kabir	162
33.	Hunter	171
34.	Hunter	175
35.	Sione	182

36.	Hunter	187
37.	Sione	194
38.	Hunter	201
39.	Hunter	207
40.	Greedy	218
41.	Levi	223
42.	Hunter	226
43.	Greedy	229
Afterword		235
Also By Abby Millsaps		236
About The Author		239

Blurb

No more running.

It's the promise I've made to myself. It's also the vow I've given to each of the four men who came together in my darkest time of need. Even when I was taken against my will and trapped in the confines of my own mind, unable to access my memories, they never gave up on me.

It's clear by the way they look at me—and in some cases, the way they look at each other—that what we have is rare. Ours is a love worth fighting for. A love worth staying for. And that's exactly what I intend to do.

I choose them:

Greedy—my first love and deepest heartbreak.
Levi—my not-so-fake boyfriend and personal ray of sunshine.
Spence—my dominating, steadfast sanctuary.
And Sione—my soul match, and my saving grace.

I choose them. All of them. In every way they're willing to have me.

It's a dream come true, the five of us together, gathered under one roof. But dreams don't always keep.

Because there's nothing my narcissistic mother won't do to get her way. Thankfully, Spence has a plan, and for the first time, every member of our group is on board.

Magnolia St. Clair is a worthy opponent, but she's no match for the British billionaire who will stop at nothing to protect what's his.

No more running.

It's time to stay and fight, and to reclaim the happily ever after we all deserve.

Sincerest Gratitude

Thank you to the following individuals who swooped in at the 11th hour to beta read and sensitivity reading for So Rare:
Adah Kruszlinski
Jen Adams
Linds Sunshine
Mica Garcia
Megan Smith

Dedication

To Beth—

For being the very best friend, the most spectacular editor, and the ultimate sounding board. Also for telling people "I'm not even writing" and asking the hard questions, like "Where's Greedy?"

Content Warning

Potential triggers for So Rare include BDSM dynamics, heavy degradation, and intense sub-drop after a scene.

Additional triggers include forced relocation, forced consumption, on page emotional abuse and manipulation of an adult child by a parent, mention of past suicidal ideation, and blood.

Chapter 1

Levi

NOW

"She's running."

Greedy chokes on the words like it's painful to speak them.

With his hands balled into fists, he presses them into the sides of his skull. "She's fucking running." The words are more despondent this time.

Kabir scowls down at his phone, still focused on the radar he claims shows him where Hunter is. If he's right, then she's just a dot—a little pink dot, traveling across a screen.

"She's moving far too quickly to be *running*, Garrett."

My best friend bristles at the scolding, at the flippant, cool nature of Kabir's delivery. Why the hell is the Brit so calm about all this?

"You know what I fucking mean." Greedy turns on his heel, and I hold my breath, bracing for impact. Preparing for him to leave, just like he's accusing Hunter of doing.

But he doesn't exit the room.

Late morning sunshine streams in through the windows, causing channels of light to illuminate every blemish and cranny in the wood floors. Tiny specks of dust dance in the glow.

Greedy marches across the room, sending the particles spiraling. "This is what she does." His tone is sharp, accusatory as he pivots and retraces his steps. "This is what she *always* fucking does."

Doubt tugs at my gut. Is he right? Did Hunter run? Honestly, I'm having trouble wrapping my brain around what the hell is going on, but my instincts are telling me he's wrong.

Would she really take off without saying a word to any of us?

Would she really leave without telling me?

I thought I knew her better than that. Thought that the connection that's developed over the last few days meant something to her. But she isn't here—that we know for sure. According to Kabir, she's hundreds of miles away. But how? And why?

Why would she leave us?

Why would she leave *me*?

Pain lances through my chest at the thought. What if Greedy's right?

My chest tightens, making it impossible to do anything more than take shallow breaths. The idea that Hunter would leave—could leave—after all we've been through?

No. She said she would come with me to meet with my mom this weekend.

She fucking promised.

"What's the math here?" Kabir mutters to himself. "I don't recall the exact conversions. Levi. Bring me your phone."

Without a second thought, I follow his command, unlocking my phone and handing it over. He pulls up the calculator app, opens it, and starts inputting numbers at a rapid pace.

"She's traveled more than six hundred kilometers so far."

"The speed limit is seventy miles per hour on that highway, at least through North Carolina," I offer.

Kabir gapes, first at me, then at the calculations. Holding the phone out to me, then to Greedy, he shakes his head in disbelief.

"That would mean she's been gone for more than five hours. You had to have just put her back in bed," he says to Greedy in an even tone, merely stating a fact.

G doesn't take it that way.

His chest heaves as he glares at Kabir. "I don't even know what fucking time that was." With another spin, he goes back to pacing, his frustration rolling off him in waves.

"What do you mean, you put her back to bed?" There's a disconnect here. I'm out of the loop. I slept like the dead after the fourway Spence coordinated last night. I didn't even notice when any of them got out of bed. And from the sound of it, I'm the only one who was actually asleep.

I survey Greedy, then Kabir, silently pleading for one of them to fill in some of these goddamn blanks.

With a sigh, Kabir puts me out of my misery. "Hunter woke during the night. I was in the living area working. We talked, the two of us. She informed me she started her period and was in a bit of pain. Eventually, she fell asleep on the couch. Garrett came down a while later—"

"Wait." Greedy comes to an abrupt stop in the middle of the room.

Kabir snaps his mouth closed, his brow furrowed at the interruption.

"We can determine when I took her back upstairs if I look at my call log," Greedy rushes to explain. "I woke up because my phone was buzzing. It was my dad. I came downstairs to talk to him."

Greedy pops his phone out of his pocket and scrolls. "3:43 a.m."

My gut sinks. What the hell? Why would Dr. Ferguson be calling at that hour?

"You talked to your dad in the middle of the night?" I scratch the back of my neck, clearly missing a lot of details here. None of this makes sense.

Nodding, Greedy studies his phone screen, as if searching it for more answers.

"He called to tell me Magnolia was freaking out. She was worried about Hunter. Said she couldn't get through to her."

"You took Hunter upstairs shortly after that call," Kabir offers. "Probably around four, then?"

Greedy nods, his lips pressed together, his eyes still on his device.

"It's nearly eleven now"—he holds out his arm, glancing at the faceplate of the massive gold watch encircling his wrist—"and we assume she's been traveling for over five hours. That means she left less than an hour after you took her back upstairs."

Greedy lets out a frustrated growl. "That doesn't make sense. She was out cold when I tucked her in." A myriad of doubt, anger, and shame cross his expression in the two seconds it takes him to blink. Then his face goes hard. "Unless she was faking it."

I don't let that idea take root.

I can't. There has to be a logical explanation. Turning to Kabir, I start with the simplest question. "Where were you once they went back upstairs?"

"I had an interview this morning, which I took out on the balcony so as not to disturb anyone."

"Who schedules an interview at four a.m.?" Greedy bites out.

I wondered the same thing—but in that tone, it's clear G is just jonesing for a fight.

"It's not four a.m. everywhere in the world at the same time, Garrett."

Rather than retort, Greedy turns on his heel and paces away from us once more.

"Wait," I reason. "G, is your car still here?"

Fury rises up and emanates off Greedy as he pulls open the door to the Juliet balcony and sticks his head outside. "My Denali's in the driveway. She must have called a rideshare or a taxi."

Sighing, I will myself not to feed into his anxious fervor. Every time we rule out one possibility, he just jumps to the next ludicrous conclusion that enters his mind. I haven't come up with a single logical explanation to counter his theory that she willingly left, but I'm still trying to stay calm and levelheaded.

For his sake and Hunter's.

"You're wrong." Kabir is back to looking at the phone as if it possesses all the answers. "There are no ride share apps on this device, nor has any Wi-Fi or data been used in the last several hours. She didn't call a car." Then, more to himself than us, he mutters, "I just don't understand why she wouldn't take her phone."

"Hold up," I say. "If she doesn't have her phone, how are you tracking her?"

A flash of panic appears on Kabir's face, followed by a hint of shame. But he schools his expression quickly and maintains eye contact. "I implanted a small tracking device under her skin while she was with me in London."

Stomach dropping, I blink at Greedy. The horror and confusion I feel mar his expression, too.

"The actual fuck?" Greedy grits out. "You put a tracking device on her? Like, inside her body?"

Kabir hits Greedy with an unamused glare. "I did. And I'd do it again in a heartbeat. When you wake up in the middle of the night to an empty bed and find the love of your life sitting in a dark office, muttering about the ideal angle with which to pull a bookshelf onto herself, you go to any means necessary to ensure you always know her whereabouts."

I gulp past the dread churning in my gut.

Hunter said things were bad when she was in London—that she was really low and that she struggled with her mental health. But hearing the specifics of what she faced... fucking hell.

Greedy's face twists, this time in pain rather than anger.

"Do you think she tried to hurt herself again?" he asks, desperately looking to me, then over to Kabir.

Spence shakes his head, chin held high. "She's been doing so well. Even this morning..." He trails off, looking from his phone to Hunter's.

"Hmm." The hum is soft, almost inaudible. "Could she have taken her other phone?"

I regard Greedy again and find him looking just as dumbfounded as I feel.

What other phone?

Chapter 2

Greedy

NOW

"What is this?" I shift the older model phone from hand to hand, only allowing my fingertips to touch the cool metal. Though I recognize it, it's hard not to handle it like it's a grenade at risk of detonating.

Levi nudges me and scoffs. "Dude, that's Hunter's phone from high school."

The logical part of my brain knows that.

But why is it here, in her bedside table at the cabin?

Spence glares at the pink device as if it's to blame for the lack of answers we so desperately need.

"She didn't take her phone. Nor did she take that." He points to the relic in my hand as if it's personally offending him. "Which she carries with her like a security blanket."

Shuffling slowly, he rounds the bed. Then he picks up two prescription bottles, rattling them, followed by a flat pill pack.

"Nor did she take any of her medication."

The meds and the phone were stashed in the nightstand by the bed in a little travel case. They would have been easy enough to grab, even if she was making a quick getaway.

It's just as hard to believe that she'd leave without her phone.

Spence stalks toward the bathroom, and as he crosses the threshold, he lets out an agitated growl. "She didn't even take her toothbrush."

My own insecurities poke at me, telling me that she left. That she's running away, like she always does. That just as we finally made a little fucking progress, she took off. Again.

But the clues Spence is revealing don't align with that theory.

"Hey." Levi touches my forearm, pulling me from my reverie. "I don't know where she went, G, but I don't think she's running."

The reassurance is one I desperately need, yet I'm terrified to hope for it.

I hold up the pink phone. "Did you know about this?"

Levi shakes his head as Kabir comes back into the bedroom.

I whirl around to the other man with the device still held aloft. "How did you know she had another phone?"

I'm being an asshole, and he doesn't deserve my ire, but *fuck*. I don't know what to make of any of this, and it pisses me off that time and time again, his knowledge of Hunter and the intimacy they share seems to surpass mine.

Instead of taking the bait and snapping back at me, Spence circles my wrist, keeping his grasp light, and takes the phone from my hand.

His touch lingers, the warmth of his hand soothing me. The contact calms me, encourages me to take in a deep breath. I focus on the shine of his gold signet ring for a moment, centering myself, before I meet his eye.

"She's kept this with her for years," he tells me softly, his expression one of sincerity. "I don't think it even has service anymore."

For a moment, he assesses me silently, as if considering his next words carefully, his piercing blue gaze keeping me in place.

"She saved it because of you. She saved your voicemails and messages. She carried it with her, always, but only allowed herself to power on the device and listen to the messages when she was at her lowest."

My heart bottoms out and sinks to the deepest depths of my gut.

Hunter saved my messages.

She kept this phone for years, holding tight to the connection we'd created.

Shivers of shame runs through me as I think about just how many desperate, pleading voicemails I left for her after she disappeared without a word. Some of them were longer, some were short, some were sweet. In one, I read each note I'd written on the paper airplanes I'd thrown at her window in a juvenile attempt to convince her to stay.

We could have figured it out, the two of us.

I convinced myself of that years ago, and up until very recently, it's what I sincerely believed. Knowing what I know now, though, causes doubt to trickle in, loosening my grip on the bullheaded ideas I so adamantly clung to for so long.

Hunter was going through so much more than I ever realized.

She was grieving, physically hurting, pushing down so much, doing what she could to protect herself and me from her mom.

I used to think that the best thing she could have done was stay.

Now that I know the details of what she's gone through, I'm not so sure I could have been what she needed back then. It wouldn't have been fair to keep her here to face Magnolia, risk her wrath.

"Fuck." The answer that's been dangling right in front of us all along finally slots into place. "Hunter's gone, and we don't think she intended to leave, right?"

Kabir lets out a huff, probably because that's what he's been saying this whole time, but I'm only now getting it.

Levi, ever the steady one, only nods.

"She's not running. I bet she didn't even leave of her own free will. Magnolia has to have something to do with this."

Chapter 3

Kabir

NOW

Try as I might, I cannot control the incessant tapping of my heel as Levi and I sit on the couch and Garrett paces in front of the coffee table.

Back and forth.

Back and forth.

My impulse is to scold him—to tell him to sit—but bloody hell, in this moment, I wish I could be pacing right alongside him.

As soon as he dialed, he tapped the Speaker button. We're all watching his device where it rests in the center of the coffee table, willing his father to pick up the goddamn phone.

By the fourth ring, I'm certain his voicemail will pick up.

But then there's a click, followed by a distracted "hello?"

"Dad." That single word is uttered with a mix of fear and relief and hope.

"Hey Garrett. Is everything okay?"

Dr. Gary Ferguson's words are calm, albeit a bit clipped. Those two simple sentences are all I need to hear to deduce that he will not have any solid information for us.

Nevertheless, Garrett looks to me as if he needs me to spoon-feed him the answer to his father's question.

I give him a pointed look, urging him to go on. Instead, a muscle in his jaw ticks.

He's torn, struggling with whether to explain our predicament.

Though the affinity he has for his father is clearly on par with that he maintains for Hunter, this is not the moment to pull punches. We must have answers, and time is of the essence.

"You there, son?" Dr. Ferguson asks. From the sound of the muffled voices in the background and the shuffling of papers, the man is busy and clearly only half paying attention to this call.

Finally, Garrett finds his voice. "Yeah, yeah. I'm here. You know how you wanted me to have Hunter call as soon as she was up?"

Dr. Ferguson chuckles through the line.

"Ah, right. I'm sorry about that, son. I may have overreacted a bit. I meant to text you this morning, but after Magnolia took off, I came up to the hospital to play catch-up."

The new information barely has time to take root in my mind before Garrett pounces.

"What do you mean Magnolia *took off*?"

"Hmm?" There's a pause on the good doctor's end, followed by more muffled chatter.

The lack of regard for his son makes my temper flare. Before I can butt in on the conversation, though, he's back.

"Sorry about that," he mumbles, obviously still distracted. "I don't know all the details, but Magnolia left a note. Said she and Hunter are heading to a spa together for girls' weekend." With a sigh, he goes on. "I'm sorry if I worried you. Turns out, Magnolia wanted to surprise Hunter and was stressed when she couldn't get ahold of her and didn't want to spoil the plans."

Surprise Hunter? My stomach plummets. *Bloody hell.*

Levi hisses beside me on the couch.

Garrett locks eyes with me, and without a single word passing between us, I'm certain we are on the same page.

Hunter would not willingly go anywhere with her mother. Especially not without telling us.

The tension in the room thickens until it's hard to breathe as a dozen new questions come to mind. I'm so lost in sorting through them that when a hand comes to rest on my knee, I startle. Levi's grip is tight but welcome in a reassuring kind of way. When I focus on his face though, he looks just as lost as I feel.

We've reached a dead end, it seems.

We have an answer, and yet, we don't actually know anything.

As I turn from him to Garrett, I'm hit with the realization that Dr. Ferguson could provide a crucial piece of information.

Quickly catching Garrett's gaze, I mouth "Where?"

With his lips pressed together, he dips his chin. "Do you know where they went?" he asks his father. "The name of the spa, or where it's located?"

"Oh... hmm."

I clench both fists to temper the urge to shout at the man. Doesn't he understand the urgency here? Can he truly not comprehend how toxic his wife is?

"I don't recall the name of it," he finally says. "I think it was some place in upstate New York? Magnolia may have included the information in her note. Honestly, I read it quickly and moved on. I was just relieved to know my worries were for nothing."

Levi huffs beside me.

"I do remember the note mentioning that they would have to surrender their phones for the treatment. It's some kind of holistic disconnect package, I believe."

Garrett grits his teeth with so much force I can hear it across the distance that separates us.

"Dad," he practically pleads. "When you get home, please take a picture of the note and send it to me. I need to talk to Hunter as soon as possible."

That finally gets Dr. Ferguson's attention. "Why are you so concerned about your sister?"

"She's *not* my sister," he snaps. Then, after an audible inhale that I assume is meant to calm his own frazzled nerves, he adds, "I'm just—I'm worried. Hunter... well..."

As Garrett continues to struggle, Levi suddenly jumps off the couch. He tips his head back and pinches his fingers together above it, as if he's dropping an object into his mouth, then holds his other hand up, pantomiming the action of drinking from a cup or bottle.

I have no idea how to interpret this charade. I'm still running through each movement, parsing out details, when Garrett snaps his fingers.

"Her meds!" he yells. "Hunter left her meds here."

"Oh my."

Finally.

For the first time since this call began, we seem to have the good doctor's undivided attention.

"I could overnight them to her," Garrett offers quickly. He continues to pace, scratching at the back of his skull, anxiety emanating from him, but he keeps his tone even. "If you can go home and get me the mailing information, even just the name of the spa, I can drop them off at FedEx."

"Yes, that works. Good thinking, son." His praise is followed by muffled speaking again. It seems impossible to hold the man's attention for more than a few seconds at a time.

"Dad," Garrett bites out. So much for keeping his cool. "Hunter needs her meds. As soon as you get home, send me the info."

"Yes, of course. Thank you for helping her, Garrett. Just put the overnight charges on my credit card."

Garrett agrees, and not a heartbeat later, Dr. Ferguson ends the call.

We all stare at the phone in a charged moment of silence. Levi has his elbows pressed into his legs, fingers steepled and forehead hidden from view. Garrett's hands are on his hips, his molars grinding back and forth audibly once more. In one quick motion, he drops his hands and lunges for the device. Then, with a scream, he hurls it at the wall and sinks to his knees.

Chapter 4
Levi

Agitation prods at me like a poker stoking a fire. I'm burning with rage, with the need to do *something*, and yet here we sit.

We're still at the cabin. Still sitting around, waiting. Still not making any moves to get our girl.

"We could have driven back to South Chapel by now," I offer up to no one in particular.

It's true. We've been immobilized by doubt, waiting for nearly three hours for Dr. Ferguson to send us the information he promised. For all we know, he's still at the damn hospital.

"We could have," Greedy placates. "But then we would have had to backtrack and drive north again. We'd be farther away from Hunter when the information from my dad came through."

He's right. But sitting around doing nothing feels awful.

This is the same discussion we've been having all afternoon. We waffle between staying and going. We consider splitting up or just jumping in the truck and heading north. We may not know where Hunter is and why, but we have a general idea thanks to Kabir's tracker.

We've tried Magnolia's phone at least a dozen times, but it goes straight to voicemail.

I reached out to Kendrick Taylor. The message has gone unread, but that's to be expected. Joey said they were heading out of town and mentioned they may be somewhere remote, without good cell service.

Fucking hell. Like Greedy, I momentarily entertained the idea that Hunter ran. Now, though, it hurts to even consider that I doubted her. Daisy had no reason to run. No reason to leave without telling us. And she sure as shit had no reason to go anywhere with Magnolia.

I'm not usually a pessimist, but every facet of this situation adds a layer to my already growing unease. Something's really wrong.

Greedy's gripping the edges of the kitchen counter, blankly looking at the food we barely touched. He made lunch, but none of us has much of an appetite.

"I could take the truck," I suggest half-heartedly. "Then you guys could call for a car service once you hear from your dad."

"And where are you gonna go, Leev?" He straightens, his knuckles white and his mossy-green eyes wild.

He's right. We have no fucking idea where Hunter is, and driving aimlessly won't help.

According to Kabir's tracking device, she's in a rural area in upstate New York. Though that aligns with what Dr. Ferguson remembered from the note, we still don't know the name of the facility or if that's really where they're going. We don't know how she got there. How she got out of the house without any of us hearing. If she even wants to be there…

"I don't know," I admit, tugging on the ends of my hair once again.

Standing around and waiting like this makes me feel so fucking helpless.

"Got her," Kabir announces triumphantly from where he's set up at the kitchen table with a laptop, a tablet, and his phone. It's the first time he's spoken in over an hour.

In unison, G and I hustle to his side and peer over each shoulder.

On the laptop screen is some sort of grid. It's mostly green, with hints of brown scattered throughout. An overhead image of a forest, maybe?

"I combined satellite data and imagery to triangulate the location of the tracker. Based on my calculations, she's here."

I hold my breath as he zooms in, but when he stabs a ringed finger against his laptop screen, I deflate.

There's nothing there.

There are treetops, what might be a grassy meadow, and maybe the makings of some sort of path or river. It's very clearly the middle of nowhere.

"What are we looking at?"

"This." With the swipe of a finger, the image disappears and is replaced with a browser window with a website loaded.

Empire Forest Retreat and Spa: New York's premier holistic psychedelic sanctuary.

"The fuck?" Greedy murmurs.

Confusion swirls in my mind as I take in the fancy web page. "What the hell is that?"

"It appears to be some sort of rustic overnight med spa." Kabir clicks through pages. "Botox with Bears. Ketamine Along the Cliffs. It's nothing more than a carefully crafted marketing ploy designed to separate middle-aged women from their money."

"Sounds exactly like the kind of place Magnolia would enjoy," Greedy mumbles.

"Despite the inability to get a clear view of the area, I am fairly certain this is where she is."

"Okay." Straightening, I clap, ready to get the fuck out of here. I clasp Greedy on the shoulder and squeeze. "Let's go."

Kabir shakes his head subtly. Greedy blows out a frustrated breath.

Before I can question their lack of enthusiasm, Kabir rises to his feet and turns to me. "We have no idea what we're walking into, champ. We can't just show up without a plan."

"Why the fuck not?" Hands balled at my sides, I take a step toward him. "Hunter's there. You know she is. She doesn't have her meds, and she's with her mother, possibly *against her will*."

"Fuck." Greedy smashes his fist into the table.

I jolt forward, quickly covering his hand with mine to prevent him from hurting himself or any more electronics. He's already cracked the screen of his phone today. Thankfully, the device isn't broken, considering we're still waiting for that confirmation text from Dr. Ferguson.

He shrugs off my touch, then meets my gaze with a pitiful, apologetic grimace. "I hate to say it, but I agree with Spence."

I guffaw. There's no way I'm hearing him correctly.

"You don't want to get her back?" At a fucking loss, I look from one man to the other.

"Leev..." Greedy pleads.

"*No*," I bark back. Fuck it. He wants us to, what, keep waiting around? Stay here and send out some thoughts and prayers that Hunter returns on her own?

He's not even acknowledging the heart of the issue: None of us are convinced Hunter left the cabin willingly. There's no way they're on some innocent mother-daughter trip.

Greedy sucks in a breath, then squares his shoulders. "Based on what my dad said about the way Magnolia was acting, her behavior could be unpredictable. We don't know what we're walking into here."

"Precisely," Kabir adds.

"I say we wait for the official word from my dad," Greedy says, "and then we make a plan. We can try to contact the facility, and we can keep trying Magnolia's phone."

"We've waited around long enough." My heart's hammering out of my chest at this point, anguish and adrenaline warring for dominance. How is it possible they're so unaffected? Why are they acting so calm?

I fold my arms over my chest and stand to my full height, regarding them both.

"I say we start driving north at the very least."

Greedy's jaw ticks as he considers. Then he turns to Kabir. "What do you think?"

What the fuck? G is siding with Kabir? *Deferring* to him? Two days ago, he hated the guy. Now it feels like my best friend and my... the, uh, guy I'm into, I guess, are ganging up on me.

Kabir studies Greedy, then me, his expression even and measured. He looks at the laptop screen for another long moment. Then, finally, he says, "I agree that sitting here does no good."

Relief floods my system. *Finally.*

"Perhaps if you drive, Garrett, I can work in the back seat, and we can come up with a plan while closing in on the location."

Kabir hasn't even finished making the suggestion before Greedy's eagerly nodding.

"Cool?" he asks me.

A renewed sense of purpose fuels me in a rush, like I just completed the perfect shallow cross and dove past the goal line. "Yeah. That works."

Greedy continues to watch me, and I see it there, too. He's still on edge like I am. Over the last few hours, though, we've found some semblance of balance and solace with one another. When he's frustrated, I have the ability to calm him. When I'm about to lose it, he's right there, assuring me it'll be okay.

"I'll button up the house and pack food. Leev, can you pack my stuff?"

"Sure." I'm already running through a mental list of clean clothes I have with me, thankful we've kept up with laundry here. "How far away is this place anyway?" I ask Kabir.

He picks up a tablet, taps the screen a few times, then grimaces.

"Approximately thirteen hours from our current location."

"God dammit," I curse under my breath.

"Hey." Greedy drapes an arm over my shoulders. "We'll get there. We just gotta be smart about this. We'll leave within the hour."

I swallow past the dread that clogs my throat every time I think about Hunter.

I hate that she's not here. That there are so many unknowns. She was in my arms just last night, for fuck's sake.

Head hanging, I give it a shake. "I just need to know she's okay."

"I know, man. Me, too." He turns so he's facing me, his Adam's apple bobbing. Then, with a long exhale, he nods and leaves the kitchen.

It isn't lost on me that G doesn't try to assure me that she's okay.

He can't.

He and I both know there's a chance she isn't.

Kabir slams his laptop shut and starts to pack up his workstation in earnest.

It looks like the urgency that's been percolating in my gut for hours has finally reached them, too.

Chapter 5

Hunter

NOW

A metallic smell infiltrates my senses when I bring my hand up to my face.

I knew I was bleeding.

There's blood and everything hurts.

There's always blood.

I've suffered from menstrual cramps, but without pain relievers or a heating pad, these are far worse than normal.

Or maybe the pain has been exacerbated by the hours I spent curled up in the back seat of a car.

Being strapped into an open-sided golf cart like this while it careens down a rocky path isn't helping matters either. Clouds of dust erupt in our wake, making it that much harder to take in my surroundings or to even suck in fresh air.

Air.

I need air.

I haven't taken a full breath in hours.

That, I'm realizing, is intentional and by design. Each time I've tried to sit up, she's noticed and then offered me a drink.

Yet I'm still so thirsty, and my mouth feels as if it's coated in sand and filled with cotton.

My tongue is so dry that its scratchy texture against the roof of my mouth is painful.

The lack of moisture makes it hard to swallow, and sometimes even breathe.

So every time she offers me a drink, I accept. It's my only option. The only small mercy I've found comes during those few seconds when a bottle is brought to my lips and I impulsively suck down a mouthful of bitter liquid.

The flavor doesn't matter at this point. I can't even bring myself to care that what she's giving me is likely the source of my lethargy and my inability to lift my head, suck in a breath, or take in my surroundings.

All I know is that for an instant, my mouth is no longer dry and I can almost inhale fully.

That is, until I'm out, and the cycle begins again.

I don't know how long it lasts.

But it happens over and over.

Now, there's a dull ache in my low back. It's different from the cramps—more acute and centralized. My bladder hurts, I realize. I desperately need to pee.

As I clamp my legs together in response to the sensation, a familiar warmth gathers in my underwear. I reach down automatically and connect the dots. My menstrual disc needs to be emptied, if not replaced.

Lifting my hand in front of my face, I squint against the dust and the glimmer of the setting sun.

There's blood on my hands.

Blood on the tips of my fingers.

I part my lips and slowly, carefully place my thumb on the tip of my tongue to peel it away from the roof of my mouth.

I'm not stealthy enough.

"Oh *darling*," my mother coos. "Here."

A bottle is brought to my lips, the promise of relief sloshing against plastic.

I can't help but drink.

One sip. I only allow myself one sip.

My brain is cloudy, my thoughts murky, but my gut screams at me, telling me that this isn't good for me.

Even so, I can't resist the temptation to take that single sip.

"You know what travel days are like," she says, her voice distant, garbled.

Dust kicks up behind us, forming a billowy haze of debris as the golf cart continues along.

The scent of limestone and the earthy scent of the forest permeate my nose. When I lick my lips, still parched, I taste the hint of salt.

I should clamp my mouth shut to avoid inhaling the dust.

But when I do, I swear I can't breathe.

There's blood.

There's blood on the beige leather seat.

There's blood on the tips of my fingers.

I close my eyes and let my head hang, despite the ache in my neck. The occasional jolt from the golf cart keeps me conscious, but just.

When I close my eyes, there's blood swirling down the shower.

There's blood coating the tiles of Kabir's water closet back in London.

There's blood.

There's blood.

There's always blood.

Chapter 6

Hunter

THEN: Spring, Year One
Follicular Phase

I'd like to say I came to Italy because I've always wanted to experience the culture and cuisine. Truth be told, I came on a whim. I only trust myself to make decisions at certain times each month, and I didn't want to reach my luteal phase and still be waffling.

So my plans to leave London came together quickly. They had to, for my sake *and* Spence's. I chose my destination based on the flights available that week.

If I thought about it for too long, I'd second-guess myself, and if I even offered so much as a hint of what I was planning to do, Spence would have stopped me.

Part of me wishes he would have.

I fear that the compulsion to run has become part of who I am. What if I never stop?

No. I can't think like that right now. I'm here for a reason, and I have to believe that what I'm seeking is also seeking me.

I square my shoulders and traverse the uneven, cobbled path leading to what I hope will be a fresh start.

With each step, I will my mind to clear. But it can't. It can't, or it won't. My head knows it's for the best, but my heart won't allow it. I miss Spence so damn much.

My departure was swift and cowardly. In my heart of hearts, I think he knew it was coming. His touches had started to linger. Sorrowful eyes followed me through the flat as if he was already preparing for my absence.

In the end, I didn't allow him the opportunity to say goodbye. Not because he didn't deserve it, but because I couldn't bear it.

I always default to self-preservation when it comes to matters of the heart.

So I left him a hand-written letter. I told him where I was going and why I felt like I had to leave. My decision had nothing to do with him and everything to do with me.

My mind is a chaotic place. That's not news to either of us.

I just hope he doesn't hate me for what I had to do.

It's poetic, really, being the one that got away opposed to the ball and chain that drags another person down. Or at least that's what I'm telling myself. Spence didn't view me that way. Not yet, at least. Though it had become a niggling worry in my mind that I couldn't ignore. He did so much for me: He cared for me in every way that was real and true. He made my happiness his purpose, day in and day out.

I don't deserve that kind of love, though. Not in the long term. Not in the way I think Spence was willing to love me. Between heartache, grief, and PMDD, there wasn't enough of me left over to reciprocate that kind of deep, unyielding care and affection.

So I said goodbye in the most cowardly way possible. I applied my favorite red lipstick—the shade I regularly wore at Splice—and sealed the letter. With my lock necklace laid over it, I left it on the kitchen island. Then I snuck out while he was in the shower.

Now I'm here. In Italy. Starting over. Again.

Taking deep breaths to soothe the pressure forming behind my sinuses, I fight back tears. I can't think about London right now. I need to focus on Italy. On what's new and what's next.

Running is my default, so it felt natural to leave before things could get too real. I'll keep the very best memories of the man I loved in London locked away in the recesses of my mind. Leaving London was both easier and harder than leaving North Carolina. Staying away from London—without an entire ocean separating me from the man I left behind—will be the real challenge.

If I'm going to stay awhile, then I need an anchor. Hence why I'm walking up this hilly pathway.

I need a job, and Villa Viola is hiring.

At the threshold of the small building, I pause and double-check the little sign confirming that I'm in the right place. Then I take a deep breath and grasp the handle of the cerulean-blue door. For three seconds, I allow myself to feel the butterflies warring in my stomach. When my time is up, I close my eyes and exhale. Then I channel my inner cheerleader, plaster an enormous smile on my face, and heave open the door.

"Hi," I chirp as I approach the older woman.

She looks to be in her seventies and is the only person in the lobby. She's tidying a little seating area, but she peers over at me as I approach. The building is much smaller than I envisioned. It's nothing more than a simple two-story residence from the outside, with not much by the way of signage.

"My name's Hunter. I was hoping to talk to the manager. To inquire about the hospitality position?"

She pauses her sweeping and straightens. Warm brown eyes surrounded by deep wrinkles lift and search my face. Her brow bone is dotted with freckles only a few shades darker than the rich tan of her skin.

Her salt-and-pepper hair is twisted into a tight bun at the back of her head, and she's wearing an eclectic lavender muumuu paired with sensible sandals.

The smile she gives me is kind, the corners of her mouth reaching high and creating deep dimples that complement the crow's feet and wrinkles all over her face.

A vision of my mother intrudes my thoughts at that moment. My mother, who abhors wrinkles. Who elects to receive an onslaught of treatments on a regular basis to keep her crow's feet at bay.

There isn't a smooth inch of skin anywhere on this woman's face or neck. Yet her smile is one of the most beautiful I've ever seen.

What's so wrong with wrinkles anyway?

I shake my head to clear the clutter. I've lost myself in my thoughts once again. "The job?" I repeat, holding my smile, despite the aching sensation in my cheeks from forcing the enthusiastic expression.

"Ospitalitatii?" she says in an accent I don't recognize, the word melodic and thick. It's not Italian. At least, I don't think it is. Although it sounds similar.

"Yes. I'm here to apply for the hospitality job."

She holds the broom with both hands, assessing me. The smile is gone—her scrutiny more intense and inquisitive than I'm prepared for. Suddenly, she releases her grasp on the long handle but doesn't look away.

I don't know where to focus—at her, or at the stick that I swear is floating between us. The broom stays propped on its bristles for one second, then two. Then three, then four, then five.

It doesn't fall. But I swear she's not touching it.

"How—"

But before I can articulate my question, she grasps the perfectly balanced broom again and resumes sweeping.

When she lifts her head and meets my gaze once more, there's a twinkle in her eye that's pure mischief.

I press my lips together, unsure whether to laugh or to remain stoic. Is this a test? Does she want me to crack?

In the end, it's useless. The longer she smiles at me, the faster I thaw. Neither of us speaks, but an unspoken warmth passes between us. A sensation akin to a comforting hug. It's as if all my worries soften around the edges and my apprehension about coming to a new place and starting over—*again*—dissipates.

"Mamaia!" A man's voice rings out from far away, joyful and boisterous.

And just like that, the spell is broken.

Although maybe broken isn't the word. Not based on the way the woman before me is grinning so wide I can't even see her irises. How is that even possible?

She moves in the direction of the voice, taking the magic broom with her. Two steps across the room, she turns to face me and holds up one finger, indicating that I should wait.

Then she's in front of me again, handing me the broom. She releases it before I even process what's happening. I'm left holding it, standing in the middle of the small space, dumbfounded. And without a word, she's gone.

Should I take over and resume sweeping like she was? Is this another test? An audition for the job?

I asked Alessia, a girl at the hostel I've become friendly with, to help me translate the ad when I found it posted outside a café in Piazza Cavour. According to the job description, the duties include cleaning, cooking, and planning activities for guests. The only requirements are experience in hospitality and the ability to speak English, both of which I have locked in.

I want this job.

No, not just want. I need it if I'm going to stay in Lake Como. I won't last in the hostel another week. And I don't want to have to pack up and leave.

More determined than ever to make a good impression, I get to work cleaning. I sweep the corners and under the seats. I sweep the threshold and move the rugs to ensure I hit every nook and cranny.

My dust pile is nearly nonexistent, hinting that Villa Viola is well cared for. Nevertheless, I persist. This floor will gleam by the time I'm done. If this is a test, then I plan to ace it.

Eventually, curiosity gets the better of me. So, craning my neck, I survey the room, confirming that I'm still alone. Then I steady the broom on its bristles and try to balance it like the older woman did. It holds, but only for a second before it falls with a clatter.

I scramble to pick it up. Then I try again.

This time the broom balances upright for one second. Then two. I clap in delight as three seconds pass. I have to hold in a squeal when I hit the four-second mark.

"Are you here to put on a magic show for our guests?" a male voice asks.

A yelp of surprise tears from my lungs, and the wooden broom clatters to the tiles, sending me jumping back.

Hand pressed to my chest, I look up, finding that the woman has returned. And she's no longer alone.

I survey the man before me, cataloging his tattoos and the glossy black hair that hangs to his shoulders.

He's grinning when I finally lift my gaze to his face. He caught my not-so-subtle ogling.

Flovely.

"I'm here about the job," I rush to explain.

I look over at the older woman, but she merely watches me with a hint of a smile on her face, as if she's happy to silently watch our exchange.

"English is my native language, and I worked as a hostess in London for—a while." I'm not keen on getting into the nitty gritty of my work history with a stranger, so I leave it at that. "Do you work here?" I look from the extremely attractive man who's close to my age, maybe a few years older, back to the woman I met when I arrived.

"I do. Villa Viola is a family business. I've been working here since I was a kid."

Okay. That makes sense. Now that he mentions it, I can see the resemblance between the two of them.

"And she's your...?" I leave the question open-ended. If I guess she's his grandmother, only to discover she's his mother or his aunt, then I can kiss my hopes of landing this job goodbye, I'm sure.

"Mamaia—Kitty—is my grandmother. I see she's already put you to work," the man teases. Then, approaching and extending a massive, tatted hand, he says, "I'm Sione."

"My name's Hunter." I shake his hand while desperately clinging to the broom for support.

When he releases me, he turns to Kitty and speaks to her in a language that's not English.

"Is that Italian?" I hedge.

His eyes flit to me, then back to his grandma, who's now replying in quick, clipped sentences that aren't as melodic as the phrases I've grown accustomed to hearing over the last few weeks.

"Romanian," he answers when she finally stops talking. "Kitty and my grandpa, Otmar, were born in Romania. They immigrated here in their twenties and started working at Villa Viola shortly after. The previous owners adored them, and when they retired, they sold the business to them. They've owned it for almost four decades now."

I nod and smile, eager to take in any little nuggets of wisdom or history that might help me secure this job.

"So is there an application I should fill out? And could you ask your grandmother when she thinks interviews will occur?"

He speaks to his grandmother in Romanian, and when she responds, carrying on for several minutes, he crosses his arms over his chest and chuckles.

I wait with bated breath, resisting the urge to ask him to translate.

Finally, she's silent, yet neither addresses me. They watch one another for a handful of heartbeats, their expressions unreadable.

"So?" I eventually hedge.

Sione grins, the expression emanating the same kind of warmth I felt when his grandmother greeted me. "She asked if your English is any good, and I assured her it is. She wants to know if you can start today, and if you'll need accommodation. There's a villa dedicated to staff. Each employee has a private room and en suite bathroom. She's also hounding me about using the good purple sheets on your bed instead of the regular white ones we use for everyone else." He arches an amused brow. "She must really like you."

"Wait, so I'm hired? Just like that?" I protest.

Why, exactly, I'm protesting, I have no idea. This seems too easy. Things never work out like this for me.

Shrugging, Sione runs one hand through his dark, wavy hair. I'm absolutely transfixed by the movement. Scratch that—I'm mesmerized by his very presence. He's got cheekbones to die for and the most gorgeous eyelashes I've ever seen.

"She said she already interviewed you."

I press my lips together, fighting a smile. That was easy. Too easy? Whatever. I'm not going to look a gift horse in the mouth, or however the saying goes.

The moment I stepped into the lobby, a comforting sensation enveloped me. I feel safe here. Respected. Not to mention amused by Kitty and her antics. Sione puts off good vibes, and if I can calm my libido for a hot second, I could see the two of us striking up a friendship.

Most importantly, I haven't thought about Spence or London or my past since walking into Villa Viola. That's a major improvement. For the last few weeks, I've been battling a never-ending barrage of intrusive thoughts. It's not often I can quiet the guilty memories that plague my mind.

I may not deserve this clean slate, but I need it.

Pulling me from my thoughts, Sione asks, "If I help you bring your things over from the hostel, can you start today?"

"Yes," I reply without hesitation, my heart leaping in my chest.

He grins. "Right on. I have two more villas to turn over. Why don't you head out and get packed up? I'll meet up with you in a few hours."

With a nod at Sione, I turn to Kitty. "Thank you. I'm a hard worker, I promise. I won't let you down."

She smiles slyly in response, and once again, when her eyes lock on me, I'm enveloped in the warmest, most comforting sensation. It's as if she's embracing me, even though she's several feet across the room. I swear the woman is magic. Just being in her presence is a balm I didn't know I was craving.

"Let me give you my number," Sione holds out a hand, and when I set my phone in his palm, he punches in his number, saves it, and winks. "You'll find me under 'The One and Only' since it rhymes with *Cee-oh-nay*."

My face heats at the twinkle in his eye and the half smile he gives me. As if I could possibly forget a single detail about this man.

"Thank you both," I gush again. "I'll pack quickly. See you later."

Chapter 7

Kabir

NOW

"You're certain?" Deftly, I pull a piece of American currency from my money clip and hold it out to the attendant behind the counter.

He snatches it faster than a viper striking its prey.

"Uh, lemme check again for you," he offers.

Unfortunately, "checking" involves flipping through a paper ledger, mumbling unintelligibly whilst sniffling, and clumsily searching through a lockbox of keys. I'm left to stand at the counter as the only employee of the Moon Mist Motel attempts to earn the hundred American dollars I just handed him.

Garrett and Levi are still out in the vehicle, so I send them a quick text directing them to hang tight. No sense in having them come in while I attempt, for the third time tonight, to find a vacancy.

We can't go any farther until a few more pieces of my plan fall into place. The boys are exhausted, as am I. Despite their insistence that we keep going, I made it clear that sleeping and starting anew in the morning was nonnegotiable.

Unfortunately, I was unable to find a single available reservation in this area when I searched online. Turns out, there's an event known as a "polar bear plunge" happening at a nearby lake tomorrow. Every hotel, motel, and vacation rental we've tried is fully booked.

"Yahtzee." With a grin, the man behind the counter procures a single key attached to a scratched-up purple plastic tag and offers it to me with a flourish.

I stare at his unkempt fingernails and rack my brain for context. Yahtzee? I have no idea what that colloquialism means. Before I can inquire, he continues.

"It's the only vacant room left on property—the Mystical Master Suite. I can give it to ya for the regular rate since you're checking in so late. It's even got a king bed." With that, he waggles his overgrown brows.

"One of the beds is king-size?" I confirm.

"There's only one bed, but it's a king. That means it's big, and the pillowcases are extra long, too."

Bloody hell.

Before I can form a proper reply, my phone buzzes in my hand.

Garrett: Levi's zonked out. Any luck?

I swear that boy could fall asleep anywhere, and under the direst of circumstances.

"Right." Reluctantly, I accept the key and produce a credit card to pay for the room. "You take Mastercard, I assume?"

I unlock the door and hold it open as Garrett helps a drowsy Levi navigate into the room.

Before either notices or comments on the arrangements, I take charge. "You two take the bed."

With the door closed behind us, I fasten the comically rusty security chain and turn the deadbolt.

"Wait, there's only one bed?"

Garrett's voice is higher than normal—from stress or nerves or anxiety, I'm not sure.

I steal myself with a cleansing breath, then I turn and lock eyes with him. "There is. This is the best I could do for tonight. Might I remind you of the annual *polar bear plunge* happening tomorrow?"

Holding my gaze, he gently lowers his mostly asleep friend onto the king-size bed.

"Pull back the comforter first," I hiss, marching across the room and stripping off the cesspool of the shared blanket.

There may only be one bed, but at least the sheets appear clean.

"Hey." Garrett brushes a hand over my forearm, stopping at my elbow, where the sleeve of my Oxford has been pushed up. "I wasn't criticizing." His eyes search my face. After a breath, his tongue darts out to wet his lips. "I can sleep on the floor, no problem."

I rear back as if I've been slapped.

"Absolutely not," I vociferate. "You've been driving for hours. He's still recovering from major surgery. I'm still on London time, and I have to be up for a call in three hours anyway. You'll take the bed, Garrett. It's not up for discussion."

Brows raised, he scrutinizes me, as if he's preparing to argue. Instead, he clamps his mouth shut, nods once, and sighs. "Thank you." His expression quickly morphs to one of sincerity, and a pain that matches the ache inside me swims in his eyes. "Thank you for everything. Try to get some rest, too, Spence. It's been a long day for all of us."

With that, he turns his back to me and heads toward the water closet.

Chapter 8

Kabir

NOW

Hours pass, or maybe it's only seconds. The boys haven't stirred for some time. Even so, I keep my computer screen dim in an effort not to disturb them.

I've rearranged my schedule for the week—canceled media appearances and interviews—and I've given my staff instructions on how to proceed in my absence.

Gerald, who despite recognizing the conveniences of modern technology, has yet to respond to my texts. He reads the messages, he just won't reply that way.

When I told him about Hunter's disappearance—the lack of note or explanation or evidence that she left of her own accord—he started calling.

Over and over again, my phone lit up, silently alerting me to his concern. Though I can understand the fear, I can't provide him with any more answers than I've already given him through text.

> **Spence:** I'm not in a position to talk. I'll call in a few hours.

To my absolute shock, and for the first time ever, he texts me back.

> **Gerald:** Might I suggest I join you in the States, sir? I'd like to be helpful in any way that may serve you and Ms. St. Clair.

Bloody hell. The old curmudgeon's down bad enough for Hunter to break his staunch no-texting rule. He hasn't even seen her for a few years.

> **Spence:** Let me find her first. Once she's secured, I'll send further instructions.

Then, because I don't want to discourage him and I genuinely do appreciate his concern, I add...

> **Spence:** Your support is very much appreciated, Gerald. It will galvanize me through this pursuit.

> **Gerald:** Godspeed.

The niggling in my gut won't settle. Hunter is gone, and she's not okay. That, I know for sure.

She's alive, and according to the information I'm receiving from her tracker, her vitals are strong.

Despite the very real situations in which she has broken down or not been herself in the past, I'm certain that what's happening now is nothing like what she experienced back then.

This isn't like London.

This isn't her pattern.

Something's not right.

Levi is the only one brave enough to voice it, but I believe his assumption is correct.

Magnolia took her.

Wherever our girl is, whatever she's enduring, it's at the hands of another person. She's gone, but she didn't leave.

We're reeling without her, but we never had a choice.

None of us did.

Not even her.

Chapter 9

Greedy

NOW

The moon-shaped headboard shifts against the wall with a dull thud as I roll over. Again. I freeze at the noise and hold my breath, hoping like hell Levi stays asleep.

He was an angry, pent-up mess until he finally nodded off in the truck, and rightfully so. Finding a place with a vacancy was shockingly difficult. It doesn't help that we're only about an hour away from Hunter.

Levi wants to go immediately, and while I understand the urge, we have to be smart about this whole operation. When Kabir suggested we find a place to stay so we could rest and he could finish whatever he's working on, I agreed with him.

Everything will be easier in the daylight. After we've all eaten and slept. Leev doesn't see it that way. He thinks Kabir and I are ganging up on him, and that's got him even more pissed off.

I've never seen him this angry, and I'm afraid he'll act impulsively or recklessly. I can barely stand the tension radiating off him. It's why I'm awake now, after just a few hours of fitful sleep.

Though it's not the only reason. Despite my efforts to temper it, the less-than-practical side of me is activated by our proximity and the desperation I feel to get her back in my arms.

It's a balm to know she's so close. Yet I'm having a hard time wrapping my head around Kabir's confession about putting a fucking tracker in her.

Just as soon as I find myself on that train of thought, though, I remember his reasoning. The very idea of Hunter in that state guts me.

There's no doubt in my mind of the severity of what she experienced in London. I've seen her on the dark nights. I've held her as she sobbed, her chest racking in an effort to pull in a full breath as she clung to me like I was her last and final anchor.

She must have been so fucking scared. Out of her head, far away from home...

I hate thinking about her like that. Particularly because I was so desperate to be with her back then. The what-ifs used to play on repeat in my mind. Hell, they still haunt me now.

If she had stayed. If she'd just trusted in me, in us...

Each time those thoughts surface, I shake them off. It does me no good, nor does it the guys or, least of all, Hunter.

She's a survivor. That much is clear. Whatever's going on at the "holistic wellness retreat," she can handle it.

I'm clinging to that notion.

Hell, maybe she's even having a decent time.

I hold in a scoff.

Yeah. No. That's not likely with Magnolia involved. Hunter wouldn't just get up and go without saying goodbye. At least not anymore.

With a huff, I roll over again, creaking headboard be damned. But when I turn to my side, a hard object jabs into my IT band. Wincing, I roll to my back, then I reach into the pocket of my athletic shorts and pull out Hunter's old phone.

My heart stumbles as I assess it. She kept this. Carried it with her. Took it to London, to Italy, and everywhere else her travels took her.

I turn the pink relic over in my hands, reconsidering the narrative she let me buy into for years. That she didn't want me. That she didn't care.

For so long, I waited for her. Hoping she'd come back. Eventually, I started to wonder if any of it had been real.

She left, but the entire time, she kept part of me with her.

I cradle the phone to my chest, equally embarrassed and nostalgic for the boy I used to be. I called this phone every day for months. Filled the voicemail box to capacity. Even after I could no longer leave messages, I kept calling. Kept trying. Just in case she needed to know I was still there. I never gave up on her—or on us.

I'm sure as hell not giving up now.

A gentle touch on my forearm startles me.

On my exhale, Levi spreads his hand wide, smoothing it down my arm, his fingertips trailing through the coarse hair just enough to tickle, until his hand is covering mine.

"You okay?" he whispers, his voice low and gruff. Shit. I was sure he was asleep. I hope like hell I'm not the reason he's awake now.

"No," I whisper into the darkness.

He gives my hand a squeeze. "Yeah..." a long breath escapes him. "I feel that." After a few breaths, he flexes his fingers over my hand. "Is this okay?"

This.

This moment.

Us.

"Yes." This is more than okay. "Try to go back to sleep," I whisper, threading his fingers with mine. I close my eyes and focus on my breathing, the sensation of his hand enveloping mine, and finally feel that elusive pull of exhaustion.

Chapter 10

Greedy

NOW

When I open my eyes again, the dingy motel room is still dark. Kabir is sitting at the small table, his sharp features illuminated by the dimmed light of his laptop.

Still lying flat on my back, I loll my head to the side and study the man who has yet to sleep. The man who hasn't stopped working since we found out Hunter was gone, who was awake for hours before any of us were yesterday.

His face is drawn, the way his computer screen illuminates him only emphasizing how exhausted he looks.

I curl up in bed, trying in vain to be quiet so the headboard won't squeak.

Doesn't work.

Spence looks my way, his blue-gray eyes tracking my every movement as I rise from the bed and shuffle over. The scowl he's wearing makes him look all the more domineering. The man's a force, even after being awake for twenty-four hours and working around the clock.

"Hey," I whisper when I come to stop before him.

He blinks, but his expression doesn't change. "Hay is for horses, Garrett. Even as a Londoner—"

I snort, fighting the urge to roll my eyes. "Don't be a dick."

He snaps his mouth shut, cocking a brow.

Huh. Interesting. Although not surprising, I guess. The man obviously favors directness.

"I can't sleep any longer. Take my place," I insist, extending my arm toward the bed.

He shakes his head once, the movement jerky. "You drove all day. You need rest. If you're—"

"Spence." I interrupt him again. "I slept as much as I can. Honestly? I need a workout more than anything. I promise I'll be okay to drive when it's time to head out."

He considers me for a breath, then eventually nods. "This motel does have a fitness center. I doubt it's of a distinguished caliber, but I do know it's open twenty-four hours."

"Cool. I'll wait a while longer to check it out. Levi will probably want to lift, too."

With a nod, Spence rises and starts to tidy up his makeshift workstation. He stashes his laptop away, casting the room into total darkness.

I use the flashlight on my phone so we can move through the room and follow him to the bed, lighting his path as he unbuttons his oxford and shrugs out of it. His belt and pants go next—unceremoniously dropped onto the floor as he steps out of them. He really must be exhausted.

Instinctively, I pull back the sheets.

Spence smirks, eyeing me as he shifts around me to climb into bed. "Are you going to tuck me in and tell me a bedtime story, Garrett?"

"Is that what you want, sir?"

My eyes widen when the words leave my mouth.

Are we *bantering*?

"Cheeky bastard," Spence scoffs under his breath. He pounds down a lumpy pillow.

Releasing the sheet, I take a step back so he can settle in. There's a deeper sense of tolerance and understanding between us now—a kinship that most certainly didn't exist twenty-four hours ago.

I hated this guy a few days ago. Loathed him, in fact.

Now? Now I'm really fucking glad he's here.

"I cannot believe he's just lying there, sound asleep," Kabir remarks, pulling me from my thoughts. I look over to Levi as the headboard once again makes its age and decrepit condition known.

Leev has his back to us, but his slow, steady inhalations confirm he's still out.

"He's always been a heavy sleeper," I remark, a warmth settling in my chest at the knowledge that he's found peace for now. "Try to get some rest."

I turn, but before I take more than a step away from the bed, warm fingers and cool metal caress the inside of my wrist.

Spence's grip startles me, though not because his touch is unwelcome. I'm comfortable with him now, I realize. Comfortable in a way I didn't know was possible with anyone outside of Hunter and Levi.

When I seek his gaze in the dark, I'm met with a steely expression.

"We're going to get her back, Garrett. I swear it to you. Rest assured; I'll stop at nothing." He releases my wrist just as abruptly as he snagged it.

This man.

There's no question as to how deeply and irrevocably he loves our girl.

"I know you won't," I assure him. "And neither will I."

Chapter 11

Greedy

NOW

I stumble back from the force of the blow but quickly find my footing and steady the swinging bag.

"Dude. Take it easy. You're going to get hurt."

That, or he'll hurt me with his sloppy footing and overly aggressive right hook. Levi's acting like this dirty vestige of a hanging bag is personally responsible for Hunter's disappearance and our current predicament.

"Take it easy?" he grits out, pulling the hem of his shirt up to wipe away the sweat dripping down his face. His whole chest inflates, then deflates in rapid, harsh breaths. He's clearly exhausted, and yet, he won't stop. "How the hell do you expect me to take it easy? We're still here. We've been awake for hours, and we're still fucking *here*."

He's only mildly exaggerating.

We've all been up for a while, but it's still early.

Spence has a plan, but he's waiting on paperwork to come through before enacting it, and it'll likely be mid-morning before that happens.

According to him, we can head in Hunter's direction the moment he gets word that everything is in place.

What "everything" entails is a mystery. But I trust him. And I trust that given the circumstances, Hunter would want us to play it safe and make smart choices.

Spence is back in the room, grumbling about the lack of coffee and tea options in the *Mystical Master Suite*. He wasn't nearly as amused by the room's official name as I was.

Levi hadn't been awake more than thirty minutes before he was practically climbing the walls, so I suggested we blow off some steam in the gym. I thought it would beat sitting around feeling useless. I thought wrong.

"Hold it," Levi bares his teeth, bouncing back on his toes. It's the only warning he gives before he rails against the vinyl cylinder between us and sends me stumbling once more. "I said hold it," he barks.

"I'm fucking trying," I bite back as I sway with the momentum of the bag.

Anger and despair radiate from him, and despite going five rounds on the tattered punching bag, he's acting like he's just getting started.

He stays light on his toes, dancing back and forth as he waits for me to reset. He's got to be fucking exhausted.

I take my time steadying the worn-out equipment, subtly inspecting him as I do. When I catch a wince and a hiss under his breath, I know it's time to shut it down.

"Let's call it."

He lets out a frustrated grunt. "No, I said hold it."

"You're spent, Leev. I'm calling it. You're done." Stepping out from around the bag, I cross my arms over my chest and stand to my full height.

"So you're back to being the boss now?" He lifts the bottom edge of his cut-off tee again, the muscles in his biceps and shoulders bunching, and wipes at the sweat dripping off his face.

"What's that supposed to mean?" I step around him to grab my water. On the pass, I put a hand on him to keep from startling him. The second my fingertips caress the warm, slick skin of his oblique, he stills.

With a shuddering breath, he jolts away from my touch and steps back to put distance between us once more.

"It *means* you're letting Spence run the damn show. I can't believe we're still here. We know where she fucking is, and we're still here."

It's the same battle he's been waging for the last twenty-four hours.

He holds my gaze through the tarnished full-length mirrors that line one wall of the gym as I squirt water into my mouth.

It takes him a few seconds, but eventually, he realizes I'm not going to answer. When that happens, he does what stubborn Levi does best: he doubles down.

"Seriously," he rages, lacing his fingers and bringing his hands to the top of his head. "He shows up, starts telling Hunter what to do, and suddenly you're okay with letting him be in control? You've been fighting with the guy since he got here."

Sighing, I scratch at the base of my skull. He's right, yet he's not. Things have changed between Spence and me. There's a new understanding between us now that we're both invested in a mutual interest. More importantly, though, I won't fight with Kabir. Now that I understand how he operates I don't mind his directness or domineering personality.

In all honestly, it's nice not to have the weight of the world solely on my shoulders for once. As quarterback, I'm used to being the one others defer to. I've always had a predisposition for leadership. Between book smarts and level-headedness, I'm pretty decent at strategizing and figuring out the best move.

In this situation, though, I'm so fucking out of my depth.

Levi's right, but he's also wrong. I'm not just okay with Spence taking the lead; I'm grateful for it. His connections and experience navigating a situation like this with Hunter makes him the better man for the job.

He put a fucking tracker in her, for crying out loud. A tracker that I'm really glad she has now. Without a shadow of a doubt, I know he'll stop at nothing until we have her back.

Levi clearly does not share my gratitude.

The real issue here is that I don't know how to explain any of this to my best friend without insulting or discounting his own desires and priorities. Even if I could find the words, he's not in a position to hear what I'm trying to say. Especially with the way he's scowling at me now.

So instead of defending myself, I hold out the water bottle in a peace offering.

His eyebrows shoot up at my clear dismissal of his questions.

I keep my arm outstretched, holding his gaze in the mirror, willing him to trust that she'll be okay.

Eventually, he stalks toward me. Just as I turn and face him, he shoulder-checks me and passes on by.

"Come on, Levi."

He lumbers away from me, limping subtly, and disappears into the locker room.

With a sigh, I grab our things and follow, and when I push through the door, I find him at the sink with his shirt off and balled in his fist. He's got his arms braced against the countertop, bracketing the sink, with his head hung low.

Sweat rolls down his torso, the reflection of the ripples and divots of his muscular chest creating a grid of glistening moisture.

He's still panting with exertion when I come to stand a few feet behind him. I want to give him space, but I can't stand to see him hurting like this.

"Leev," I try again, my voice cracking with desperation.

His head snaps up, the fury in his gaze pinning me in place. *Stop following me.*

"I can't do that." I take a single step closer. "Even if we don't agree on the play, we're still on the same team."

Understanding flickers over his expression. Before he can respond, though, both phones in my hand—his and mine—vibrate, distracting me.

"Hold up," I murmur, unlocking my screen to read the message.

My heart beats double-time—then it sinks into the pit of my stomach.

> **Spence:** The plan is in motion, but there's one more component that needs to fall into place.

> My lawyer needs two hours. I requested late check out. We'll leave here at 1 p.m.

"What is it?" Levi asks.

Bracing myself, eyes closed, I hold out his phone and let him read the message for himself.

"Is this a fucking joke?"

By the time I open my eyes, Levi's thrown his phone on the counter and he's pulling back as if he's about to smash his hand into the mirror over the sink.

Heart lurching, I burst into motion, hustling forward to tug on his arm.

His fist makes contact with the glass before I can stop him, but he's still holding tight to his T-shirt. Thankfully, the mirror doesn't crack.

"Dude. Chill." I step up to his side, then briskly pull his hand closer to inspect it for damage. "You went five rounds on the punching bag, Leev. You think by now you'd be out of steam."

Standing this close, I can feel the heat of his body. Carefully, I unfurl his fist, finger by finger. As each one uncurls, he grows more tense. Finally, when his fist is open and the shirt he's been holding drops to the floor, I instruct him to flex his hand.

As he obeys, I watch his face, looking for any sign of discomfort.

"Now make a fist," I instruct.

Once again, he complies.

"Any pain?"

Steely blue gaze locked with mine, he shakes his head. The urge to break contact is strong. He's so intense right now, his every emotion palpable, so I give in and blink first.

Focusing on his hand, I test the joints and search for any tender spots.

"I love Hunter," I tell him, my attention still averted. "You know that. Nothing has changed. I'm not stopping until we get her back. We have to be smart about this, though. Spence and I can't be worried about you blowing a gasket and hurting yourself—or worse, reinjuring your leg—because you don't know what to do with your feelings."

"Fuck you." The insult carries far less heat than the words he spoke to me moments ago.

After completing my assessment, I keep a hold of his hand and, gulping past the hesitation brewing in my gut, stand a little taller. Slowly, I lace my fingers with his and seek out his reaction in the mirror. He's not looking at me—he's staring at our joined hands in the reflective glass.

"Hunter's not the only person I care about," I confess, voice husky as I push down my self-doubt. "We'll get her back. But I need to know you're going to be okay, too. What can I do to help you?"

His blue eyes float up to meet mine in the mirror, and his whole body freezes.

We're both holding our breath.

"Levi." I speak his name slowly and deliberately low.

It's an invitation. It's a risk I'm not sure he's willing to take with me. But now that the idea has presented itself in my mind, it's all I can think about.

"Let me help you." I trail my fingers over his wrist and up his forearm.

As I touch the taut, fatigued muscles, his bicep jumps. When I reach his shoulder, I rest my hand there and squeeze. Then I keep going.

Cuffing his neck, I force myself in between his body and the countertop. My fingers sink into the damp wavy blond hair at his nape. I use my grip on the strands to tilt his head to one side, then bring my lips close to his ear.

"Let me fucking help you, Leev. Help you work through what you're feeling. Help you pass the time. Let me help you now. Then, in a few hours, we'll go get our girl."

I scrape my teeth along the tendon bulging in his neck, pulling a sharp breath from him, and nip at his earlobe.

"Lock the door, Levi. Meet me in the shower."

Chapter 12

Levi

NOW

It takes me several heartbeats to process what just happened—what's about to fucking happen. I stare at my reflection in the mirror, my chest heaving with exertion.

Exertion mixed with a shit ton of nerves.

I give myself a few more seconds to dwell on the unknown, because, fuck, are we really doing this?

His touch still lingers. The gentle way he inspected my hand for damage. How he grabbed the hair at the back of my head and tugged so hard I felt it in my balls.

Then there was last night.

I'm a deep sleeper, but my subconscious nudged me awake. Before I fully came to, I knew Greedy was awake and that he wasn't okay. I covered his hand with mine out of instinct. The moment my fingers found his, I felt it.

He settled. I settled.

The physical connection was exactly what we both needed. I thought it would be enough to hold me over until Hunter was back in the fold and we could determine where things stand for us as a group.

This morning, though, he figured it out before I did.

I need a release—an outlet; a reset—if I'm going to get through this day without having an anxiety attack.

Beyond that, beyond the tension and attraction, Greedy sees me. He really fucking sees me, and clearly knows what I need even before I do.

Before I can talk myself out of it, I push away from the counter, turn the lock on the door, and stalk toward the showers.

There's only one stall running.

Only one place he could be.

I step out of my shorts and add them to the hook where Greedy's clothes are already hanging.

Then, after one last deep breath, I pull back the curtain to the stall.

Fucking hell.

I couldn't have dreamed up a hotter image if I tried.

Greedy, naked and soaking wet, his hair clinging to his forehead, water cascading down his face and chest. Soap suds still cling to his calves and feet. With one hand, he gives his cock long, lazy pulls, his forearm flexing in a way that makes my mouth water.

When I force myself to meet his eyes, he gives me the most sincere, dazzling smile. Then, in the space of a breath, he grabs my arm, pulls me into the stall, shoves me under the stream of warm water, and drops down to his knees.

"I knew you'd come. I can't wait to taste you," he murmurs, both hands traveling my thighs as he looks up to me expectantly.

He's a fucking sight to behold.

Greedy, on his knees, for *me*.

Never in a million years did I think this would be our reality.

He licks his lips, those bright green eyes darting from my hardening cock to my face.

"Hold up." I clutch his wrist.

He freezes in place, his expression turning wary.

"Let me wash real quick." I reach over his head for the generic shower gel and pop the cap.

With one hand raised, he says, "Let me do it."

Without hesitation, I squirt a dollop into his palm. Then I watch, enraptured, as he rapidly slicks his hands together to create soapy suds.

He lifts those hands and uses both to encase my entire length.

"Fuck, G," I grunt, overwhelmed by the sensation. His big hands running up and down my shaft send sparks through my extremities. "Just like that. That feels so fuckin' good."

Greedy's eyes widen at my reaction, his grin growing as he continues to stroke me. He gives a few more healthy strokes with a twist of his wrist. I'm throbbing by the time he moves on to washing my pubic hair and lower abs, then working the soap gingerly over my balls and between my thighs.

He rubs the remaining body wash up and down my legs and over the backs of my calves. My heart stutters when his touch softens and he takes extra care to wash around the scar on my left leg.

"Turn," he murmurs, gently guiding me farther into the stream of water so he can rinse away the bubbles. Once the suds are gone, he leans forward, hovering between my thighs, then dips his head and plants a kiss on my surgery scar.

"Is this still okay?"

My gut clenches and emotion rises in my throat.

This.

Us.

Him on his knees, licking his lips and waiting for permission to put his mouth on me.

Nothing has ever been this okay in my whole damn life.

"Yeah, G," I confirm, my voice low and barely recognizable from the lust coursing through my veins. "More than okay."

"I can't wait to taste you," he repeats. His eyes stay glued to my face as he opens his mouth, sticks out his tongue, and gives my cock a slow, methodical, tentative lick.

I blow out a shaky breath the second his warm mouth envelops me. When he closes his eyes and lavishes the ridge of the crown with his tongue, the visual is so erotic I swear my knees are going to buckle just from the sight of him.

When he skirts a hand up my thigh and grasps my length at the base, I have to slap a hand to the shower wall for support. He squeezes, giving me the perfect amount of pressure on the shaft as he makes a fucking meal out of the tip.

With my free hand, I cup the back of his head, but as I do, he stalls.

"You okay?" he asks, peering up at me through dark, wet lashes.

I chuckle, but quickly reassure him. "Yeah, man. More than okay."

His eyes stay glued to mine, curiosity and determination shining behind the bright green irises. His Adam's apple bobs in slow motion, as if it's taking concerted effort to work up the courage for what he's about to say.

"I've never done this before. Talk me through it, Leev. Teach me what you like."

Understanding and affection wash over me. The hesitation isn't because he's unsure about us. Lack of confidence is the issue here. I'm the first man he's ever been intimate with. Shit. That makes me feel like a fucking champion. I can help him out there, no problem.

Bringing my hand around to cup his jaw, I tilt it so I can look directly into his eyes.

"You're doing so fucking good for me," I praise, stroking his hair. "I love how tightly you jerk my cock. How fucking strong you feel, jacking me hard while sucking on the tip."

His eyes light up.

"Do it again, just like that, but try to take me deeper this time."

Nodding eagerly, he tightens his hold and brings his focus back to my dick.

I move both hands to his head to guide him. "That's it," I encourage. "Relax that gorgeous throat for me, G. Relax and let me in."

He takes me deeper this time, hollowing his cheeks and digging his short nails into my ass as he works to take my length.

The second I hit the back of his throat, he gags, his throat spasming around me. God dammit. I just about blow it right there. The sensation is exquisite.

"Fuck," he pants, popping off to catch his breath. "You're so big." A half-laugh escapes him.

There's no fighting my grin. "You've got this, G. You can take it."

The hint of amusement vanishes from his face, and his eyes darken, the color of a thick, overgrown forest.

He opens wide for me, this time tipping his head back and granting me even deeper access.

Groaning, I gently thrust into his mouth again and again.

With every plunging motion, he loosens up and takes me a little deeper.

"Fuck, G. You're doing so good for me. Keep going. Just like that."

Fuck any doubts he had about not knowing what he's doing. The guy's a fucking natural. He was made to suck my cock.

With a fist wrapped around the exposed length, Greedy jerks in tandem with the rhythm of his sucking, giving firm, intense tugs while lavishing me with his tongue. My vision narrows and tingles course through my legs with such force I have to brace my other hand against the wall to remain upright.

This beautiful fucking man is open so wide for me and jacking me hard, just how I like it.

Saliva smears along the side of his mouth as I fuck his face, and the visual of me marking him nearly sends me over the edge.

Spine tingling, I throw my head back. "Just like that, baby. You were made for me. You're doing so fucking good. Suck me harder and make me come."

When I look down again, I realize not only is he working me over like a champ with his mouth and one fist, but he's also tugging on his own hard, weeping cock.

That's it.

That's what does it.

The sight of my best friend, on his knees, attempting to deep-throat me while giving his first ever blowjob, so fucking turned on that he has to touch himself at the same time? That's what sends me over the edge.

My vision tunnels, and I lose it. I'm a beast finally out of his cage.

I fuck Greedy's face so hard I have to cradle the back of his skull to hold him in place.

He moans around me, encouraging me, taking his fucking pounding like a good boy.

"I'm close," I warn, though I'm fully intent on painting his throat with my cum.

Eyes full of tears and face red, he hums around my length and double-fists his own cock, wanking himself in time with my thrusts.

My insides are on fire, my abs tensing and every nerve in my core furling up in anticipation.

"Take it," I grunt, driving myself into his mouth a final time. "Take it and swallow every drop of me."

Intense, burning pleasure rips through me. Every limb. Every muscle. Every part of me ignites and pulsates, thrumming with the heat and fire Greedy cultivated with his hands and mouth.

He moans, his eyes rolling back. Then he groans and gasps as he comes in long jets without pulling off me.

I stroke his head with both hands, appreciation and admiration washing over me as my body comes down and I start to relax.

I needed that. He *knew* I needed that.

Slowly, he licks my softening length, as if savoring it, before finally releasing me.

With one hand still planted on the wall to steady my shaking legs, I hold the other out and help him to his feet.

"That was—"

Fuck. I don't have the words to describe just how satisfying and soul-aligning this moment of intimacy with my best friend was.

"Yeah," Greedy agrees. "Yeah it was."

Rising to full height, he angles in, his movements slow, as if he's still unsure. He pauses for a breath. Then another. Finally, he closes the gap between us and ghosts his lips over mine.

I return the kiss, tasting myself on his tongue. Instinctively, I wrap my arms around him and hold him close, relishing the way his heart hammers in time with mine.

His chest is slick and warm as he hugs me back.

"Is this okay?"

The question steals the air from my lungs. It's the same one I asked him last night when I reached out in the dark and wove our fingers together.

Nodding, I wet my lips. I'm more nervous than I've been in a long time. My chest is on fire from holding my breath in anticipation.

When he kisses me a second time, stars erupt behind my eyelids and the world tilts off its axis. The sensation of his tongue teasing mine and the more assured way he kisses me this time rocks my fucking world. His tongue dips out to tease mine, a soft caress, followed by a more intense, probing stroke.

I find myself leaning in, desperately craving more.

More of him.

More of us.

I can't believe this is happening.

I'm kissing Greedy—and he's kissing me back with just as much fervor.

I'm kissing my best friend.

I'm kissing my girlfriend's first love.

With that thought, the joy and excitement drain from me.

Fuck.

Daisy.

A choked sob escapes me as I pull back abruptly.

I haven't thought about Hunter once since I stepped into this shower stall.

What kind of boyfriend am I, getting sucked off and locking lips with someone else while my girl is out there waiting for me?

She could be hurt. Scared. Yet here I am, fooling around with Greedy. Shame percolates low in my belly, replacing all the lightness and joy that inhabited the space just moments ago.

"Get washed up," I say, exiting the shower and grabbing a thin, scratchy towel off the pile. I grab one for him, then think better of it.

I don't want to waste another minute waiting.

Dropping the towel back onto the stack, I toss my own to the floor. "I need to ask Kabir about that text. Meet you back in the room."

Without waiting for a reply, I tug my sweat-soaked shorts on, sans boxers, then unlock the door and leave.

Hunter.

My sole focus right now needs to be Hunter.

I walk back to the room with a renewed sense of purpose. We need to get on the road and get our girl. Greedy mentioned last night that the truck still needs gas, and knowing that Kabir wasn't satisfied with the beverage options this morning, we'll probably need to stop for food, too.

But I'd be lying to myself if I didn't admit that my heart is still pounding so hard I'm afraid it might beat right out of my chest.

The image of Greedy on his knees for me will be etched into my consciousness for the rest of my life.

My stomach plummets, and another wave of shame swamps me.

Fuck.

In my haste to get to Hunter, I left him in the shower. Ran off without explanation. Without even a backward glance. He deserves so much more than that. Especially considering that was a first for him.

I'll apologize as soon as he gets back to the room. He's probably worried that I have regrets. Dammit.

If anything, it was too much, but in the best way. Every sensation from the erotic to the sensual to the brief kiss we shared after we came was incredible. Fuck. Maybe it actually was too much. Otherwise I wouldn't have totally lost my sense of place and time. I forgot where we were, why we're here, and what we need to do.

I'm not upset with Greedy at all, I realize, as I insert the motel key into the keyhole. If anything, I'm frustrated with myself for allowing even one second of my energy and attention to deviate from Hunter.

My heart is beating double-time as I enter the room. The curtain is still drawn, and none of the lights are on; Kabir must be asleep.

Quietly, I pad to the bathroom so I can get ready without disturbing him. Hell, I could probably use another shower with the way I'm feeling now. A cold one, this time.

It isn't until I turn the handle and push that I notice the steam billowing out from under the bathroom door.

Heart lodged in my throat. I clench the handle, ready to silently shut it again. I'm hoping he hasn't noticed me when his words reach my ears.

"Are you well, champ?"

Fucking hell.

My eyes dart up to meet his. Instead, I'm met with the smooth, broad expanse of muscle and dark skin of his bare back.

A dingy white towel clings to his hips, riding precariously low.

I'm still staring at it when he turns to face me.

"Levi. I asked you a question."

His commandeering tone sends a shudder through me.

"Are you well?"

Slumping against the bathroom door, I close my eyes and breathe deep, trying to get my shit together.

"No," I croak.

When I open my eyes, I'm startled by his proximity.

He's inches from my face, the warmth of his body soaking into me. He cups my cheek, the gentle move encouraging me to exhale slowly. I didn't even realize I was holding my breath.

"You're not well. Noted." He turns my face slightly, as if inspecting me. "You are, however, freshly showered. Freshly fucked, as well?"

My stomach lurches at the callout.

"Freshly fucked, but not entirely satisfied, perhaps? Do you need more, champ?"

"What?" I gape. I don't need more. I've already taken things too far with Greedy, all while Hunter's waiting for us to get a move on.

"We—I—" I search for the words to articulate my concerns but come up comically short.

"Hunter," I finally force out. "We need to get going. We need to find Hunter."

His eyes soften. I've got a couple of inches on him, so he has to look up a little to catch my gaze. Despite the gentleness in his expression, his grip on my face tightens, reminding me of exactly who's in charge in this moment.

"Did you receive my update? Everything is in motion, but not yet in place. We need to wait just a bit longer, and then we'll be on our way. Now," he continues before I can interject or argue, "answer my question, champ. Do you need more?"

"What—what does that even mean?" I pant. I'm hot. Uncomfortably so. It must be the steam from the shower. Or Spence's body heat warming me with his proximity.

"Hunter always needs more. One orgasm isn't enough for her to truly let go," he explains.

Hunter.

The mention of our girl is the reminder I need.

"N-no," I stammer, taking a step back. "No, I'm good. We have to go. Hunter is—"

"Levi."

My name is a two-syllable command.

I snap my mouth shut and will my breathing to level out.

"You need to be honest with me if this is ever going to last. You just came. By way of Garrett, I presume?"

My cheeks heat with shame as a bead of sweat rolls down my spine.

I'm not embarrassed about what Greedy and I did. I'm ashamed that, even for one second, I let myself feel anything but sorrow and despair.

"You're angry." Spence examines me, his piercing blue-gray eyes reading every emotion I'm fighting like hell to hide from him.

He leans closer, bringing his mouth to my ear.

"I can be the outlet for that anger. I can take it. But I can also give you more if needed."

I close my eyes and turn my head, desperate to shut out the temptation his offer creates.

He nips at my earlobe, then runs his nose along my jaw. On a husky whisper, he murmurs, "How would you feel if I put you on your knees right here, right now?"

"*No.*" My answer escapes before I can even process it. It's an immediate, guttural reaction. I don't want to be dominated or degraded by Spence. Not now. Maybe not ever.

Experiencing that dynamic when Hunter's here, even dabbling in it, is sexy. I like bantering with him and following his instructions with her by my side. But without her, if it's just him and me, the lack of control is too sickeningly familiar. The power exchange is too distinct.

Even in a drunken stupor, my father was cunning and brutal. I shudder at the very thought of being at the mercy of another man.

"No," I repeat, calmer this time, but still just as sure. "I'll safe-word if you try it."

Spence stands up straight, looking me directly in the eyes. "Then I wouldn't dare."

I gulp past the trepidation threatening to rise up my esophagus and look right back at him, nodding my appreciation.

"Very well, then," he says, not the least bit upset by my rejection. "You don't want to be degraded, and I don't bottom. But I do believe I can still help. Although a plethora of options exist, one in particular comes to mind that I'm quite certain will meet both our needs nicely."

"Wha"—I clear my throat, confusion and curiosity getting the best of me—"What option is that?"

"May I?" Spence asks, teasing a long finger along the seam of my athletic shorts.

My whole body lights up from that one simple touch, my abs rippling and my heart rate picking up again.

Spence wants to help. We're not leaving this place until he says so, and that alone is enough to bring my agitation to the surface again.

I'm too in my feelings to resist his offer.

Too raw to try to pretend that I don't want him.

Eyes closed, I nod once more. I'm afraid if I speak, he'll mistake my painfully rigid reply for hesitation.

The sensation is the opposite of hesitation. I'm burning up on the inside, desperate to let go and accept what he's offering, shame and guilt and worry be damned.

He read me exactly right. I need more. I'm still reeling from the unknowns with Hunter and Greedy and all that's transpired over the last twenty-four hours.

A firm hand brushes over the outside of my shorts.

"There he is," Spence murmurs. I open my eyes to find him smirking at me. He grips my cock tighter, pulling a sharp gasp from me.

"I knew your refractory period was impressive," he praises. "You don't even know what I have in mind, yet you're already hardening. I love your enthusiasm, champ. Your zest for life. I want to make you feel so fucking good."

"What do you have in mind?" I rasp, pressing myself harder into the closed door at my back. Not because I want to get away, but to counteract the heady, lust-drunk feeling coursing through my limbs with something solid and tangible.

"I want to make us both feel good. Together. I want to seek mutual pleasure with you as my equal. With your permission, I'll reach into your short trousers, wrap my fist around your cock, then stretch my foreskin over the smooth glands that make up the head."

At the mental image his words conjure, I groan.

"Would you like that, champ?" he pushes. "Because I think I would like it very much."

I gulp, but I don't have the courage to answer. I've never done this before. I want it, I want him, and yet I'm trembling with nerves.

As if sensing exactly what's holding me back, Spence squeezes me gently, then ghosts his lips over my ear once more.

"You are worthy, Levi. I see you. I respect you. You need to see yourself that way as well in order for this to work. I'm at your mercy. I won't move another inch until you give me consent. Say yes for me, champ."

"Yes," I grit out, shoving down my shorts and exposing myself to him.

"Bloody hell." With one look at my angry, pulsing cock, he whips off his towel and lets it fall to the floor.

The breath leaves my lungs as Spence tugs on his length, then lines up the slit of his slick penis with mine.

"I'm already leaking for you. Look how intensely you affect me."

On contact, I moan, and my hips piston forward of their own volition, desperate for more.

"Easy," Spence advises. "Breathe for me, champ. You have to be still while I line us up."

I shakily nod and force oxygen into my system, unable to tear my attention away from the sight of our cocks nudging and bumping at the tips.

Spence hisses as he pulls on himself, gathering enough foreskin to cover his glands and encase me as well. "Fuck. You're stretching me so beautifully, champ. Look at the way we fit together."

Look? I don't think I could blink if I tried.

His dark, velvety foreskin is pulled taut over my aching cock. But he doesn't stop there. He keeps working it farther along my shaft, stretching himself to cover as much of me as possible.

"Last look," he teases.

That comment finally breaks my focus. Lifting my gaze to his face, I frown, confused.

"I have to hold us together to make this work." With one large hand, he encircles the place we're joined.

My knees threaten to buckle as he adjusts his tight grip over the heads of our dicks.

"Ready?" he asks, his voice the shaky one this time.

I search his face, drink in the way his pupils are blown out and his gaze is focused on the union of our cocks.

"Ready," I tell him confidently. "Make me feel good, Spence."

He gives a tentative stroke. Warmth surrounds my length, then exquisite tightness leaves me lightheaded when he pulls away.

"Fuck," he hisses as I grit out a "fuck yeah."

It's the most sensitive, stimulating sensation: wet and wanton, intimate, and deeply deprived. Our cocks kiss and stroke each other in a beautiful dance, guided by the grip of Spence's hand. Every pulse of his head spurs me on. Every nudge of my tip against his inspires a physical reply that leaves me weak in the knees.

We are joined. We are equals. When one of us moves, we both benefit. When one of us takes, we both gain.

On the next stroke, Spence slams his free hand against the door near my head. His chest heaves with exertion, and a moan rumbles from deep within him before escaping as a roar. His upper body trembles as if he can't hold himself upright and jack us off at the same time.

"Whoa. Easy." I wrap one arm around his back, supporting some of his weight.

Wild eyes lift and search my face, so full of need. He's just as engrossed in this moment as I am.

"I've got you." I lean in until my lips brush against his.

It's our first kiss.

The sweetest, simplest gesture, offered in reassurance and paired with the most erotic, intoxicating sexual experience of my life.

Pulling back, he mindlessly brings his fingertips to his lips. "Thank you," he murmurs. On a long exhale, he angles in farther, letting me support more of his weight. With his forehead pressed into the top of my shoulder, he ruts against me and resumes his mission, jerking our cocks in unison.

"Bloody hell, champ. I didn't expect it to feel like this."

That makes two of us. The fire he sparked inside me erupts, warming my core as flames lick up my spine.

"I'm going to jerk us hard and fast now. Are you ready for me?"

"So ready," I pant, balling my free hand into a fist as I cling to his low back and hold on like my life depends on it.

Without hesitation, Spence pulls on our lengths in quick, rapid succession. Every tug feels incredible enough to send me into the abyss, but the blaze he's stoking inside me just keeps building as our cocks fuse together from the friction.

"I'm close," Spence grunts into my ear.

Thank fuck. My control is practically nonexistent.

"Get ready, champ. First, our cum will seep into the sanctuary I've made for us. Then I'll release my hand, and we'll stay united as we glide together in our combined release."

Spurred on by his exquisite, detailed dirty talk, hot flames of arousal shoot up my legs and spasm low in my core. "Fuck. Coming." The words have barely passed my lips before the first wave of pleasure rips through me.

"Me, too. Come with me, champ. Come with me as my equal."

He releases us, as promised, then wraps his arms around my neck and lets me hold him. We stand like that together, panting, reveling in the unexpected intensity of the experience we just shared.

Together. As equals.

Chapter 13

Levi

NOW

One last stop, Kabir assured us.

One last stop, and then we can take her home.

Greedy pulls over at a gas station ten miles out from where we suspect Hunter to be. According to Kabir, there's not much between here and our destination. He also warned that we may have to wait a bit once we arrive at the facility.

Nothing is fast or easy about any of this, apparently.

But we're almost there. We're almost fucking there.

With a huff, I unbuckle and slide out of the passenger seat. Kabir steps out of the back seat and sidles up next to me. Unsurprisingly, he's dressed in a three-piece suit and expensive-looking shoes. The aviator sunglasses perched on the bridge of his chiseled nose complete the look.

"Right. I assume we're responsible for refueling the vehicle ourselves? What's the difference between the green pump and the black pump?" He points between the gasoline and the diesel.

Greedy comes around the bumper to join us as Kabir steps up to the pump.

"I suppose we want the green one, for less environmental impact?"

"*No*," Greedy and I yell in unison, shooting horrified looks at Kabir before turning to each other.

"We got it," I insist, reaching for the proper pump.

Greedy stands beside me so we're shoulder to shoulder and swipes his card, effectively shooing Kabir from the area.

"Right. I'll see what sort of nourishment I can find inside the"—he surveys the sign above the station—"Quickie Deluxe Mart and Deli." With a shake of his head, he pulls a face. "Who the hell is in charge of naming these things?"

With that, he saunters into the mart.

Greedy leans back, letting the cab hold his weight. With his arms crossed over his chest and one leg crossed in front of the other, he tips his chin my way.

"Wouldn't want to end up with diesel in the combustion chamber, huh, Leev?"

I try to hide my smile—but dammit. Nostalgia and the depth of our shared history sweep over me like a horse collar tackle I never saw coming. We've been through so much together, Greedy and I. He's seen me at my lowest, and he's stood by me at my worst.

I shouldn't be surprised by the recent turn of events. He's always been one of the most important people in my life. Even during the years we barely spoke. Emotion clogs my throat momentarily before I clear it, desperate to make a joke and bring a little levity to this situation.

"Leave it to the British Invasion to not know how to pump his own gas."

Chuckling, Greedy rights himself and glances over his shoulder, back to the convenience store. His gaze lingers there for a few seconds.

In that span of time, I miss his attention something fierce. A tightness settles in my chest once more, this time motivated by longing laced with jealousy.

"I've got this," I assure him, lifting my chin. "If you want to go check on him—"

He closes the space between us in two strides, then confidently hooks one arm around my shoulders.

"He's not the one I'm worried about." The words are soft, just for me.

I stiffen in response. Judging by how he lingers, he isn't the least bit thrown off by the intimacy of the gesture. Isn't he scared? Confused? Why isn't he demanding we talk about what happened in that locker room?

As if sensing my spiraling concerns, he wraps his other arm around my waist, then plants his chin on my shoulder. "We're okay," he whispers, his breath on my neck as warm and soothing as his touch. "Whatever we are, and whatever we're going to be, we'll it figure out. Right now, we're okay."

Through the sleeve of my T-shirt, I feel Greedy kiss my shoulder. I squeeze the pump as hard as I can to distract myself from overreacting to the gesture. To keep myself from spinning him around, pinning him against the truck, and kissing him for real, right here, out in the open.

I nod silently to acknowledge him, then let my eyes fall shut and inhale deeply to calm my nerves. Greedy's familiar scent, leather and sweet vanilla, infiltrates my senses. The pungent smell of gasoline joins the mix, too, snapping me back to the moment.

"I'm going to grab something to eat, too. Can I get you anything?" Greedy shifts back, putting an arm's length between us.

I miss the heat and solidness of him immediately.

"How about a slushie?" I suggest, my voice cracking from the unsteadiness I've been navigating for hours.

When I lift my gaze to his, he gives me that cocksure grin that hits me like a punch to the gut. His eyes light up like it's the best damn idea we've had all day. Which isn't true. Because that blowjob was actually his finest moment. And I'm the one who had to go and ruin it all by freaking out and running off.

"G. wait." I grasp his hand, using it as an anchor to pull him back to me.

"Thanks. For earlier. It was—" I dip my head and focus on our joined hands, rubbing my thumb in small circles over his knuckles while I dig deep for the courage to spit the words out. "It was amazing. So fucking good."

When I peek up at him, he's watching me, gnawing on his bottom lip.

"You don't have to thank me, Leev. I wanted it, too."

He wanted it, too.

Those words almost bowl me over. What the fuck do I say to that? How the hell am I supposed to react when my best friend shares a confession so simple, yet laced with the power and potential to change everything?

Though has anything really changed? We've been friends for years. He only ever had eyes for Hunter, and I respect the hell out of his commitment, even if it was shockingly intense for a kid fresh out of high school.

Greedy is next-level attractive. He's also generous and kind and loyal. I've never allowed myself to consider him as anything more than my best friend. His heart belonged to Hunter, even after she was gone. Yet he's standing here telling me he wants me.

When I allow myself to think of him in that way? There's no doubt in my mind. I want him. I've never given myself permission to want him before these last few days. Now that I've had a taste? There's no way I can deny him or myself any longer.

Not only am I attracted to him and connected to him in a way I've so rarely experienced with anyone, but I want to care for him, grow with him, support him and be by his side for all the ups and downs life will surely throw our way.

Because I can see it. A future.

"I mean it," I tell him, squeezing his hand. "So. Fucking. Good."

A small smile turns up the corners of his mouth. "Thanks, man. Appreciate it. When you took off like that—"

"That was stupid." I lower my head and give it a hard shake. "I shouldn't have taken off. I got in my own head about Hunter. I was worried about her, and honestly feeling guilty that we were..." I trail off, not ready to voice the complexity of my shame and concern. "Doesn't matter. We'll have her back in a matter of minutes, right?"

Greedy raises his eyebrows, but he doesn't argue with me. Kabir warned us that today's recon mission could take several hours. Even so, I prefer to remain delightfully delusional about the whole thing.

"Strawberry slushie," G confirms with a nod. "Anything else?"

I shake my head. There's no way I can stomach anything else until we have her back and I know she's okay.

Greedy takes a few steps back and gives me a once-over, green eyes full of warmth. It feels fucking good to be noticed like that—to be so seen.

I watch him too, and when he makes eye contact, I hold it, forcing him to be the one to finally break it when he has to turn around.

When he emerges a few minutes later, Spence is at his side, harping on the contents of the cups in Greedy's hands.

"I don't understand why anyone would put something that color into their body. How would one even describe that? Highlighter pink? That cannot be natural—"

With a grin, Greedy holds up the tall slushie cups and says, "Watch out, Leev. Spence is jonesing to try one. If you're not careful, he might steal your slushie right out from under you."

"I most certainly *will not*. And I'm not 'jonesing' for anything," Spence argues, looking down his nose at Greedy. "Except perhaps a proper cup of tea and visual confirmation that Hunter is truly well."

His dramatic declaration is all the reminder I need.

Blowing out a long breath, I replace the pump and turn to Greedy, who's holding my cup out to me. I reach for it, my warm hand connecting with his ice-cold one. For a moment, we linger like that, watching one another, his somber expression matching the way I feel.

That implication—that she may not be well—has eaten at me since we discovered her missing. Now that we're so close, my anxiety is tenfold. I just want her back. We all need to lay eyes on her, and to make sure she's okay.

"She loves these," I murmur, finally taking my drink from Greedy and ripping open the straw with my teeth.

"She does," Greedy laughs under his breath. "Want to know a secret?"

I nod, and he grins.

"I never liked strawberry-flavored anything until that summer. But I love the way it tastes on her." Then, wistfully, Greedy adds, "We'll stop and get her one on the way home, okay?"

Fucking hell.

It's bad enough I miss her so much my chest physically aches. That ache becomes a sharp pain when I have to witness Greedy and Spence each reeling without her, too.

I flip the fuel door closed, more determined than ever. "Let's go get our girl."

Chapter 14

Hunter

NOW

"Isn't it neat? How fast it spins? And voilà!" The nurse holds out two tubes as if they're cute little bunnies she just pulled out of a magic hat. "Perfectly separated platelet-rich plasma."

My mother claps and squees with excitement.

Not for the first time this hour, I think I'm going to be sick.

It doesn't help that I was woozy before I had my blood drawn.

I haven't slept at all. Haven't eaten much of anything, either.

Stomach churning, I fight back the bile scorching my esophagus and rub at the cotton wad and bandage wrapped around my elbow. The small vial she's holding contains a lot less blood than if felt like she took from me.

I've been here for two days—I think—and it's all I can do to keep my wits about me and piece together any and all clues that'll help me determine where I am and how I can get the hell out of here.

I've lost hours. Chunks of time. I don't remember how I got here. I don't know how long we're staying. I don't even remember what I'm missing—pieces of me, people and places I know I should long for but can't quite recall.

Home?

I try to recall an image of home.

Wisps of places I once loved dance around the periphery of my mind, just out of reach.

I remember what home feels like. I remember who feels like home.

I just don't remember coming here, or much of what's happened since we've arrived.

Apparently, we're "glamping" in the private villa of some new-age woodsy med spa. My mother has the staff convinced we're enjoying a mother-daughter bonding weekend. I have yet to discern whether these people are in on the bit or just really, really stupid. It's possible, I suppose, that they can't fathom a reality where a mom, what? Kidnaps her adult child and brings her to a spa? Conceptually, it's preposterous. Yet I'm intimately familiar with the audacity of Magnolia St. Clair.

It doesn't help that she does all the talking every time a service technician or hospitality host ventures in. Originally I thought I could befriend one of them. Make nice, then ask to borrow a phone to make a quick call. Frustratingly, it seems like we never see the same person twice. This place must have a significant number of people on staff. There's always someone new introducing themselves when they bring meals or show up to perform a service.

This afternoon's service? My mother is about to receive a "vampire facial" in which the blood they just took out of me will be injected into her face.

It's the newest craze.

The hottest trend in the med spa world.

And, in an unsurprising move, it's uncommon for one person's blood to be used for another person's facial. It was my mother's idea. Since we have the same blood type—and likely because she's paying a lot for these people to do whatever she wants—the staff has agreed. Buzzwords like "cutting-edge" and "total rejuvenation" keep being thrown around.

All I can do is try my best not to throw up.

I close my eyes and rest my head against the taut natural fiber canvas that makes up the side wall of the tent.

Perhaps while my mom's getting her treatment, I could close my eyes and take a break.

I'm so tired.

So very, very tired.

My head has ached for so long that I don't remember what it feels like when it isn't throbbing.

I peek one eye open, trying to keep my wits about me as she settles in for her treatment.

My mom is sitting on a pop-up massage and facial table in the middle of the room, and the technician is holding a mirror in front of her. They're chatting animatedly about the procedure and how lucky I am to have her genes.

My nose tickles with the threat of tears as they blather on.

Yes, how *very lucky* am I.

How lucky am I to have a mother who drugged me and guided me out of the comfort of my own bed.

How lucky am I to have been born to a woman willing to stop at absolutely nothing to get what she wants.

How lucky am I to have a mind that's working overtime to put up mental walls against the trauma of the last forty-eight hours.

How lucky am I.

How lucky am I.

How lucky am I.

Chapter 15

Kabir

NOW

I glare at the square mail application on my phone, willing the notification we need to come through.

The vehicle is shut off. The boys are ready. Beyond ready, honestly. By all measures, it should be a quiet moment: the calm before the storm. Yet the incessant bouncing of Levi's leg provides an annoying rhythm whilst also shifting the stationary vehicle ever so slightly.

Turning fully in the passenger seat, I reach back and grip his thigh. I dig my fingers roughly while offering him a sympathetic but pointed look.

"Levi."

That's enough to halt his movements.

"We're here," I say. "It's all working out. Just—what do you Americans say? Chill fucking out?"

Garrett snorts. "It's chill the fuck out."

I hit him with an unamused glare, then focus on the man in the back seat again.

"We're close. I swear this is going to work, and then we can—"

"Why aren't we in there already, then?" Levi yanks himself from my hold, scrubbing both hands down his face. "What are we waiting for? Let's fucking *go*."

Mercifully, my phone dings, the sound piercing in the now silent cab.

A quick glance confirms the final piece is in place. "We were waiting for this." Quickly, I open the message and scan the contents. Finding it satisfactory, I close out of the email and navigate to the phone app.

"Now?" Levi lurches forward.

"One more call," I promise, tapping on the correct contact icon, then on the Speaker button.

"Is she there?" the voice on the other end of the line asks by way of greeting.

"Hello to you, too, Crusade."

"Jo wants an update," a second voice says. "I can see your current location, but I assume the paperwork just came through?"

Clever man.

"Correct," I reply to Kylian Walsh, bypassing Crusade's question completely. "It's all in order. I'm calling to confirm that the press is on standby, should we need to deploy that option."

"Megan's up to speed and ready to run with the story, if needed," Crusade confirms. "Two of the paps we keep in our pocket are on a chopper now, headed your way. There ETA is—"

"Seventeen minutes," Kylian Walsh supplies.

"Very good. Although I'm fairly confident it won't come to that."

Though I work to remain levelheaded, my appreciation for the well-developed and fully supported backup plan provided by Walsh and Crusade can't be measured. They're a dynamic duo, those two. Together, they've got enough intelligence, money, and influence to put a plan in place in half the time I could have done it on my own here in the States.

"Jo wants you to have Hunter call as soon as you have her." Walsh repeats his earlier sentiment.

I pull a face, but don't outwardly object to his request. "Noted."

Looking to Garrett, then back at Levi, I'm met with questioning glances, but steely resolve. They've waited long enough. It's time to go get our girl.

"Got to go. Thank you both for all your support and contributions to this effort, especially given the circumstances."

"You don't have to thank us. We're happy to help. Kylian especially." Crusade laughs. His words are lighter, his tone playful.

Kylian scoffs. "You're the one who dragged us to this godforsaken island."

"Wait, are you still on your honeymoon?" Garrett frowns at the phone.

"We are," Decker confirms. "Kyl's just salty because there's too much sand."

"No," Walsh bites out. "There's not *too much* sand. The entire land mass we're inhabiting consists of sand. Only. Sand. It's inescapable. Unavoidable. It's fucking everywhere. The moment I step out of the bungalow—"

"Right. We'll be in touch." I tap the End button, cutting off their bickering in the process.

"What the hell?" Levi's leg is once again bouncing with rhythmic precision. "Why do we need paparazzi flown in on a helicopter?"

"It won't come to that," I assure him, stashing my devices and adjusting my sleeves.

"So what's the plan?" Garrett asks.

I flit my gaze to the man in the driver's seat. He's just as tense as Levi based on the way his jaw ticks and he keeps mindlessly scratching at the back of his head.

Evenly, I tell him, "I can sit here and explain it to you, or we can go in and get our girl."

Garrett blinks, gives me his back, then pushes open his door.

Levi follows suit.

I exit the vehicle, dust my front, adjust my lapels, and button my jacket.

It's colder here than I expected—the mild temperatures of North Carolina replaced with the biting chill of upstate winter air. New York feels an awful lot like London, despite being on the other side of the ocean.

Clouds cast shadows around the gravel parking lot, but I leave my aviators in place. Best to look the part.

"Come along, boys. Time to check in on my latest investment." I lead the way to the door to the Welcome Center and hold it open so Garrett and Levi can pass through first.

New-age music plays from speakers hidden around the reception area. Scents of lavender and sage waft through the space. Everything is cream and white and professionally decorated.

Side by side, Levi and Greedy stop in front of a white marble desk and turn to me for direction.

I bite back the smile threatening to take over. Then, without pausing, I walk around the back of the desk and assume command of the computer station.

A young man who had previously been seated quickly rushes to my side. "Sir. Excuse me, sir."

Turning, I scan him from head to toe and back up. White scrubs. Clean-cut appearance. And a nametag that reads *Troy*. Very well, then.

"Hello, Troy. Please pull up the client manifest and all of today's appointments."

When he gawks, wide-eyed, I wave one hand at the computer. "Now."

"I'm sorry, sir, I'm going to have to ask—"

"What are you doing?" Garrett hisses, clutching the edge of the marble counter between us with so much force his knuckles are white. "You can't just walk in like you own the place."

A low chuckle rumbles out of me. If the situation wasn't so dire, I'd quite like to drag out this moment and enjoy a bit of fun. But as it stands, there's one goal to this entire charade. One purpose: one person.

"Au contraire, Garrett." I eye both boys, then an exasperated Troy, chin lifted. "I do, in fact, own this place."

Levi and Greedy gape, mouths ajar and eyes wide, and beside me, Troy sputters. But I don't let him get a word in before I dive into a condensed explanation.

"As of one p.m. local time, Spencer Enterprises acquired ownership of Empire Forest Retreats LLC. I own this facility, as well as the land it sits on. I also own the parent company, and, in a strange but necessary twist"—keeping a straight face here is a challenge, but I manage—"I am now part owner of the South Carolina Cougars professional football team, as well as the lead investor in a Formula 1 start-up set to replace Mulligans Racing next year."

Two more employees outfitted in white emerged from the back somewhere during my introductory speech. I'll leave it to Troy to catch them up to speed. For now, I square my shoulders with his and stare him down.

"Show me today's appointments. Now."

Side-eyeing me, Troy gingerly leans across the front of the workstation I'm partially blocking to pull up the client manifest for the day.

It only takes a moment for me to locate the full-day block for "M.F. and Guest."

"Here." I tap a knuckle to the screen. "These two. Where are they?"

Troy's eyes dart from the screen to me and back again, but he doesn't speak.

"Might I remind you that as the sole owner of this establishment, I hold all the cards. Additionally, I have reason to believe the alleged 'guest' noted on this reservation is being held against her will. Kidnapping. Human trafficking. An entire myriad of possibilities exists. Failure to comply with my request will result in charges against every staff member who has been on the premises in the last twenty-four hours. So, I'll ask again, Troy. But I'll only ask once more. Where are they?"

One of the boys emits a low whistle.

I have to bite the inside of my cheek to hold back a smirk.

Troy clears his throat and swallows audibly. "That reservation is a mother and daughter duo, sir. I assure you, no one is being held against their will. They're out in the Namaste Bungalow, which is only accessible by cart."

"Bring them both here. Now."

"But sir, they're scheduled for back-to-back treatments all day. We don't want to—"

I hold up a hand, cutting him off. Clearly, Troy hasn't grasped the concept of being under new management. Looking beyond the contrary young man, I tip my chin to the two employees who are watching us with wide eyes.

"Bring them here, right now, or you're all fired. That will be just the start. I can assure you, your employment status will not protect you from the media on standby, ready to break this story."

"What story is that?" a woman with a dark complexion, thin braids, and flawless skin asks. She crosses her arms in front of her, clearly prepared to stand her ground. Her name tag reads *Naomi* and indicates that she's a nurse practitioner.

"The story about the predatory, experimental, often unsanctioned treatments being performed here at Empire Forest Retreat and Spa without the proper medical staff in place. According to the New York State Medical Board, any facility administering ketamine therapy must have a licensed psychiatrist and an MD on staff. Let me ask you, Naomi; is a good doctor available to chat with me?"

Silence lances through the room.

Lowering my voice, I take a single step closer to the woman. "Are you the most senior medical staff at the facility right now, Naomi?"

Her eyes widen with realization, her chest rising and falling in quick breaths.

"As the senior-most member of the staff, that means you're in charge. It's not just your job you should be concerned with. It sounds like your medical credentials may be on the line."

Rather than respond, Naomi storms over to Troy. "Send the cart. Get them up here now," she hisses.

With a nod, Troy pulls a radio from his pocket, then gives the order.

Before the person he's directing can confirm, I hold up one finger, garnering everyone's attention.

"You have twenty minutes." With that, I turn on my heel before anyone objects.

Chapter 16

Kabir

NOW

Levi's leg is once again jiggling out of control. I don't bother trying to soothe him this time. The frantic rhythm of his movements matches that of the kinetic anxiety coursing through me.

I won't rest until she's with us. My lungs won't properly inflate or fully deflate until I have her back in my arms.

Mercifully, my twenty-minute time limit was taken seriously.

I sense her before I see her.

Sucking in a steadying breath, I look to the boys and nod once. Then I rise to my feet and wait. One minute. Then two.

There's a kerfuffle outside the welcome area. As the noises get louder, I prepare myself to storm out there. Before I can, though, the door swings open.

Magnolia storms in first, but I pay her no mind.

It's the woman behind her—the shell of a human with her head down, whose every movement is stilted—that captures my attention.

What I see is the exact opposite of how one should look after more than a full day at the spa. She's haggard. Ill. Pale and hollow, without any of the ferocity and spirit that lives inside my firecracker.

"The fuck?" Levi growls, lurching to his feet. "Who did that to her?"

I cuff his neck and give him a silent look of warning to ensure he won't do anything stupid before I turn back to Hunter.

There's a bandage wrapped around her elbow. The slightest hint of bruising is just visible along the border of the cloth. Was she injured? Has she been physically harmed by Magnolia or someone on staff?

"Hunter."

She freezes, and her head snaps up—instinctively, but also defensively.

The emptiness in her eyes causes a piercing pain in chest. She holds my gaze, her brow furrowed slightly. As if she's trying to figure out where she is, who I am, and what's going on.

She's looking at me, but she doesn't see me. She's standing right there, and yet she's a million miles away.

"What is the meaning of this? To be interrupted in the middle of a service, no less."

Hunter flinches at the sound of her mother's voice. Magnolia is so focused on sorting out the apparent interruption of her treatment that she hasn't even noticed the three of us hovering in the seating area.

With her hands balled into fists, Magnolia marches over to the desk and drones on, raging against the hosts who have been made powerless by my hand.

Hunter just stands there. Staring. Searching.

She's looking at me like she has absolutely no idea who I am.

"Hunter..." I hedge, keeping my tone soft.

Levi attempts to lunge for her, but I tighten my grip, keeping him in place. This time, his desperation having clearly reached a boiling point, he shrugs off my hold, shoots me a surly glare, and takes a step forward.

I'm not about to come to blows with him, but my gods, is he dense. Hooking one finger through the belt loop of his denim trousers, I halt him once more.

"Give her a moment," I plead.

Something's not right. Something's not registering. I can see it—or the lack of it—in her eyes. She's not with us. Not really.

The tension rolling off Levi is thick enough to slice with a knife. He could easily break away from my hold, but he grants me the power to tread lightly.

"Tem…"

At the sound of Garrett's voice, it's as if an electric current zaps through her body and jolts her back to life. Hunter's head snaps over, and when her gaze locks with his, a heartbreaking, hollow cry fills the room.

Then she's rushing toward him with her arms outstretched. She slumps against Garrett, letting him take her weight, sobbing. As he holds her tight and whispers to her, relief floods my mind. A wave of bitterness shoots through me, too. But relief dominates. Relief. Relief. Relief. We have her. She's okay. We have her back.

"Daisy?" The nickname is a hoarse cry, choked out with the same kind of desperation still plaguing me.

When Hunter doesn't acknowledge him, Levi stiffens.

I keep a grip on his hip—firm, but reassuring. "She's okay," I murmur low, hoping to soothe the agitation that radiates from him more violently with each breath. "He's got her," I assure him, tipping my chin toward Garrett.

I stand tall, addressing the room, including the staff and Magnolia, who's red in the face as she argues with the concierge, growing more irate by the second.

"Effective immediately, Empire Forest Retreat and Spa is closed. Employees found to be in good standing and not morally corrupt—" I pause for dramatic effect, regarding Troy, Naomi, and the other woman, the concierge, according to her name badge.

Troy gets the hint. Clearing his throat, he crosses his arms over his chest, then he subtly distances himself from the others.

"—will receive severance and reassignment assistance."

"When did you three get here?" Magnolia demands, finally noticing our presence.

Her ability to go this long without realizing we were in the room only confirms every awful, self-centered, narcissistic truth I've come to learn about Magnolia St. Clair-Ferguson.

I look at Hunter's mother, really look, and really let her see me.

This isn't a game. Even if it was, she's in no position to win. Her hold on my woman stops now. Either she lets this go, or I'll tear Hunter from her grasp one perfectly manicured finger at a time.

I stride across the room, plant my feet so we're inches apart, and glare down at the awful excuse of a human I'd love to be rid of once and for all.

"We've been tracking you since the moment you coerced Hunter out of her bed and *relocated* her to this facility."

Magnolia gapes, her mouth opening and closing like she's searching for an argument. Slowly, methodically, I press two knuckles to the underside of her chin, closing her mouth for her.

"You're done. You're done here, and you're done with Hunter. This is over, Magnolia."

Her bottom lip trembles, but the rest of her face remains frozen, emotionless. When tears begin to well in her eyes, I know I've fucking got her.

Yet she doesn't know when to give up.

"You can't announce this facility is closed. You're not even *from here*," she hisses, looking from me to the staff behind the desk, then finally over to where Garrett is still clutching Hunter to his chest.

Her expression flickers, but she looks away quickly.

It's on-brand for Magnolia. She's never taken a genuine interest in her daughter. She's never truly cared about anyone but herself.

Tsking, I draw her attention back to me. Standing to my full height, I assess her up and down and say my final piece.

"I'm Kabir Spencer. I'm from everywhere. I own everything. If I don't own it, I can make that happen, as proven by my recent acquisition of this facility. Do not question my power, my abilities, or my devotion."

A glance at Hunter confirms she still has her face tucked into Garrett's side. It's for the best. At least for now.

"You're done," I warn Magnolia once more, menace lacing my tone. "If you know what's good for you, if you care at all about your daughter or your own well-being and longevity, you'll heed this warning. Any attempts to contact Hunter from this moment forward will be viewed as a direct threat to what I love most in this world."

"That's *my* daughter. You can't tell me—"

"*Was*. She was your daughter."

I inspect my fingernails, noting for the first time a smear of blood coating two knuckles. I whip out a handkerchief and make quick work of ridding myself of the bodily fluids. If I'm going to have Magnolia's blood on my hands, it will be intentional, and a lot more productive than this encounter.

"Clear out all the remaining guests and perform all the closing duties as assigned," I tell Troy over my shoulder. "My people will be in touch."

Chapter 17

Levi

NOW

We couldn't get away from that place fast enough. Somehow, I'm the one behind the wheel now, despite the rage simmering just below the surface.

Someone—multiple people, in fact—hurt Hunter.

They hurt Hunter so fucking badly that the woman buckled into the back seat only remotely resembles her.

Honestly, I shouldn't be driving, but Spence is busy taking care of business related to his, well, new businesses, I guess, and Greedy is comforting our girl.

One glance in the rearview mirror is all I can manage before I have to direct all my focus squarely on the road.

Her entire body is turned into his, her head burrowing into his shoulder. He's got both arms around her, holding her and soothing her in a way I physically ache to but can't.

I've never felt like this while witnessing the two of them together. They were each other's firsts. I know they love each other, just like I know that whatever she's going through isn't permanent.

Yet I can't keep my teeth from grinding or my grip on the steering wheel from getting tighter with each mile that races by.

I want to be back there. I want to be in the thick of it, holding and comforting them both.

After a thorough assessment, Greedy determined Hunter did not require immediate medical attention. Kabir was satisfied with Greedy's evaluation but claimed he had several emails to send.

It made sense that I drive.

But I really fucking hate being stuck behind the wheel.

"Wait," Greedy says through a yawn. There's no urgency to his tone, and yet I still find myself easing off the gas. "We never called Decker."

Hunter shoots up like a shot. "Do Joey and her guys know what's going on?"

The question grates on my already frayed nerves.

"They're aware." Kabir turns in his seat to hand Hunter his phone. "Here, love. Call this number. It should connect to Kylian Walsh."

"Why do you have Kylian's number?"

"We needed his help," Kabir offers by way of explanation. "He's quite clever, that one. I like how his brain works."

Greedy snorts. "You would."

I accelerate, frustrated as all get-out that they're all like we're on a casual road trip back to North Carolina.

"Hunter!" A feminine voice fills the otherwise silent car. "What the hell? What happened? Are you okay? We've been so worried!" Joey's words come out fast and frantic.

An uncomfortable laugh stutters out of Hunter. "Girl, you're supposed to be on your honeymoon. I don't know whether to be flattered or concerned that you've got time to think about me."

There it is.

There's the fucking rub.

Hunter remembers Joey. She remembers Joey's partners. Hell, she even remembers that Joey is supposed to be on a tropical island, enjoying her honeymoon.

But she doesn't fucking remember me.

I stomp on the brake harder than necessary as I approach a toll booth.

"Easy." Kabir braces himself against the dash. In my periphery, he's staring me down, but I do my damn best to ignore him. "Let's pull off at the next rest area. I could drive for a stretch."

My head shakes of its own volition, my whole being adamantly opposed to the idea of giving up the last shred of control I have in this situation.

I don't want to switch. I don't want to be in a position where I'm not occupied with getting us safely home. If I'm available and she still doesn't remember me or need me? Then the rejection will hurt that much worse.

Before I can verbally object, Spence rubs my thigh firmly. "No worries, champ. It was a shit idea, anyway. I'd probably have us careening down the wrong side of the highway."

I let out a silent sigh of relief.

Spence squeezes my leg once more, lighter this time, then leaves me be.

The girls chatter on, and then another voice joins their conversation.

"Decker has an idea," Joey announces through the phone. "Are we on speaker?"

"You are," Greedy confirms.

"Hey, Hunter," Decker says, his voice deep and serious. "I'm glad you're okay. Listen, we won't be home for another five days. And I can only assume you don't want to go back to Dr. Ferguson's house. Am I right?"

Fucking hell.

My gut twists into a painful knot. I hadn't even thought about that. Which is especially ridiculous, because I'm the one transporting the group to North Carolina.

Decker's right. There's no way we can go back to the Ferguson residence. Kabir's warning was direct and to the point, but Magnolia is unpredictable. If she also returns to South Chapel, there's no way any of us could stand to cohabitate with her.

"I think I can safely speak for all of us when I say we most definitely do not want to go back to the Ferguson residence," Kabir replies.

"Why don't you stay at our place? At least until you regroup and figure out what's next."

We're all silent for a breath, then another, as we take in Decker's offer, eyes pinging from one person to another around the cab of the truck.

"I assume the accommodations are adequate?" Kabir asks.

Greedy snorts, and Hunter assures Kabir that the Crusade mansion is, in fact, more than adequate.

Decker rattles off a few more instructions about the marina and getting to the isle. And just like that, we have a destination in mind.

Once the girls have said their goodbyes, Kabir hands the device back to Greedy and asks him to put in the proper coordinates.

"Starting route to Exit 27, North Marina, Lake Chapel, North Carolina."

Chapter 18

Kabir

NOW

I turn halfway round in my seat, craning my neck until I lock eyes with Garrett. "Is she asleep?"

With a silent nod, he combs his fingers through her hair. His face is illuminated every few seconds as we pass streetlamps positioned over the downtown district of Lake Chapel, North Carolina.

He mouths a silent "thank you," my way, sincerity shining in his dark green eyes each time the light catches on the iris.

I offer a tight smile and a nod. I appreciate the sentiment. Truly. Though he may not be thanking me in a few moments.

"There's something I need to tell you both, and I'd like to do it now, whilst Hunter is asleep, so we can discuss next steps."

Levi sucks in a sharp inhale, and the tension in the vehicle skyrockets.

I'm not aiming for dramatic effect, so I cut to the chase. Still half turned in my seat, I look from Garrett to Levi once before I try to explain.

"The night before she was taken, Hunter mentioned someone to me. Another man. Someone she met in Italy."

The air crackles, thick with apprehension. I'm used to high-pressure, stressful situations, but even this is a bit much for me.

Clearing my throat, I carry on. "I thought perhaps he knew her whereabouts. Or that he could be involved, somehow."

Garrett lays a protective arm over Hunter. Whether he's conscious of it or not, we're all still carrying a heavy load of anxiety from the last few days.

"Obviously, we know now that the charade was all Magnolia."

"Why are you telling us this?" Levi demands, his tone sharp.

Clearly, my attempt to soften the blow isn't going all that well.

It's now or never. I just have to admit to what I've put in motion.

"Because that other man is on his way here now."

"What, like to America?" Greedy whispers.

"To Lake Chapel."

"Fuck it all to fucking hell." Levi smashes a fist into the steering wheel, blasting the car horn in the process.

He's practically levitating above his seat, his anger and frustration a living, breathing beast among us.

"You're serious?" he demands when neither Garrett nor I react to his outburst. "You're really fucking serious right now?"

Though a heavy weight settles in my chest, I keep my posture straight. "I am."

"What the fuck is wrong with you?" he whisper-yells.

"Shh," Garrett reminds him from the back seat, though Hunter, miraculously, hasn't stirred.

"I thought he might have information that could help us."

"And you're just mentioning him to us now?" Levi counters.

I flop back in my seat and unbutton the top two buttons of my Oxford. "I didn't intend to keep it from you. Nor did I find the information relevant once we had a solid lead on Hunter's whereabouts."

"Why is he coming here, then?" Garrett asks.

Sighing, I confess, "I had to tell him enough to pull the truth out of him. Unfortunately, he was unnerved. This afternoon, I let him know we had her back. But he informed me he was already on his way to the States, waiting on his layover out of Heathrow."

Silence ensues. I typically prefer silence, but not when I know there's more to be said.

"So what now?" Garrett asks.

I have to hand it to him. He can be exceptionally reasonable when he wants to be. His composure under pressure is admirable.

"That's what we have to figure out. Why I'm bringing it up now."

Levi scoffs. "So *now* we get a say in the matter?"

His attitude grates on my nerves. If I weren't so attuned to his emotional anguish, I would consider some sort of punishment to absolve the Brat Mode that's been activated inside him.

With a sigh, I garner all the patience I have left. "As I already stated, I did not intend for the situation to escalate to this point. It's clear the man cares about her."

Levi shoots daggers at me. "This guy's a stranger."

"To her he's not."

"What's his name?" Garrett interjects.

"Sione," I supply. "Sione Tusitala. According to my research, he studies alternative medicine and has been accepted to four chiropractic colleges. His mother is Romanian. His father, Tongan. He has four younger sisters, and he's originally from Utah, which I wasn't aware was a real place until I looked it up on a map. He's spent the last few years working at his grandparents' villas near Lake Como." Clearing my throat, I add in the one detail I always suspected but have only recently confirmed. "He and Hunter were together in Italy for even longer than she was with me."

The truck is engulfed in silence as Levi takes the exit, drives down a gravel road, and eventually comes to park at a lakeside lot with a sign overhead that reads *North Marina*.

He puts the vehicle in park, unbuckles his safety belt, and turns to face us. "Look. The last thing Hunter needs is someone else showing up and adding to her confusion."

"Hey," Garrett says softly, putting a hand over Levi's where he's bracing it on the center console.

The blond man pulls away, clearly rejecting the advance.

With a small frown, Garrett sits back. "She just needs time, Leev. A good night's sleep. A few days' rest."

Levi scoffs. "You're only saying that because she remembers you. What she *needs*—"

"Enough."

Both men fall silent at my command.

"I don't believe any one of us is in a position to dictate what Hunter needs. That's why I shared this information. For consensus. We're all doing the best we can, and we all have the same goal in mind. We have to come to terms with the reality of the situation. A man will be arriving in Lake Chapel in the next day or two. Under no circumstances do I intend to keep him from seeing Hunter. I can put him up at a hotel nearby. We can delay their reunion, if that's what we decide, but I will not allow myself or either of you to interfere."

"Fuck," Garrett mumbles. "Have him come here. To the isle. To her." He glances down at the girl still curled up in his arms, sound asleep. "She deserves all the support and love she can get right now."

Levi storms out of the car and slams the door shut before I can ask whether he agrees.

Chapter 19

Hunter

THEN: SUMMER, YEAR ONE
OVULATION PHASE

Smooth pebbles shift underfoot as I make my way to the edge of the water. Villa Viola guests—and by extension, employees—have privileges at several lidos and clubs around Lake Como.

Although there are plenty of sandy beaches, I prefer the rockier options, like here along the shoreline that stretches along Lido Di Luminosa.

The rocky beaches are reminiscent of those surrounding Lake Chapel. So it makes sense that this is where I feel most at home. Where I go when I need to forget.

I've been in Italy for nearly four months, but I've yet to find a remedy to soothe the ache that flares to life in my chest twice each month.

Tears well in my eyes and heat scorches me from the inside as I try to calm my breathing and cool my nerves.

This feeling will pass.

This is PMDD. Nothing more.

I know these things, and I'm fighting against the darkness that threatens me at regular intervals. I take the minipill and an SSRI religiously, and I still attend bi-monthly telehealth appointments with one of the counselors I met in London. Even so, the same feelings creep in twice a month, each month.

It's like clockwork.

Like painful, emotional, anxiety-laced clockwork.

I swipe a tear off my cheek. It's no use. Instantly, more tears fall without my permission. With an angry huff, I scrub at my eyes with the back of my hand.

Though I have no reason to be sad—no new reason, at least—I can't stop the emotions whirling through me. It's as though my brain is conspiring against me, searching the recesses of my mind and conjuring up every sad, stressful, heartbreaking mistake I've made over the last few years.

A spark of self-loathing ignites inside me every time I ovulate. A painful reminder of what happened. Of the person I used to be. The man I used to love. What we lost. How I ran.

Despite my best efforts, that spark will continue to smolder over the next few weeks and eventually grow into an inferno of rioting emotions.

My body and mind are gripped with tension between ovulation and menstruation. I become more irritable. Apathetic, too. Especially right before my period begins.

My emotions and anxiety tighten around me like a vise, squeezing until I can't help but wonder if I'll ever feel "normal" again.

Joke's on me, it seems. The answer is yes, because this is my normal now.

Mercifully, menstruation is like an emotional cleanse.

The physical symptoms wreak havoc on my body. My low back aches. My upper thighs tense up and cramp unexpectedly. A fogginess that can't be cleared by sleep or rest settles over me.

I welcome it all with open arms.

Because once the physical symptoms hit and I start to bleed, hope returns.

Once I feel the contractions of my low belly, the signal that my uterus is shedding its lining, I know relief is on the way.

This is the worst of it: my darkest night of the month, when I bloat and I'm cranky and I hate everything. When nothing soothes me.

Ironically, it's also the brightest night of the month, at least this time around.

As I stand barefoot on the water's edge, I lift my face and take in the glow of the full moon.

"Hunter?"

Startled by the sound of my name, I yelp.

With my hand on my chest, I turn away from the lake. Away from the moon.

Sione stands about ten yards away. He's barefoot, like me, and wearing an obscenely small pair of fitted athletic shorts—yoga shorts, he calls them—with a tight sleeveless tank that clings to his chest and puts a whole lot of muscle and ink on display.

Breathing deeply, I will my pulse to steady out and my eyes to refrain from ogling him.

"You scared the shit out of me," I pant.

He tilts his head, his brows pulling together in concern, taking me in.

"Why are you crying? What's wrong?"

Leave it to Sione to bypass all the niceties, stumble upon my secret pity party, and not even give me the grace of pretending that I'm not visibly upset.

"I'm fine." It's a lie, but I follow it with a partial truth in hopes that he'll believe me and let it go. "Just not feeling my best. I came out here for a bit of privacy." I add that last part as a hint that he should leave me in peace.

He watches, waiting for me to go on.

My stomach flips as I assess him in return. I don't want to open up to Sione. We've become friendly, and that's close enough. I want to keep this job—keep up appearances. Allowing him to see me grappling with the extreme low I'm dealing with today could put my employment in jeopardy. Or worse: it could make him pity me.

A full minute passes before he speaks.

"Right. Okay. We don't have to talk about it. How did you find my secret spot anyway?" He comes closer and squats, swinging his drawstring bag off his shoulder.

"Your secret spot?"

This is *my* spot. This particular beach is far enough away from the Villa Viola property that I don't have to worry about bumping into guests who might recognize me.

Turns out, the guests aren't the problem.

"I come down here at least twice a month," I defend. I find solace in the cool water lapping the pebbled beaches. A reprieve I crave when the PMDD symptoms get louder and I feel as if I could burn alive from the inside.

When the darkness is close to taking over, I stand at the edge of the lake and let the water lap at my feet.

I let it soothe me, and I let myself remember. The more I think of the men I've left behind, the hotter the memories burn and the ache in my chest blossoms into a beast all her own, the easier it becomes to convince myself I'm better off. To remind myself that they're all better off without me.

The water helps me keep my cool.

"You must not have come at the full moon before," he says plainly.

Face lifted to the inky black sky peppered with infinite stars again, I drink it all in. Despite the size and grandeur of the night sky, none of the stars visible tonight hold a chance against the splendor of the full moon.

"No," I relent. He's right. "The moon has never been here when I've come to this spot."

He freezes, still in a deep squat that makes my inner thighs burn just to observe. "The moon is always here." The confidence emanating from him contrasts sharply with his typically easy-going nature. "It's with us now, and it'll be out there still in two weeks. Even on the darkest night. Even when you can't see it. It's with us always. That, you can count on."

Emotion burns behind my eyes and nose. I understand what he's saying on a conceptual level. I know how moon cycles work. But his tone brooks no argument. His words are a simple promise. An assurance that though tides ebb and flow and the view of the moon changes each night, it's always there.

The melancholy weighing heavily on me quickly morphs into anger.

How can he be so sure of something he can't even see?

Heat creeps up my neck and into my cheeks. The emotional heaviness in my chest tugs hard against my rib cage like a corset pulled just as my lungs have fully deflated.

I don't want him here. Not when I'm feeling volatile and sad, angry and unhinged.

I don't want Sione to see me like this. I don't want him—anyone—to know me on my bad days. Truth be told, I wish *I* didn't know me on days like this. It's not fair to ask others to tolerate me when I can't even tolerate myself.

If he can sense my displeasure with his presence, he doesn't show it. He busies himself emptying the contents of the bag, taking out the small items one by one and arranging them among the rocks.

Annoyance flashes through me, and I let out a derisive huff. "Did you bring rocks to a pebbled beach?"

Gaze lifted, he swipes a long strand of jet-black hair behind one ear. "These are crystals," he states, his tone calm, his words direct. "I come here every full moon to charge them."

There it is. The shakeup that breaks through my intrusive thoughts and reminds me that this world consists of so much more than me and this night and my irritation.

I may be wound up, anxious, desperate to peel my skin off my body and leave it on the shore to cleanse, then come back in the morning and start anew.

But this isn't my spot.

Not *just* my spot.

What are the chances that Sione and I share the same secret place?

I take a tentative step toward him. "What do you mean charge them?" A few feet from where he's crouched, I stop and survey the crystals. "Like a cell phone?"

He homes in on me, his eyes dancing with playfulness. He looks so much like his Mamaia in this moment: mischievous and soulful, earnestly focused on me. "Exactly. They get better reception when they're fully charged."

I know he's teasing. But now I'm intrigued.

Curiosity races through me, momentarily dulling the pain that's plagued me for hours. "What do you do with them once they're charged?"

"I don't do anything with them; they just are. As am I. I focus on them when I meditate. I hold them when my worries feel too big for my body." My heart clenches, and my throat tightens. With a hand at my throat, I whisper, "What kind of worries?"

His hand freezes over a shiny white stone, carved into an elongated pyramid. His brows pull together, his gaze intensely serious as he meets my gaze.

"All kinds. Big worries. Small worries. Fleeting thoughts. Murmurs that grow louder and more persistent when I close my eyes at night."

"I have those sometimes, too," I confess, my knees suddenly wobbly.

Without asking if I can join him, I sit. Against the smooth but hard support of a million little rocks that make up this beach, I settle directly across from Sione and invite myself into his space.

"I think most of us do," he states.

He doesn't understand.

"Not like mine," I insist. "Mine are loud. Angry. Mean. They get worse during certain times of each month..." I trail off then. He doesn't want to hear about the intricacies of the hormonal imbalances caused by PMDD that plague me. "I do all I can to prepare. To silence them. But it never gets any easier," I confess.

Instead of placating me, Sione sits quietly. Absorbing my words. Allowing me space to work through my thoughts.

Eventually, once he's arranged the crystals to his liking, he rolls to sitting, crosses his legs, and presses his palms into the stones. His biceps and shoulders flex as he holds the position.

Without my permission, my eyes devour the sharp planes of his body illuminated by the moon. I don't ogle too long, though. Because on the next breath, Sione is pulling me out of my head and back to reality.

"Which one speaks to you?" He studies me, then lowers his focus to the crystals in front of him.

Mirroring his position, I lean forward, assessing the dozen or so rocks juxtaposed against the smooth, earthy pebbles of the beach.

"They're all pretty," I murmur, uncertainty whirling in my belly.

He shakes his head and tuts. "I asked which one speaks to you, Hunter. Look at them and listen. Or don't even look. Just let them speak."

With a shaky inhale, I do as I'm told. I survey one crystal after another, listening, pushing away all thoughts, taking each one in. Stones of all shapes and colors contrast against the dull gray, brown, and beige rocks of the pebble beach. They're stunning. All of them. So unique and special. No wonder Sione likes them.

"This one," I say, ghosting my fingertips over a hazy purple stone.

"Amethyst." He looks up at me, his eyes round and eager, as if this excites him as much as it delights me. "It's often used in healing, especially self-healing and inner work. That one is yours, once it's charged."

"How long does that take?" A thread of impatience works its way through me. It's ridiculous. Juvenile, really. But I'm itching to pick it up and hold it.

"At least a few hours. I plan to be out here for a while."

Sighing, I settle back, clasping my knees. "What do you do when you're waiting for the crystals to charge?" I've never seen Sione play on his phone or mindlessly scroll through apps. He's the most present, settled person I've ever met.

"Sometimes I meditate. Sometimes I nap. In the summer, I swim to cool off."

I cock a brow. "In the dark?"

"It's never dark on a full moon," he corrects. "The temps have been brutal this summer, and no number of showers can compare with the way the lake cools me off."

It makes sense, I guess. I've taken two showers already today, and yet I'm sticky and cranky and overheated once more, even long after the sun has set.

"You could swim, you know. Skinny dip if you're feeling brave."

The suggestion shocks me. At first, I'm sure he's teasing, but one glance at his expression disproves that assumption.

"I used to skinny dip all the time in a quarry back home in North Carolina." I don't know what compels me to say that. It's not polite or professional. Thankfully, the modicum of modesty I still possess kicks in and I leave out the part about being accompanied by my boyfriend. And sometimes his best friend.

"There's no new water on this planet."

The subject change is as random as it is jarring. I scowl, thrown off. Every time I think I have Sione figured out, he says or does something to remind me of just how complex and avant-garde he really is. "Is that some sort of doomsday prophecy?"

"It is not," he states matter-of-factly. "It's the truth. Water holds memory. Water has wisdom. Water can take literally any form. Water can settle and soothe the way no other natural resource can. The quarry water of your past is the same water before us now. There's no new water on this planet," he repeats. Then, softer, he says, "If stripping down in front of the moon and swimming in the lake might help, you owe it to yourself to try."

The sincerity of the suggestion shocks me to my core. I never would have considered it, especially out here on my own. I was lost, consumed, festering in my anxiety and despair. I haven't tried anything new to ease the symptoms of PMDD in months.

I consider the suggestion for a moment, then another. The longer I think about it, the more I agree. It's worth the try. I'm worth trying for.

"What about you?" I say, the words scraping out of me more harshly than intended. I don't want to take away his opportunity to swim. I also don't know how I feel about undressing in such close proximity to him.

It's abundantly clear that Sione isn't attracted to me. But I enjoy his company, and he seems to enjoy mine. We seek each other out often, moving through our daily chores and activities together, even if they take longer that way.

I like him. A lot.

I'm intensely attracted to him.

But I've given all the hints I can. He's not attracted to me, full stop, and I have enough self-respect to know better than to throw myself at him.

We are friends and nothing more. And that's okay. I just feel... strange, I guess, undressing, swimming naked, putting myself in such a vulnerable position, while he's so close.

Gulping past the trepidation mounting inside me, I search his face.

Kind eyes meet mine. A stoic, assured nod confirms his consent. "I will sit here. Wait with the crystals. Turn my body and give you my back. This way, so you can be sure I am not looking, and I can be sure no one will catch us by surprise."

Oh. My heart thunders in my chest as I watch him, transfixed.

"Go, Mahina. Let the water help you. Let yourself accept the support you deserve."

Mahina.

It means moon.

He's called me that a few times before, but it's never felt quite like this.

He turns as promised, so with a nod to myself, I stand and undress. Tears stream down my cheeks as I fold my clothes and leave them in a tidy pile on the shore. Sobs rack my body as I take the first step into the lake. The farther I move into the water, the more the pressure in my chest grows. I don't bother glancing back. Sione is a man of his word. I don't have to see him to know he's sitting patiently with his back to me, offering the privacy and serenity I need.

My feet shift and slip on the silty lake bottom, causing me to throw my arms out and gasp.

Steady once more, I move farther from the shore, letting the chill of the water cool my limbs and kiss every curve of my exposed skin.

By the time I'm submerged to my neck, the tears are flowing so freely, I feel nothing but wet, from my head to my toes.

No new water on this planet. No new tears inside me now or ever again.

Chapter 20

Hunter

NOW

I wake up in a disoriented haze and prop myself up on my elbows slowly to get my bearings. I'm on a boat. A boat that's knocking into the side of the dock hard enough that the impact ricochets through the cushioned seat and makes my whole body jolt.

"Shh, you're all right," a deep voice soothes.

It's a voice I recognize, but in a removed, distant kind of way.

It's a voice I should know, but it's one I can't quite place.

It takes another moment to realize I'm leaning against the source of the voice. Gingerly, I sit up and scoot a few inches away.

Once I'm no longer touching him, I lock eyes with the boy beside me.

My head knows who he is immediately.

Levi.

I'm with Levi.

He's one of my oldest friends. He's Greedy's best friend.

Greedy. My heart stumbles. "Where's Greedy?"

A flash of hurt crosses Levi's face. Sitting up straighter, he nods toward the dock. "He's helping Spence tie off the boat."

His words are clipped and cool, like he's upset, but I don't know why. I duck my head, trying to meet his gaze, but he won't look me in the eye.

I search his profile, willing him to turn back my way. Instead, he focuses on his feet, his hands steepled and his forehead resting on them.

"I hate boats," he says quietly.

Instinctively, I run my hand along his cheek, the need to soothe him innate. He closes his eyes, and with a long breath out, he sinks into my hold. There's a desperation churning inside him, and it emanates from him as if it's a silent plea.

I don't know what he's asking. I don't know what I'm missing.

After another breath, it all feels like too much. I pull away and clasp my hands in my lap.

Finally, Levi meets my gaze. His denim-blue eyes are filled with anguish. They're accusing in their hardness, like this is all my fault.

Defeat and shame wash over me. "I'm sorry."

He's hurting. *I'm* hurting him.

I shift over again, putting a bit more space between us.

Based on Levi's response to the move, it's the wrong thing to do.

With a frustrated growl, he rises to his feet and stalks to the other side of the boat. It's only a few feet, but it's as far as he can get from me. It might as well be miles for the crater of loneliness that's growing between us.

I watch, helpless. Despite how badly I long to, I can't console him. Not when I'm the source of his pain.

For a moment, I consider faking it. Calling out to him. Telling him it's all coming back to me.

I've never lied to him before, though. Or at least, I don't think I have. I hate the idea of upsetting him like this, I hate the idea of being disingenuous even more.

As I rack my brain for what could have happened between us to cause such a rift since I came back to town, another thought hits me.

Levi is here. In North Carolina.

"Levi."

His head snaps up, and he meets my gaze.

"Why aren't you at school?"

His terse expression only hardens, morphing into something fiercely troubled. He stares at me for a breath. Then another.

Pain rolls off him in waves, his frustration so palpable I can feel it from the tip of my head to the soles of my feet. Rather than smooth things over, it's obvious I've just made things worse.

Finally, Greedy appears by Levi's side, skirting past him and coming to stand in front of me. "Let's get you inside, Tem. You need rest."

I do. But Levi is struggling more than I am right now. Though apparently I can't give him what he needs. So, defeated, I sigh and sit up straighter.

Greedy offers me both his hands, which I grasp and use to pull myself up. The boat sways slightly as we exit.

Kabir holds out one hand to help me step onto the dock, and when we touch, an intense energy rises between us. Tentatively, I meet Spence's eyes and am met with patience. Compassion. Understanding. This expression is the antithesis of the one Levi fixed on me.

Without another word, Levi brushes past us and storms up the dock toward the Crusade mansion.

As I watch him go, I wrap my arms around my front and shiver. It's brisk, the breeze off the lake damp and cold.

I don't realize I'm frozen in place until Kabir gently tugs on my arm. "Give him time, love. A bit of space. He'll be all right."

As I find my footing, Greedy rests a hand on my low back, guiding me along the rocky beach.

If space is what Levi needs, he's about to get that in spades. The mansion looming ahead of us is absolutely massive. The Crusades have more than enough space for all of us.

Spence emits a low whistle once we've entered the house and reset the security system.

"Right. I believe this qualifies as adequate accommodations. Well done, Kylian Walsh."

Greedy squeezes my hand, the two of us in on the joke. Technically this is Decker's house, but it's entertaining to let Spence think Kylian is the mastermind around here.

"There's a gym," I tell him. Lights turn on automatically as we move from the great room to the kitchen. "A theater room. I think there's even a hot tub."

"You hear that, champ?" Spence calls to Levi across the kitchen. "They've got a hot tub."

The statement is infused with innuendo that only seems to piss off Levi more.

Greedy sighs, clearly tuned in to Levi's frustration.

Shrugging—my mind is still far too muddled to work through what the issue is, so I may as well move on from it for now—I rest my forearms on the quartz countertop of the kitchen island.

"Kendrick's mentioned it before. I've never been in it, though."

Dense silence settles in the air, yet another moment, another reaction I don't understand.

"What am I missing?" I eventually ask when the room remains silent.

"You remember this place?" Levi asks, his brows low and his voice tight.

I nod. "I do."

"Because Joey lives here?" he pushes.

"Yes. Joey lives here with Decker, Locke, Kendrick, and Kylian." My chest fills with pride at the ease with which the names come to me. I'm still myself. It's all still in there. I'm just... foggy right now.

Levi pushes off the massive kitchen island and grips the roots of his mop of blond hair.

"Come on, Leev," Greedy hedges. He looks from me to his best friend, then back again. "Give it a rest for tonight."

But Levi doesn't let up. Gripping the edge of the bar once more, he clenches his jaw, icy eyes narrowed on me. "So you remember all of them—"

"I've known them for years," I fire back, uneasy.

He pushes off the counter and explodes. "You've known *me* for years, Hunter. You've known Spence for years longer than you've known Joey." He paces toward the great room, only to pivot and storm back into the kitchen. "This is bullshit. Total fucking bullshit."

When he turns around on his second pass and gives us his back, I panic. Because as he storms away, I'm hit with the deeply seated fear that's lived inside me since my dad left me alone with my mother.

Everything I love leaves.

"Wait! Don't go."

I make it all of three steps around the island before Spence intercepts me. A moment later, Greedy hovers close behind me.

Overprotective assholes.

"Levi," I plead, desperate to get through to him.

Forlorn blue eyes reluctantly meet mine, then look away just as quickly. As if he can't stand to look at me. As if I'm the root cause of all his pain.

With an exasperated sigh, Levi crosses his arms over his chest. "I'm not leaving. But I can't stand here and pretend this isn't fucking killing me."

The last two words come out broken.

I'm hurting him, and I don't know how to stop.

"I'm sorry," I sob. "Levi, I'm sorry."

Head lowered and focus averted, he turns and heads for the great room again. "I'll take one of the second-floor bedrooms."

Greedy hugs me from behind, and I crumple into a heap of sorrow.

"I'm hurting him," I cry. "I don't *not* remember. I just—"

"It's all right, love," Spence coos. "Your well-being should be your only concern tonight. Though Garrett says you're okay, and I trust his medical assessment."

I nod. I trust Greedy, too. And like I said: I don't *not* remember Levi or Spence. There are just foggy spots in my mind, tarnished memories living below the surface of my consciousness.

I hate that my mother took me the way she did, lying to everyone—including herself—that we were enjoying a mother-daughter trip.

Even more, I hate what she took from Levi. From Spence. I hate what they've endured because of her. *Because of me.*

"We all need rest. We'll regroup once you're feeling up to it, then we'll go from there," Spence determines. His features are etched with resolve, but there's an underlying bit of sadness present in his face, too.

Seeing him mask his pain on my behalf hurts almost as much as Levi's outburst.

Spence is right, though. There's nothing more we can do tonight.

"I'll go up to Joey's room and see what I can find to change into," I tell the guys, though I don't move. I can't. It's as if my shoes have been superglued to the floor beneath my feet.

Because, I realize, I don't want to be alone. Not even for one second.

Decker's house is as secure as the Pentagon, I'm sure, and the isle itself means no one can access this place without a boat or swamp vehicle.

Still.

I shudder at the thought of Magnolia attempting to come here. Of her finding me. Of being taken against my will yet again.

As if reading my mind, Spence steps forward and places a tentative hand on my mid-back. "You're all right, love. You don't have to do any of this alone. I'll escort you upstairs. Wait while you gather some things. Would you prefer to sleep in the same room as Garrett tonight?"

A glance at Greedy confirms we're on the same page.

"Decker said we could use the primary," he offers gently.

Nodding, I reach out and squeeze Greedy's hand. I hate to be away from him, even for a few minutes. "I'll be right back down."

"After you," Spence says coolly, holding out an arm toward the central staircase.

Chapter 21

Kabir

NOW

Bloody hell.

This is torture. Pure personal torture.

I don't begrudge Levi for his big, bad attitude in the slightest. I wish I could rage and verbalize the dejection that plagues me as a result of Hunter's memory loss.

She doesn't remember me. She doesn't remember *us*. She hasn't said as much, but we can all feel it.

It's in the way she hesitates. In the way she flinches at the slightest touch. I'm not a stranger—she knows my name, and hints of familiarity dance behind her irises. But our intimacy is gone. She doesn't remember the connection, our dynamic.

What if she never remembers?

The reality of the situation is an unexpected sort of trauma I wouldn't wish on my greatest enemy.

Scratch that.

I would gleefully transfer this type of pain onto Magnolia St. Clair-Ferguson.

I wouldn't, however, wish this on any other nemesis, rival, or casual acquaintance. It hurts. It bloody aches. Nothing about this feels right.

Regardless, I won't give up. I'll give her space, and I'll give as much support as I can muster for the one man she does seem to be intimately acquainted with in her mind.

Garrett joined me in the upstairs hallway a few minutes ago. Though he said his intent was to check on Levi, I assume he feels the need to check on her as well.

"Let's discuss how tonight will go." I brace my hands on the open doorframe across the hall from the room Hunter is currently occupying.

Garrett leans casually against the opposite wall. To his credit, he doesn't gloat or taunt me with the advantageous position he's found himself in. Instead, he crosses his arms over his chest and nods. "Sure. What are you thinking?"

"I'll stay up here on this side of the house and keep an eye on Levi. You"—I meet his gaze, willing him to feel the sincerity of what I'm requesting—"take care of her. Comfort her. Shower her. Wash her hair thoroughly. Leave the conditioner in for at least two minutes before rinsing."

"Is that necessary?" he probes. "She's exhausted. We're all exhausted..."

As if I'm unaware.

She deserves to feel clean. Cared for. Nurtured and looked after. I can't do it, dammit, and now I'm getting pushback from the one person who can?

Still braced against the doorframe, I press harder, holding myself back from launching at him and getting right up in his face. "It *is* necessary. We don't know what she's been through. What she's endured. Just because she remembers you, Garrett, does not mean she is well."

He raises both brows in challenge, the look causing my blood pressure to spike far beyond what's healthy.

"For fuck's sake." I slam my palms against the molding around the door. "Do as I say, Garrett, or I swear to gods—"

"Okay, okay." He holds up his hands. "I've got this. I can handle it."

With a harsh breath in, I will my anger to dissipate. It won't do any good if I lose my shit right now. Levi's already cornered that market.

I push off the doorframe, resigned to leave him to wait for Hunter. "I'll be close by. Just text. Or holler, if you must. I can be available at any time if you need backup."

"Thanks, man." He straightens and crosses the hall, arms outstretched. I don't read his intent immediately, but after an awkward few seconds, I realize he's offering me a hug.

Reluctantly, I wrap my arms around him, surprised by the aggressive *thump* he delivers to the center of my back.

Goddamn American boys and their machoism.

On the next breath, he pulls me closer and squeezes.

"Spence." My name is a whisper, a quiet invitation to a truth I'm not entitled to yet am desperate to hear. Staring right into my eyes, he says, "It's going to be okay. *She* is going to be okay. She didn't experience any sort of blunt impact or physical trauma to the head. She's cloudy, but she's there. The memory loss won't last forever."

"You don't know that," I argue like a petulant child.

Despite my obstinance, what I want more than anything is for him to repeat that sentiment. To reassure me. To promise me, even if it's not his promise to give, that the woman I love isn't destined to fade away just as we were reconnecting.

Garrett takes a step back but keeps hold of my shoulder and gives it a squeeze. "I do. I know how deeply she cares for you. How much she respects you. Loves you. Our girl's a fighter. She won't let any of it fade away."

I swallow down the overwhelming lump of emotion suddenly clogging my throat.

Our girl's a fighter.

That she is.

She won't let any of it fade away.

Gods, I hope he's right.

I let his reassurance hang between us for another breath. Then I nod, straighten, and break the spell of hope he's cast over me.

Getting back to business, I point one finger at the closed door. "Make sure she cleans her teeth for a full two minutes. And remove her earrings if she doesn't do it herself before bed."

With a mock salute, he replies, "Yes, sir," then hits me with that cocksure smile.

"Good night, Garrett." With all the willpower I possess, I force myself to walk away.

Chapter 22

Greedy

NOW

After what feels like a lifetime, the door I've been staring at swings open and the girl of my dreams steps through it.

She looks so much better: freshly showered, her skin clean and glowing. Her eyes are brighter somehow, too.

Working to steady my breathing, I rub at the tightness coiling in my chest. It's futile, though, to temper this response to her. After all these years, a single look at her still gets me all hot and needy. Every time. In every situation.

"Look what I found," Hunter singsongs, stepping into the hallway and pulling the door closed behind her.

When I finally get my wits about me, I scan her from head to toe, and I'm just about blown over by what I see.

Fuck. Me.

She's wearing a teal jersey, the oversized garment emblazoned with a white *2* across her chest. On her, the hem of the shirt rests mid-thigh. Her tan legs are bare, and the jersey is loose and flowy except for where it stretches over her hips and accentuates her curves. I've never seen anything more erotic in my life.

She's not just wearing teal; she's wearing South Chapel Sharks teal.

She's not just wearing any South Chapel Sharks jersey; she's wearing number 2.

She's wearing *my* jersey.

"Spin for me," I husk out. "Let me see the back."

She obeys, doing a half turn while she sweeps her hair to one side, revealing *Ferguson* scrawled across her shoulder blades. Her ass cheeks peek out from beneath the hem of the jersey when she lifts her arms to hold up her hair. Her *bare* ass cheeks.

I can't help but reach out. Touch her. Confirm this is real. Reverently, I smooth my palm over the 2. Then I take my time tracing each letter of my name where it's proudly displayed on her back. Finally, I use that same finger to glide down the curve of her spine. The smoothness of the path confirms what I'm desperate to know.

Nothing beneath. Nothing between us but my jersey.

"You're killin' me, Tem." Groaning, I pull my hand back and run it through my hair, just to give myself something to do.

She spins around, her eyebrows knitted together in concern as she studies me. "Do you want me to change?"

"Hell no," I rush out. I want to commit every detail of this moment to memory. I want to take a goddamn picture. She looks so fucking good wearing my jersey. Nothing but my jersey.

"Get over here."

She's in my arms a moment later.

Running my hands down the length of her back, I breathe her in. I pause above the globes of her ass, and in response, she leans into me farther, squeezes around my neck tighter. With that silent cue, I continue my exploration. Cupping her cheeks, I lift her up, stalk forward, and pin her to the wall.

I hold her just like that and drink her in. In this moment, I swear my heart might beat out of my chest. My reaction to the sight of her, the proximity, is visceral and overwhelming.

My brain is working overtime to commit this moment to memory. Her body pressed against the wall as I support her weight. Her toned legs wrapped around mine, holding me just as tightly. The soft skin of her thighs and hips against my fingertips where I hold tight to her.

My cock is weeping with want. But it's my heart that aches the most.

This is all I've wanted for so long. This woman. Our connection restored.

"Do you know how crazy I feel right now? Seeing you in this jersey? Holding you in my arms?" I clear the emotion from my throat, then bury my face in her neck. "I want you to wear this all night."

I take in a deep inhale but am surprised when the scent assaults me.

"This doesn't smell like you." I press a kiss to the side of her neck, then gently set her back on her feet.

"It's Joey's."

I cough in surprise. "Any idea why your best friend has my jersey in her bedroom?"

Biting down on her plump bottom lip, Hunter leans back against the wall once more and extends her arms, inviting me in.

I situate myself between her legs and wrap both arms around her shoulders, soaking in the feel of her.

"I *do* know why," she finally says when we're wrapped up in each other once more. "Locke and Kendrick have a wicked sense of humor and like to regularly remind Decker of that time Joey wore your jersey to the shore week game. They gave this to Decker for Christmas. Joey wisely confiscated it and stashed it up here for safekeeping."

Heart in my throat, I search her face. Christmas was only a few days ago. "You remember all that?"

Surprise passes over her expression. "I do." She tilts her head back to meet my gaze, confusion and frustration swimming in her eyes. "Joey texted me all about it on Christmas. We laughed, and she even sent me a picture. I remember other things, too," she says. "I'm just missing a lot of details. I know who Levi is. I know Spence and I were involved. But the personal stuff, the stuff that matters, feels like it's just out of reach."

I rest my chin on top of her head, smoothing both hands back and forth along her back. "Spence thinks you were drugged."

"I was," she states matter-of-factly.

Shock ripples through me. The simplicity of her confession is gut-wrenching, but the way her face morphs as she comprehends her own words is what threatens to send me on a personal rampage against her mother.

"Shit. I was. I was drugged. I—I didn't remember until just now."

Tears well in her eyes, and her bottom lip trembles with emotion.

"She kept making me drink from a bottle. She forced me to take little sips, and each time, I'd fall asleep again. I couldn't shake it. Everything was sluggish. I couldn't wake up. I tried, Greedy." Her voice cracks on my name, and tears fall in rapid succession down her cheeks. "I swear, I tried."

I wrap her in a hug so suffocatingly tight I fear I'll hurt her. But I can't quell the pulsating anger that's taken over. It's like a living, breathing beast has been awakened in my chest. I couldn't tame him if I tried.

"Shh, you're okay, baby." I will her to feel all the love and comfort I'm mentally pouring into her as she sobs in my arms.

Her body heaves with emotion, trembling in my arms as she processes the memories coming back to her. I struggle to keep my shit together, but I do. I breathe deeply and use every ounce of energy I possess to whisper reassurances and hold my girl safely in my arms.

Once I'm sure I have a grip on my own emotions, I pull back and search her face. "Want me to go get the guys? You might feel better if we're all together."

If she remembers being drugged, I surmise it won't be long before other memories reemerge as well.

She snuggles closer, shaking her head against my chest. "Would it be okay if it was just you and me tonight?"

A surge of pride and protectiveness rises in me. "Of course." I kiss the top of her head, then step back and take her hand. "Let's go to bed, Tem."

I exude calmness as I guide her down the stairs.

In reality, I'm anything but calm.

Tonight, she wants only me. It won't last. Her memories will come back, like the one that hit her just now. She'll remember and embrace what she shares with Spence and with Levi.

But for tonight, it's just her and me. I'm going to savor it while I can.

Chapter 23

Greedy

NOW

Nostalgia swirls with the present moment, creating an all-consuming sweetness as I lie wide awake, holding my girl and watching her sleep.

For the three years she was gone, I'd wake in the night, disoriented and desperate to see her lying by my side. I never got used to the harsh reality of waking up and remembering she was no longer mine.

When she came back, I'd relish the monthly visits to my bed, despite her pain. I do my best to be a good person, but I can't deny that I was exultant once I recognized the pattern and became stingy with the limited time I spent with her. I craved her monthly retreat into herself because it was the only time she'd allow me to hold her. Even then, I'd cling to her until the sun would rise, knowing I had hours, then minutes, then only heartbeats, before she'd wake and leave me once more.

Holding her like this is reminiscent of these sacred hours. I'm exhausted, but I couldn't sleep if I tried. Not now. Not when I get her all to myself like this.

For the first time in a very long time, I know that when she wakes, she'll still want me. There will be no sneaking out. No pushing me away.

I brush a few loose hairs off her forehead and let the silky strands slip between my fingers, taking care not to wake her.

There's so much history between us. So much heartache and so much pain. But losing her this time—knowing it was against her will—has changed my outlook on everything.

Hunter's not who she was when we fell in love at eighteen. I see that now. I see that so clearly. She's endured. She figured out how to keep going when it would have been easier to give up.

Beyond her bubbly personality, sharp mind, and genuine kindness, and hidden underneath her natural playfulness and the vivacious spirit of the girl I fell in love with, is a survivor. She had to be tough, because it was the only way to survive. She had to be cold, because it was the only way to separate herself from Magnolia and the damage the woman leaves in her wake.

Hunter couldn't fight for me back then because she was fighting like hell to hang on to herself.

The girl I loved is gone. I accept that now.

The woman I'm holding tonight is a survivor, and she's perfect beyond all comprehension. Her poise. Grace. Resilience. Strength. She's never looked more beautiful.

Every month, she goes to battle, waging war on the hormones and intrusive thoughts that come with PMDD. Every month, she holds on during the dark moments and fights like hell to keep chasing the light.

I refuse to let her fight alone ever again.

Another thing I've come to learn? It's something I wouldn't have been able to accept before, but that I can and gladly will now, both for her sake and mine.

I'm not the only one she needs.

Tonight should have felt like a dream. I thought it would, actually, when we crawled into bed and cuddled up under the covers, just the two of us, before she fell asleep in my arms.

Tonight, I have her back, and I'm all she wants. It's what I've craved since the moment she moved back into my dad's house at the start of the fall semester.

Now? I'm man enough to admit it's not what I want. Not everything, at least. It's not all she deserves, either.

I'm enough on my own, but Hunter deserves it all.

I want her to have everything—and every person—who fills her cup and makes her feel whole. I want to remain open and be willing to explore whatever sort of future makes sense for us as a unit.

With a kiss to Hunter's head, I breathe her in, so fucking glad she's finally able to rest.

As I continue to relish this moment, I can't resist texting the guys. I don't want to gloat, and I especially don't want to hurt Levi more than he's already hurting, but we're in this together, and I want them to feel like they're still part of this in every way.

G: She's sleeping soundly.

Spence: Very good. Thanks for the update.

I hold my phone up and stare at the screen, willing Levi to respond so I'd know he's okay. When the screen goes dark, I drop the device and let it bounce on my stomach, defeated.

An instant later, though, it vibrates against my lower abdomen, startling me.

Leev: Thanks, G. I appreciate the update more than you know.

Another text comes through less than a minute later.

> **Leev:** I'm sorry for earlier. I was hurt and pissed off, but I shouldn't have lost my cool. This situation sucks, but it's no one's fault. I shouldn't have reacted that way.

Relief sweeps through me. Thank fuck. It feels good to know he isn't holding on to his anger. Honestly, I would have reacted the same way had I been in his situation. For what feels like the first time, though, the Universe was on my side.

> **G:** No need to apologize. It's been a really hard day for all of us.

> **Spence:** Speak for yourself. Had he not apologized of his own volition, I would have had to force it out of him.

I snicker, and when Hunter stirs, I hold my breath and tip the screen against my chest to block out the light. The device continues to vibrate in my hand as Levi and Spence banter. Once I'm sure she's still asleep, I hold the phone above me again to catch up.

> **Leev:** You wouldn't dare.

> **Spence:** Try me, champ.

> **Leev:** Don't tempt me, sir.

> **Spence:** Temptation will be the least of your concern if you choose to activate your own version of Brat Mode again.

I can't tell whether they're flirting or fighting. Maybe both. I feel compelled to interject.

> **G:** Chill, you two. She remembered some things from her time at Empire Forest. I think her memories will be fully restored sooner rather than later.

> **Leev:** Good to hear. But however long it takes, I'm not going anywhere.

> **Spence:** Nor am I.

I release a soft, satisfied sigh. It's been a hard fucking road to travel, but it feels like we're all finally on the same page.

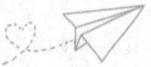

Chapter 24

Hunter

NOW

I wake with a start. Heat courses through my body, setting every nerve ablaze.

Sucking in a breath, I roll over. Instantly, I lock eyes with Greedy.

We don't speak. We just take each other in, our faces inches apart, our bodies a tangled mess of limbs and sensation, memories, and desire.

I lick my lips on instinct, my gaze drifting from his eyes to his mouth, and cup his face, encouraging him to bring his mouth down to mine.

"You need sleep," he says, his voice low and husky.

With a single shake of my head, I bring my lips close enough to touch his. "I need you."

With a low hum, he relents, letting his eyes drift closed.

The first kiss we share is tentative and tender. Slow and languid, unhurried and sensual. His tongue teases mine. I capture his bottom lip and suck on it, desperate to show him just how much I need him. I want to crawl into his body and take up residence in his chest. I want him to plunge inside me, reuniting us in the most physical and emotional ways.

We exchange slow, steady caresses as we reacquaint ourselves with every inch of one another in the sanctuary of this bed. We savor each other, taking time to explore and build up the fiery frenzy stoking deep in my core.

Greedy ignites a sensation inside me that I thought I'd have to give up completely once upon a time. His desire for me is heady and intoxicating, and it's made all the more sweet because of the history we share.

He wants me.

Despite who I am now, and how I've changed over the years, Greedy wants me still.

An urgency fills me at the thought. Fueling me. Taunting me. I can't kiss him hard enough. Fast enough. Long enough. Panting, I break away to kiss his stubbled jaw and suck on his throat. Our mouths fuse together in desperation. Our bodies gyrate and meld together under the sheets in a needy, frantic rhythm.

That's how I feel.

Desperate.

Needy.

Untethered from every excuse I've relied on since I returned to South Chapel.

Unable to function or think of anything but uniting with him, mind, body, and soul.

I've waited so long to love this man out loud.

I can't wait another second.

In a frenzy, I claw at his T-shirt. Shove down the athletic shorts slung low on his hips. When he's stripped down to his boxer briefs, I reach for my own top.

"Stop," he demands, circling my wrists.

I freeze, panting.

"This stays on," he tells me, smoothing the hem of his oversized jersey where it brushes against the tops of my thighs.

Big hands explore beneath the fabric. Then, rolling me to my back, Greedy mounts me, bracketing my head with his forearms and situating his lower body between my thighs.

I buck my hips, searching, writhing, pleading. "*Greedy.*"

With his solid form hovering above me, he nuzzles into my neck, kissing me so hungrily the fervor travels right to my clit.

"Need you," I pant, clawing at his boxer briefs until his cock springs free and there's nothing left between us.

With a groan, he lifts his head, and in tandem, we shift until the crown of his length lines up perfectly between my legs.

For several heartbeats, we stay like that, watching one another, breathing the same air, our bodies humming with desire and carnal need. Our souls stitching together, creating a beautiful tapestry of hope.

"Please," I murmur, craning up to kiss him once more. "Please, Greedy. I need you."

Bright green eyes sparkle with unshed tears as his gaze finds mine. "You have me, Tem. Always. I've been right here"—he bends low, kissing the fabric of the jersey over my heart—"this entire time."

I close my eyes, my breathing hitching in my chest.

Then, as I exhale, look up, and lock in on the first man I ever loved, he slides into me and begins to mend the sharp, jagged edges I had long accepted wouldn't ever heal.

Chapter 25

Hunter

NOW

I peek my eyes open, only to close them again quickly. The room is blindingly bright, which confirms what I suspected. There's too much light for it to still be morning. I've been asleep for a very long time.

With a yawn, I stretch my arms overhead and take my time coming back to the land of the living.

The next time I open my eyes, the last few days flood my mind.

Magnolia shushing me and keeping me loopy. Lying in the back seat of a car through the entirety of a long, bumpy ride, followed by being strapped into a golf cart for an even rougher ride.

The blood on my hands. The blood from my veins.

I shudder at the memories but force myself past those thoughts to brighter ones.

To Greedy. Levi. Spence.

They came for me. They saved me. And they got me out of there so quickly, I didn't have time to question how they located me or pulled any of it off.

"Hey, sleepyhead." Greedy's sitting up beside me, scrolling on his phone.

"Hi," I croak, scooting up the bed and climbing into his lap. "Where are the others?" I ask through another yawn.

His face pinches but quickly softens again. "They're here," he assures me. "They were just giving us space."

Why? Space and distance are the last things I want from my guys after everything we've been through.

More memories rush back.

Greedy tucking me into bed. Greedy holding me in his arms as I drifted off to sleep. Greedy telling me to leave his jersey on before he slid home and made love to me so passionately my belly flip-flops from the recollection alone.

"Thank you for taking care of me last night."

"Always, Tem. You don't have to thank me. I want to spend the rest of my life caring for you." He smooths his large, calloused hands over my legs and up my sides. "How are you feeling today?"

"Sore," I admit, stretching out my arms and legs to get a bit more movement in my joints. "My head hurts, too. Probably because I haven't taken my meds for a few days."

Greedy hums. "You took your SSRI yesterday, as soon as we found you. Spence made sure of it."

"I did?" I don't remember that.

"How... how long was I gone?"

Greedy releases a pained sigh. "Two days. From what we can tell, you left the cabin around five a.m. Maybe we could have gotten to you sooner, but we had to be smart about it. We couldn't just go in without a plan."

My heart lodges itself in my throat as emotion bleeds into every one of his words. "I'm so sorry you guys had to go through all that." With my arms around his bicep, I snuggle into his side. He doesn't need to assure me they did everything in their power to find me. I know that down to the very core of who I am.

"What else do you remember from your time with Magnolia?" Greedy hedges.

I give myself a few breaths to collect my thoughts, ignoring the discomfort gnawing at my stomach. "A lot of it is blurry. Like I watched it happen to someone else instead of experiencing it firsthand. The time closer to when you found me is clearer. One minute, they were drawing my blood—"

His body goes rigid beneath me. "Are you serious? *Why*?"

"My mother wanted a vampire facial, I think? It's where they draw blood, separate the platelets, then take the platelet-rich plasma and inject it into the skin. Although my mom wasn't having her own blood drawn for the procedure," I add flippantly.

Greedy gapes. "Wait. She was taking *your* blood to inject into *her* face?"

Nose wrinkled, I shrug. "Are you actually surprised?"

With a sigh, he pulls me tighter, as if holding me close can erase the hell I've been through. He kisses the top of my head. Then kisses my temple, too.

"I guess not," he finally admits, his tone full of defeat.

"One minute, the technician was drawing my blood and I was trying not to pass out, and the next, two staff members were coming into the tent and telling us we had to go immediately. That it couldn't wait. I don't know what you guys said or did to make them react like that, but it worked."

Greedy's jaw ticks, but for once, it's not in agitation. He looks like he's trying not to smile. "Spence bought the facility."

All the air is stolen from my lungs as I stare at him.

"That's why it took so long to get to you. He bought the whole place, and he had to make sure all the contracts and paperwork were in order before we barged in and started making demands."

God dammit. I fucking love that man. "Classic Kabir."

Greedy hums. "Sure is." Then he stiffens again. "Wait, you remember them? Spence and Levi?"

"Of course I remember them." What kind of question is that?

I peek up through my lashes and search Greedy's face. The pity in his eyes has me instantly on edge.

"You didn't remember them yesterday. Not really."

Oh.

Shit.

My stomach rolls with worry as I try to recall any encounters I've had with the other two men in my life over the past few days.

I saw them, spoke to them. I knew I was safe in their presence. But when I really focus on the time between leaving the facility and now, all I really remember is Greedy.

"Were they upset because of me?" I ask, heart squeezing.

"Spence was fine. Or he acted like he was. Barked orders at me about what to do and how to take care of you. By the way, if he asks, please tell him I made you 'wash your teeth' for two full minutes before bed."

I snicker and fight back a smile.

"Levi, on the other hand..."

My thoughts drift to my sweet, easy-going boyfriend. A memory nags at the back of my mind, but I can't pull it to the forefront. I know it has to do with Levi. Maybe his mom was involved, too?

"*Shit*. What day is it?"

"It's Tuesday, but it's still winter break. School doesn't start up for another week."

That's not what has me reeling.

"I missed Levi's meeting with his mom. It was supposed to be Sunday, after church. Oh god. He's going to lose his health insurance because of me."

"Hey, hey, hey." Greedy pulls me back into his arms, wrapping me in an enormous hug and holding me steady as my mind riots with panic and worry. "Relax, baby. We'll figure it out."

"How?" I demand. I've blown it. I promised Levi I'd go with him, and I let him down.

With his hands on my upper arms, he eases me back and ducks his head, forcing me to make eye contact. "Levi doesn't need to worry about insurance. My dad has been covering the cost of his rehab. Plus, I don't think it would be a hard sell to get Spence to step in if needed."

Of course it wouldn't. Not with Spence. Levi, on the other hand?

"He's not going to want to accept anything from anyone," I hedge.

"I know. We can talk some sense into him. I don't want him to have to depend on his mom for *anything*. The last thing we need is another mother meddling in our lives."

"Agreed."

We fall into silence, but the air in the room thickens with tension. Greedy is obviously stewing over something else. I can always tell when he's working up the courage to share a confession or admit a secret. I've developed this deeply seated sense of knowing over time, I suppose. So I wait him out, give him space to put into words what's on his mind.

"I need to tell you something," he eventually says.

Eyes locked with his, I nod, encouraging him to entrust me with whatever he needs to say.

"While you were gone, Levi and I..." He trails off, letting the charged silence linger between us.

Greedy and Levi—*together*? My heart trips over itself when the implication clicks.

"What did you two do?" I tease, grinning up at him.

"I, uh, well, we slept in bed together at a motel. Nothing really happened that night. But then, the next morning, after we worked out... I sucked him off in the shower," Greedy confesses.

Greedy was the giver?

Surprise and delight wash over me. Never would I have guessed that's what transpired. And damn, Levi is absolutely massive. What I wouldn't give to bear witness to them exploring each other in that way.

My grin only widens as I envision it. "Did you like it?"

Greedy considers me, his expression stoic, then nods. "I liked that it was Levi. That I could help him work through some of the stress weighing on him. It made me feel closer and more connected to him."

That's a much more insightful answer than I expected.

"Would you do it again?"

"For sure," he says without hesitation. Quickly, though, he backtracks. "Is that okay with you?"

Eager to reassure him, I reply just as quickly. "It's more than okay." I crawl into his lap, straddle his hips, and loop my arms around his neck in an effort to show him just how okay I am with his confessions. "I want us all to be together, whatever that looks like. Levi's my boyfriend. You're..."

Greedy cocks one brow, egging me on.

"What am I, Tem?"

"Well, you're *not* my brother..."

"No," he laughs. "I'm most certainly not."

I rest my forehead against his and for a moment I just breathe. Then, cupping his face, I look him in the eye and share my truth. "You're my sanctuary. My anchor. My first love. My first everything."

He grips the back of my neck and brings me to him for the sweetest, most sincere kiss. Before it builds to anything more, I pull back. I'm inspired to make sure he knows the depth of my love for him and the sorrow I still carry.

"I'm sorry I didn't trust in us before," I whisper against his lips. I caused so much pain, my actions motivated entirely by fear.

Greedy shakes his head. "Don't be sorry. I didn't get it before. Now I do. Now that I see how she is, how she acts, what she's capable of? Your mother fucking kidnapped you, Tem. She drugged you, kept you sedated. For what? So she could take your blood and inject your platelets into her skin?"

I shudder at the reminder. Sadly, I don't think Magnolia's scheme was that simple. "I assume her primary goal was to have my blood tested for the partial transplant."

Greedy sits ramrod straight, jerking up so quickly he almost dislodges me from his lap. "Are you serious?"

I shrug, both defeated and embarrassed by my mother's actions. "They took multiple vials of blood. Knowing Magnolia, I can't help but suspect that the whole point of whisking me away to a med spa in the woods was to get my blood. The facials and whatever other services she had lined up were a front. Or maybe a secondary benefit."

Greedy shifts us again, clearly prepared to rise. "We have to tell the guys."

My stomach dips, but he's right. I never intended to keep this information from them, anyway. "Okay."

"Like, now," he emphasizes.

I falter at that. Burrowing into his chest, I make my case. "How about today, but later?"

I gulp past the dread that sinks in my stomach.

"Once we leave this room, everything changes. We have big-picture decisions to make. Plans to discuss. It'll be time to set it all in motion. Right now, though, none of that can touch us. In here, it's just you and me. We waited so long for this." I curl into him farther, looping my arms around him like I'm clinging to a life raft after being swept out to sea. "I want it to be just you and me for a little while longer."

He cups the back of my head, kissing me softly. I return the kiss, trying to block out all the noise in my head. All thoughts of what's happened and what may still be to come.

My best friend Joey has a saying she uses to center herself when her anxiety starts to kick into high gear: *I am here. This is now.*

The only place I want to be at this moment is right here, right now, with the first boy I ever loved.

I run my hands through his hair, toying with the dark strands along his neckline. He tips his head back to give me better access. He hugs my hips and holds me close, granting me the serenity of a few more private moments.

"Hey, Greedy?"

"Yeah, Tem?" he says softly.

"I think I love you."

His eyes widen in surprise, then well with tears.

My confession is only partially true. I don't just *think* I love him; I know it with every fiber of my being. With every cell in my body. I need him to know that the love never left. It was dormant, and I tried to ignore it for years, but it was always there, waiting just below the surface.

My words today, though, mirror the way he first shared his heart with me all those years ago, and from his reaction, I'm confident he senses the underlying meaning.

Wrapping his arms around my shoulders, he curls forward and rests his head on my chest. Then he whispers against my skin, right above my heart, "I think I love you, too."

Chapter 26

Hunter

NOW

Greedy and I stayed hidden away until mid-afternoon. The time together to reconnect and just be was invaluable. I'm certain he was texting with the guys to keep them updated. He allowed us to stay hidden away longer than I expected him to, honestly.

Now, though, we're both anxious to talk to Spence and Levi. Me especially, after learning how everything went down over the last few days.

We don't have to go far to find Levi. He's stationed in Decker's at-home gym, straddling a bench as he does a set of bicep curls. He looks intense, sweat-slicked and scowling, his gaze focused on his form in the mirror.

Until this moment, I haven't been sure how to approach him. But the second I lay eyes on him, knowing how badly he's struggled over the last few days? I'm desperate to ease his worries, to make damn sure he knows just how important he is to me.

Forget easing into anything. I just need to act, for his sake and mine.

Catching his attention in the mirror, I saunter forward. When I'm close enough to reach out, I place one hand on his shoulder.

He freezes, tension bunching in his muscles, and I swear he's holding his breath, too.

I straddle the bench behind him, scoot forward until my thighs press into his ass, then wrap my arms around him from behind and rest my cheek against his back.

"Daisy?"

Peering over his shoulder, I smile at his hopeful reflection in the mirror.

"I'm back," I whisper, kissing his cheek and squeezing his hot, hard abdomen from behind.

The moment it registers, he sinks back into my hold.

Relief hits me so hard I wobble on the bench. "I'm so sorry, Duke." I hold him tighter, willing him to feel my sincerity.

"Wasn't your fault." Voice husky, he rests his hands over mine on his abdomen.

"I know. But you still suffered because of it."

As if he can't let another second pass, he jumps up, turns, and repositions himself so we're face to face. I swing my legs over his thighs, then circle my arms around his neck. Anything to be closer, to make sure he knows how much I care.

"I'm sorry I missed the meeting with your mom."

He shakes his head. "I didn't go. Couldn't. Not without knowing you were okay."

"I'm okay," I swear, chest aching. "I'm so sorry I worried you, but I swear, I remember everything now, and I'm okay."

With a nod, Levi offers me a sad smile. "It was just hard, ya know? Seeing you run into G's arms, knowing that what you two have is so much stronger than—"

I press my fingertips to his lips, silencing him. "Please don't finish that sentence," I beg. "If we're doing this..." I look over my shoulder to where Greedy's standing in the doorway. I need him to hear this just as much as I want Levi to understand.

With a chin lift, he approaches, and when he gets close, I shift forward, pressing my front to Levi's body and making room for Greedy at my back. Once he's settled, I put a hand behind my back, offering it to him. Then I ghost my fingertips up Levi's forearm and cup his face.

"I know what we have is newer, Duke, but it's no less potent than what I feel for Greedy. It's different, but it's not less. I could tell parts of me were missing, but I think my mind was in survival mode, and I didn't have the ability to focus on much of anything that was important to me." Sniffling, I shrug one shoulder. "I hate how my brain works sometimes. Always have."

"I love how your brain works." Greedy moves in closer and kisses my temple. "Despite the darkness and the foggy parts. I love it, because it makes you who you are."

I sniffle again, wiping away the tears that trickle down my cheeks as I sit between these two boys I love with my whole damn heart. I have to believe that even though I'm flawed—even though things are never easy for us—what we have is worth it. That I'm worth it. Because at the end of the day, they're so damn worth it to me.

"I care about you so much, Duke. I—" The confession is on the tip of my tongue. I love Levi. I love him with every fiber of who I am and who I hope to be. But if I tell him that now, I worry it could distract from his pain and allow him to mask his true emotions. He deserves to process what happened.

"I want you." I run my nose up his jaw and plant a kiss below his ear. "I want to be with you. And Greedy. And Spence." I lean back then, pulling Greedy's arms around my middle. "I want all of us together, in whatever way feels natural and good and right."

Levi's pupils blow out and his brows shoot into his hairline. He looks past me and locks eyes with Greedy. "You told her?"

Greedy squeezes my hips, then reaches past me to place his hands on Levi's thighs. "I did," he admits. "I hope that's okay."

Levi searches Greedy's face before focusing on me again. He licks his lips, then sucks in a steadying breath. "You're not upset?" he asks on the exhale.

"What? Of course not. Unless by *upset*, you mean horny..."

Greedy barks out a laugh, nipping at my neck.

"You're sure you're okay with us being together?" Levi hedges.

Sure doesn't even begin to cover it. I rest my head on Greedy's shoulder and tip it back, pressing my teeth into my bottom lip. "I'm sure. But maybe this is one of those situations where it's easier to show him rather than tell?"

A matching grin lights up his expression. "I'm game if you are."

Grinning, I rise and offer Levi my hand. "Come on, Duke. Greedy and I want to show you just how sure we are."

Chapter 27

Levi

NOW

"Wait. Hold up." I'm flustered and confused, following a giggling Hunter and a determined Greedy down the hall. "If we're going where I think we're going, I can't. There's no fucking way I'll be able to get it up in Decker Crusade's bed."

Greedy barks out a laugh, then turns to lock eyes with Hunter over his shoulder. The look he gives her is pure sex. Clearly he didn't have the same issue last night.

"Fine, in here." Hunter opens a door in the hallway that leads from the gym to the kitchen and scurries inside.

It's a walk-in closet.

No, wait.

It's a small storage room filled with dry goods. There are ingredients for baking and an impressive selection of protein powders lined along one shelf.

Along with an entire shelf dedicated to perfectly lined-up and labeled nuts.

"Are we in a pantry?" Greedy asks, standing closer than I realized.

No one bothered to flick on the lights. We're relying on the dim glow from the glass block windows along the top of the far wall.

"Joey says this is where they keep all the best snacks." Her tone is pure tease. Closer now, she says, "Tasting you is all I can think about, Duke. Especially knowing that with Greedy's help, we might finally be able to handle your massive cock."

"Teamwork makes the dream work," Greedy quips.

I brush my hands up the length of her spine, exploring in the dark until my fingers weave through her silky blond hair. I pull her toward me, desperate to taste her, too. Only the kiss turns out to be more of a peck and far too innocent for my liking.

Before I can pull her back in to remedy the situation, she sinks to her knees, dragging her hands down my legs as she goes.

Calloused fingers grip my neck, turning my head. Then Greedy's lips are at my ear. "Hunter wants this. I'm desperate to show her everything I've learned." His mouth tips up in a smile.

Fuck. The guy's given me head once, and already he's so confident. My thighs clench from his promises.

"Do you want us both to suck your enormous cock, Leev?"

In response, I smash my mouth against his, pouring every bit of my answer into the kiss. Our teeth clash and our tongues war for dominance. My cock hardens at such a rapid rate it aches.

My pulse is so loud in my ears I almost don't catch it. But Greedy freezes, and the second time, Hunter's moan fills the space.

"I want you both," I consent, pulling Greedy's head back by the hair at his nape. "Make me feel good, G. Show our girl what you know."

With a cocksure grin, he sinks to his knees beside Hunter.

I'm a mess of anticipation as they murmur to each other, strip me of my shorts, and explore my rigid, throbbing length in tandem.

Soft hands caress me first, though they're soon replaced by bigger hands that grip me so tight my knees threaten to give out.

"You can be firmer with him, Tem. He likes it rough. Let's make him feel how badly we want him."

Mewling, Hunter grips me harder, her fist not even big enough to fully encircle my crown.

"Lick him, baby. Open wide and suck the fat head of his cock into that perfect mouth while I jerk him hard between your pouty lips."

Greedy uses firm, even strokes to work most of my length while Hunter does exactly what she's told, suckling on the end of my cock, swirling her tongue around the head, and moaning as she laps at the beads of precum leaking from my tip.

Throwing my head back, I give in to the sensations of the two of them working together.

Together. They're doing this together, for me.

Although judging by the way Greedy occasionally groans and Hunter whimpers, they're enjoying this moment as much as I am.

"Kiss me," Hunter pants as she pops off my dick.

I mourn the loss of her hot, skilled mouth immediately. Though a moment later, a new sensation shoots arousal straight to my balls. Because god damn. Now both their mouths are on me, licking and lapping around the end of my cock.

"Fucking hell," I moan. They're making out on my cock. Around my cock? Fuck, it feels like they're making out *with* my cock.

Two mouths. Two tongues. It's incredible how they've come together to make me the center of their goddamn world.

"I could suck on Levi's dick and make a fucking meal of your sweet kisses all day, Tem. You both feel so fucking good. Go lower," Greedy instructs. "I want to feel our boy in the back of my throat."

He repositions himself behind Hunter, and she dips lower as instructed, peppering my shaft with kisses as G works me deeper into his throat.

I try to hold back, to resist fucking their faces, but when Hunter sucks my nuts into her mouth—both at the same fucking time—I snap.

"Fuck, fuck, fuck," I chant, thrusting and aching and trying so damn hard to keep it together.

"He's close," Hunter murmurs, the words reverberating through my balls.

"I know." Greedy pulls off long enough to taunt me and shoot me a mischievous wink.

I don't even have time to come up with a retort before he's back to work, relaxing his throat and swallowing around my length, then taking me so deep I'm sure I'm cutting off his airway.

Gripping both their heads, I hold them to me, uniting the three of us, as tingles of warmth and undulating pleasure zap up my legs and gather deep in my core.

Now that my eyes have adjusted to the dimly lit room, I can see them working me over. Hunter suckling and rubbing my nuts. Greedy deep-throating me like a fucking pro.

It's the sight of them that does it.

My best friend and my girl. Together. On their knees. For me.

"Coming." I barely grit the word out before the first wave of release racks through my length. Eyes squeezed shut, I use every ounce of energy to remain upright as my orgasm rips through me.

I tense and contract, spasm and moan until I lose touch with reality. I can't keep track of who's hands are on me and where or whose mouth is sucking and prolonging my orgasm.

"Don't be a cum hog," Hunter whines, Brat Mode clearly activated.

Greedy's responding laugh vibrates through my shaft, sending another jolt of pleasure through me. Then he releases me, kisses the tip, and makes room for Hunter.

Quickly, he grasps my length and jerks me hard.

In front of me, they've got their faces tipped back, mouths open, needy and eager and hungry for *me*. I'm transfixed by the visual of long ribbons of cum shooting from my tip and covering their tongues with my seed.

Hunter whimpers each time G's tongue gets coated instead of hers.

"Greedy girl," I tease, tapping my cock against her cheek a few times. I position the tip at her lips, then wrap my fingers around G's hand, tugging on my length in tandem to ensure she gets every last drop she craves.

Moaning, she smiles up at me, her eyes dancing with mischief. She swallows down my cum then grins.

"Levi's girl, too," she corrects.

Chapter 28

Kabir

NOW

To my knowledge, Hunter and Greedy haven't emerged from their room yet. Though Garrett did text our newly created group chat to confirm they're okay, and that he believes Hunter's memories are far less foggy today.

Good thing. Levi needs the assurance more than anything. Plus, we have guests arriving soon. I would hate to spring this on Hunter without memories or context for what either of these men means to her.

I'm standing outside on one of the myriad of balconies and decks, casting my gaze out over the lake as I wait for their arrival. Phone in hand, I check for updates, but when the sliding glass door off the main living room opens with a soft *whoosh*, I turn.

Garrett, Hunter, and Levi file out, their dispositions light-years from what they were yesterday.

Garrett turns to offer Hunter the opportunity to pass him. He rests a hand on her low back and guides her forward whilst also turning over his shoulder to speak to Levi.

The blond man barks out a laugh in response.

I fight back an instant smile that surprises even me.

My firecracker is back.

Anticipation courses through me as I watch her watch them. Levi bends low to whisper in her ear and says something that makes her smirk, then smack his chest playfully. Grinning, he slings an arm over her shoulders and kisses the top of her head.

Relief joins the emotions stirring in me. Greedy looks love drunk and sated. Levi appears calmer than he's been for days. All my worst fears dissipate as I take them in. All is right in his world once again.

She did that for him. She does that for all of us.

There was never any doubt in my mind that I'd share her. I'm willing and eager to participate in whatever version of a polyamorous relationship we land in. But this feels so much deeper than attraction and sex.

Garrett and Levi clearly need her just as badly as I do, but for different reasons.

She obviously needs them, too. Dare I say that I may need these American boys as well? I sure as hell hope they see value in what I bring to the dynamic.

I keep watching. Waiting.

When she finally looks my way, every hardship and struggle we've suffered since I arrived on the doorstep of the Ferguson house dissipates. Face alight, she ducks out from under Levi's arm, brushes past Greedy, and practically runs to my side.

Turning, I grip her neck, pull her to me, and kiss her. Hard. I've waited far too long to be gentle. I've worried far too much to hold back.

One of the boys—Garrett, I can only assume—clears his throat beside us.

But I take my damn time snogging my woman and making sure she knows exactly how deeply and irrevocably I need her. When I finally do release her mouth, she whimpers. That's my fucking girl.

"Are you well, love?"

She bites her lip and shakes her head. "No. But later, when you wrap my hair around your fist and put me on my knees, I will be."

A zap of electricity races up my spine as I take her in. There she is. My firecracker.

She pulls me into a hug, one that's tight but also tender. I wrap my arms around her low back and hold her just as tightly.

Tipping her chin up, she murmurs, "Greedy told me what you did."

In an uncharacteristic moment of panic, I dart a look at Garrett. Hunter doesn't know about the tracker. I had every intention of telling her, but I wasn't planning to do that today. If he's already disclosed that information...

Thankfully, my assumption is off base. Garrett meets my gaze, holds it, then quickly shakes his head. With that assurance, I focus on the woman in my arms once more.

"And what is it I did?" I ask, tone teasing.

"He told me that you're the one who pieced together clues and found me. And that you bought the entire facility. You saved me, Spence. Again."

My heart clinches at the sincerity and gratitude in her words. As if it was any hardship or even a question of how far I'd go when it comes to the safety and wellness of this woman.

I run my knuckles along her jawline, then gently squeeze her throat once more. "We're endgame, love. No matter what obstacles get in our path or what forces try to keep us apart, I'll never stop fighting for a happily ever after with you."

"I assume that's who we're waiting on?" Garrett's question pulls us out of the moment.

I home in on the boat as it slows on approach. "Right. Well, then. We've got a bit of a surprise in store for you, love."

No time like the present to admit to the cascade of events I've set into motion.

"Please remember: we were terrified. All of us," I add, because although I was the one who made the calls, I did so for the benefit of the entire group. "Early on, when we were trying to figure out where you had gone and who you were with, I contacted everyone I could think of. I was determined to leave no stone unturned, no lead unpursued."

A quick inhale catches my attention.

Hunter is literally flying out of my arms a moment later, then racing down the stairs that lead from the deck to the rocky beach below.

I resist the urge to charge after her. Or at the very least shout demands for her to slow down and be careful.

I tug on my shirt collar, suddenly finding it hard to breathe. As I undo the top button, anxiety spikes in my chest. I should have told her earlier. I should have attempted to explain last night, despite her foggy memories.

When I refocus on the beach, my heart falters, and my breath catches in my chest.

"Gerald!" she exclaims as she barrels into his arms and practically knocks the old man off his feet.

Bloody hell.

That was *not* the individual I intended to warn her about.

Chapter 29

Hunter

NOW

"*Gerald*." I pull back, suddenly aware of just how close I came to knocking an eighty-year-old man over. "You're here. I can't believe you're here." I wrap my arms around him.

Chuckling, he drops his luggage at his feet. "Hello, lass. Fancy seeing you here."

His deep voice and melodic accent instantly transport me back to my time in London. I can't believe Spence convinced Gerald to come all this way.

"Are you well, love?" he asks, holding my shoulders at arm's length as he inspects me.

I blush at the phrase Spence uses so liberally but in a much different context.

"I'm okay," I tell him honestly. "It's been a tough few weeks." Understatement of the year. "But I'm feeling wonderful now that you're here."

That's the truth. When it comes to the people who wholeheartedly and genuinely care about me and those I love, Gerald is one of the good ones.

"How is your wife?" I ask, weaving my arm through his and hugging his side once more. "Gone, I'm afraid."

My heart plummets, and my breath catches.

"She passed the winter after you left London," he tells me solemnly.

Throat tightening, I hold him more firmly. "I'm so sorry, Gerald."

With a sniff, he tips his chin, alerting me to Spence's approach. "We've both been suffering from heartbreak since then," he remarks quietly.

I squeeze his arm, then turn to face the others.

"How's it, Gerald?" Spence greets as he and the other guys step onto the rocky beach.

"All is well, Mr. Spencer."

"Very good." Spence sidles up to my side. "I take it you're in need of a rest and a hot meal?"

"Both would be most welcome," the older man says. With a glance at the mansion, he lets out a low whistle. "It's even larger than it looked on the boat. Your friend and I were surprised to discover that this was to be our final destination."

Greedy and Levi step up to either side of Spence then, and introductions are made, hands shaken. Greedy takes Gerald's bags for him, which just about bowls him over.

Smiling, I grasp Levi's hand and start to follow Greedy up to the house.

Before I make it more than two steps, another voice snags my attention.

"Mahina."

My lungs seize, and my every cell freezes. Slowly, I peer over my shoulder. The sight that greets me is one I never thought I'd have the privilege of beholding again.

Sione.

With a lake spread out behind him. Standing on a dock. Reaching out his arms. Calling out to me.

"Si?" The name is as much an exclamation as it is a question.

What in the world is he doing here?

I stride toward him, then break out into a sprint when he does the same.

We collide at the edge of the lake. He sweeps me up into his arms and spins me around and around, holding me tight.

His enormous hands press into my back and ass. Laughing uncontrollably, I have no real choice but to wrap my legs around him and hang on for dear life.

Eventually, he slows and places me back on my feet. His hair is loose around his shoulders, his dark eyes smoldering as he looks down at me wearing that gorgeous, familiar smile.

"What are you doing here?"

He tucks my hair behind one ear. Like he can't resist touching me. "I thought the Brit told you I was coming," he says, his voice low and melodic.

Reminded that, *oh yeah*, we have an audience, I turn and find the four men along the beach watching me interact so casually and lovingly with an outsider.

My chest tightens, and nerves skitter through me. Oh boy. This is going to be a lot for everyone to process. And just as it felt like we were finding our footing.

With pursed lips, Spence searches my gaze.

He was supposed to tell me. Honestly, though? He never stood a chance. I've barely seen him all day, then when I finally did emerge to check in, I let myself get all sorts of caught up in Gerald's arrival.

I thought Gerald was the surprise visitor.

I blow out an exasperated sigh. Spence catches it, shakes his head, and shrugs.

We all have a lot of explaining to do, it seems.

With Sione's hand in mine, I guide him up toward the house to introduce him to the others.

I'm delighted he's here. I'm also high-key worried that all the progress Greedy, Levi, Spence, and I have made is about to crumble down around me.

My first love. My boyfriend. My European lover. Now my other European lover. All here. All under one roof.

Flovely.

"What are you thinking, Mahina?" Sione probes as we navigate the rocky shore.

"I can't believe you're really here."

He halts, stopping me with a slight tug. Tenderly, he cups my face, bows his head, brushes his plump lips with mine, and says, "You know you're where I always want to be."

Chapter 30

Sione

THEN: FALL, YEAR TWO
LUTEAL PHASE

"Breathe, Mahina. Lean into it and open for me."

Hunter releases a shaky exhale, her thighs quivering, and gives me another inch.

As she straddles the yoga mat we're sharing, sweat drips from her nape and along the curve of her spine. The single bead of moisture disappears beneath her sports bra before it has a chance to make it to where my tatted hand is splayed wide on her back.

I'm mesmerized by that single droplet of her essence.

I'm jealous of the fabric that has the honor of absorbing it.

I yearn to peel her out of her clothes and lick it from her salty skin.

Months and months have passed.

With each cycle of the moon, my body awakens further.

What started as companionship blossomed into friendship.

But friendship didn't keep.

It wasn't enough. I want to possess her. Consume her. Claim her as my one and only.

My soul has made its choice. My mind, heart, subtle body, and, most recently and surprisingly, my physical container, have all followed suit.

The cordiality and civility I felt toward her has been replaced with yearning and desire.

I feel reborn.

I feel *unhinged*.

No longer can I linger in her presence without battling the unrelenting desire to have her. To hold her. To take her and keep her and discover where this unprecedented sexual attraction could take us.

I want to tell her. I *need* to tell her. It would be a disservice to the heart, and an actual crime to my soul, to keep my feelings to myself any longer.

But will it be enough? Can *I* be enough?

After more than a year of friendship, how do I explain the shift I'm still coming to terms with myself?

My attraction to her grew slowly. It took root and it bloomed. It gathered in my core, drop by drop, until my desire and desperation became parts of who I am. Now, I can't imagine not feeling like this.

"Si. It hurts," she whimpers, jettisoning me back to this moment.

This moment, where it's just the two of us, working through a private flow in the heated yoga studio.

This moment, where the warmth and sweat and energy of the room have nothing on the insatiable flames licking up my spine.

"I know, Mahina. I know. You're doing so well."

Shifting, I reposition myself directly behind her and place both palms on the small of her back.

Hunter swears this helps when she's cramping—the deep stretching and the hot yoga. Sure, she could do it on her own, but I tell myself she needs the counterpressure to really open up and relieve the worst of her discomfort.

She's been open to trying so many new things over the last year in an effort to counteract the symptoms of PMDD. My curious, inquisitive, soulful girl.

She still takes her meds and meets with her therapist regularly, but she's added yoga to the regimen. She meditates. She drinks raspberry leaf tea the week leading up to her menses. She works hard to take care of herself from the inside out. To alleviate the symptoms she can, to honor the situation she's in, and to accept that she's doing her best.

I'm so proud of her.

"Lift up so I can move the roller," I encourage.

Without hesitation, she pushes into downward dog.

It takes all my strength not to give in to the temptation to stare at her backside, which is now perfectly positioned in my line of sight.

Quickly, I reposition the foam roller she was pressing her pelvis into, turning it parallel with the yoga mat, hopeful that if she can stretch out her groin muscles, she'll find another pocket of relief.

Holding it steady with one hand, I swipe at the strands of sweat-drenched hair that have escaped the elastic on top of my head.

"Lower," I murmur, expecting her to flow through chaturanga like usual.

Instead, something wholly unexpected happens. She slips, likely physically spent and mentally foggy, and plops onto the foam roller with an *oof*.

My natural instincts take over, and I place one hand on her hip to steady her while I use the other to hold the foam roller in place.

"Hunter."

Her reply is an airy, wanton moan that echoes off the walls of the studio.

Despite the temperature of the room, the true heat of the moment radiates through me, sending a surge of unprecedented desire straight to my core.

Still straddling the roller, which is positioned perfectly between her thighs, she rolls her hips forward and whimpers.

My heart takes off at a sprint. Is she...? Heavens. She is. She's deriving pleasure from the sensation of the foam roller pressing up into her core.

I want her to feel good. But I don't know that I can remain calm if she moans like that again.

"Hunter," I plead, her name as much of a warning as it is a prayer.

She lifts her head, her chest heaving, wisps of sweat-slicked blond hair clinging to her forehead.

We lock eyes in the floor to length mirror in front of us.

A new kind of heat consumes me.

It's desire. It's attraction. It's lust and want and *need* in a way I've never experienced with another human.

The energy of a supernova bursting into existence erupts between us. Around us. *Because* of us.

Maintaining eye contact, she grinds against the foam roller.

"It feels so good." She whimpers. Hands planted on the mat, she spreads her thighs even wider.

"Then do it again, Mahina. Chase that feeling. Do what feels good."

My words are as much an encouragement for her as they are permission for me.

Chase the feeling, follow the light.

Do what feels good, lean into the newly illuminated path. The path that feels so rare, but also so right.

My inner warrior is awake, standing at attention, yearning to see this through.

Every atom that makes up my physical body vibrates with virility.

Without looking away from her reflection, I rise to my knees and shift, angling my pelvis to show her the reciprocated arousal I'm experiencing.

"Look at what you do to me, Mahina. Do you see how I react? How I grow just for you?" I grit out, smoothing one hand along the outside of my yoga shorts, over the erect, throbbing proof of my attraction.

A small gasp catches in her throat, and her pupils blow wide as she watches me touch myself—confidently and proudly—showing off just for her. Her eyes leave mine, drifting and searching. Taking in my physical state as I slowly stroke myself again.

For the first time in this lifetime, I wish the hand touching me belonged to someone else.

Her breaths quicken and her focus remains locked on me as I touch myself through my shorts. This moment is more erotic and satisfying than any solo session.

"Can I?" she asks on a whisper.

Can she. *Can she?* I honestly do not know.

I haven't been sexually active with a partner for years. I've never derived pleasure from a sexual exchange with another person.

But this is different. She is her, and she is it for me.

Despite the intensity of my emotions and how much I want to feel her skin against mine, insecurity slams into me. My chest tightens with the fear of underperforming and disappointing her. I want to make her feel good, but I must be mindful of my subtle body and her delicate disposition. She's physically hurting. Emotionally vulnerable.

"Si..."

Breath held, I home in on her reflection.

"I just meant, can I... get myself off. In your presence. Right now. Like this?" She grinds her core against the foam roller once more, exhaling sharply.

A bolt of desire travels up my spine. In all my conscious days, I've never been more jealous of an inanimate object.

"I would never do this in front of you without your consent," she explains, her eyes soft, her concern palpable.

My brilliant, beautiful girl. She knows me so well. She cares for me so deeply. She can interpret my worries before they even fully form in my own head.

"You have my consent," I assure her. "But now I must also ask yours."

Her gorgeous green eyes widen in surprise. She searches my face, then she scans the length of my torso and thighs as I proudly remain on my knees.

"Yes. God, yes. You have my consent to do whatever feels good."

Joy radiates from my soul. It's incredible, receiving her permission so easily. Before I lose the nerve, I reposition my body behind hers, splay my hands on her low back, and encourage her to fully sink down on the roller between her thighs.

"Feel it, Mahina."

She moans. I shift closer.

"Feel how powerful you are." With both hands on her hips, I guide her to grind forward.

With a long, drawn-out roll of my hips, my body connects with her. Her ass to my groin, where a throbbing, newly awakened warrior greets her in full salute.

Teeth gritted, I press my cock between the mounds of her ass. "Feel what you do to me."

"Si," she whimpers, her head bowed.

"Don't think, Mahina. Just feel. Feel it and own it. Let it encompass all you want to release."

She does as she's told, working the apex of her thighs against the foam roller, then rolling her hips back so her ass brushes against my erection.

We find a rhythm, though we abandon it quickly. We're a mess of movement, both desperate to connect and inspire pleasure in one another.

"What you're seeking is seeking you," I remind her. But the words are in vain, for both of us, really. My body wants to bond with hers in ways it has never yearned for another.

Hunter picks up the pace, her pants and whimpers, too, increasing in speed. In neediness. In volume.

"It's going to feel so good, Mahina. Look how exquisite you are." I remove one hand and push my fingers through the hair on the back of her scalp, guiding her head to lift.

Another whimper. Another boiling hot moment of eye contact. Then, with a shaky breath, she corrects me.

"Look how exquisite *we* are. Look how perfectly we fit together."

Physically. Mentally. Emotionally. Spiritually.

Every part of who I am is sated in this moment.

"I've been waiting for you, Mahina," I whisper, my lips against her ear. "You were worth it. You *are* worth it. Through this moment and every lifetime we have yet to live, I will wait."

Her movements become more erratic and hungry. I steady her hips and slow her speed, drawing out the build-up, ensuring she feels it all.

"You are my soul match," I murmur. "I am complete with you by my side. I will spend the rest of this lifetime making sure you know how worthy and wanted you are."

Boldly, my fingers explore beyond the safety of her hips, cupping her inner thighs and stretching her to the max.

"Yes. Fuck. Si..."

She's close.

I pull her thighs apart, supporting more of her weight, and use all my strength and final strands of composure to keep the foam roller still.

"Si," she moans. "Si. Si. Si."

The desperation of her chant takes root deep in my chest, feeding my inner warrior and provoking a chemical reaction that builds in my core.

"Feel it, Mahina," I beg. Once she comes undone, our subtle bodies will align and our souls will fuse together in a web that can never be untangled. I need her to feel it all.

"I'm coming," she moans. Her thighs shake under my palms. Her body trembles with anticipation, then quakes with release. "I'm coming, I'm coming, I'm coming."

I watch her face in the mirror, desperate to witness the sanctity of this moment. The sweat. The tears. The undulating pleasure that possesses her, that has wiped away every ache and every pain that lived inside her minutes ago.

When she lifts her head, and her eyes lock with mine, my body reacts so viscerally it burns.

A moan escapes me. Tingles peak into mountain tops and sink into valleys as my cock pulses and I fill my shorts with warm, fresh seed.

I'm not just coming.

I'm *becoming*.

My highest self accepts that I have not fully lived in this lifetime or any other until now.

I have not fully lived until her.

Chapter 31

Hunter

NOW

Introductions were as awkward as expected.

Greedy is tellingly cool and almost too calm. Levi is clearly frustrated but trying to keep his shit together. Spence apologized over and over again, but after the dozenth time, I pulled him aside and asked him to please stop.

Sione's here. He traveled all the way from Italy to be with me. There's no sense in making anyone feel shitty about the situation we've found ourselves in. Particularly because I'm the root cause of all the drama.

We fumbled through dinner, then Greedy and Spence helped Gerald get settled in one of the guest rooms on the second floor.

Si's luggage is conspicuously still taking up space in the middle of the living room. As if no one has decided—or accepted, perhaps?—that he's also here to stay.

Levi's washing dishes. He insisted he doesn't want or need help, so I left him to it. Better to work out his frustration on a crusty baking dish now than to detonate when we all sit down to sort things out.

Once Gerald is settled and the dishes are done, the five of us agreed to gather around the bonfire pit down near the shore.

Sione and I ventured down here first. He built and started the fire quickly. Now, we're settled back in two of the chairs, watching the flames dance as we wait for the others.

"You're too far, Mahina," he teases, reaching out and coaxing me to join him. "I come all this way to see you, and you think I'm going to waste a single second not holding you?"

Fucking swoon.

I'm in so much trouble.

Just like I was in Italy, I'm drawn to Sione like a moth to the flame. Rising to my feet, I cross the few steps between us, then allow him to guide me onto his lap.

"Lay back. Let me feel you."

There's nothing overtly sexual about his request. Rather, he wants to relax and hold me. Yet warmth spikes low in my belly all the same. He's always had this effect on me. The ability to soothe my sharp edges. An innate knowledge of what I need, whether it be time, space, comfort, or assurance.

"When will the darkness come?" Si tenderly ghosts his fingertips over the left side of my rib cage where my one and only tattoo resides. I haven't thought about the ink under my skin for months. But as soon as Sione touches it, awareness and connection surge to the forefront of my mind.

"My period started a few days ago."

"You're still so tense," he remarks. He grips my shoulders and kneads into my muscles. "The Brit told me about your mum. About how she took you. And here I always thought your father was the shitty parent."

It's a fair assumption. My dad is the reason I left Italy—and by extension, Sione. When my father called last summer and gave me a "use it or lose it" ultimatum regarding my college fund, I made a choice that rocked both our worlds.

"She's definitely worse now than she used to be." I groan when Si hits a particularly tight spot between my neck and my shoulder blade. "That feels incredible," I tell him, leaning forward to grant him more access. He works me over for a few minutes, his touch growing more sensual and reverent with every pass.

It's the reminder I need, the nudge to address what he deserves to know.

"Before the others join us," I start.

Sione stills, my low back putty in his very capable hands.

"I need you to know that I'm with them. All of them," I clarify.

He hums in understanding, then resumes his ministrations. After a long, silent moment, he clears his throat. "I assumed as much. But what about us, Mahina? Does your soul still match with mine?"

Fucking swoon. Again. The heat in my belly warms further.

With a deep inhale, I allow myself several heartbeats to truly consider his question.

Greedy was my first love. Spence my partner, Dom, and lover. Levi is my boyfriend. Sione has always been and will always be my soul match.

"Nothing could unbraid my soul from yours," I promise, grasping one of his hands. I guide it across the front of my body, then place it over my heart. It's the truth. Like a phoenix reborn from the ashes, I came back to life during my year and a half in Italy with Sione. The fabric of who I am—the strongest, bravest, most lively parts of this version of Hunter—was cultivated with him by my side.

North Carolina broke me.

London irrevocably changed me.

It was Lake Como, Italy, under the light of the moon, with this sensual, spiritual man by my side, that truly brought me back to life.

"Is there room for me here as well?" Sione's fingertips dance over the fabric of my T-shirt, right over the spot where my heart beats in my chest.

"There is," I hedge. "As long as you're okay with not being the only one for me."

Sione glides his hand up and weaves his fingers in my hair, tilting my head back until he's staring directly into my eyes. "I guess they don't know about my nickname."

I snort. "No. Although I'm pretty sure you're the one who put yourself in my phone as The One and Only when we met."

Sione's laughter pierces the otherwise silent night, delighting my soul and bringing about a lightness I've so desperately craved.

"It was to remind you how to pronounce my name, Mahina. It's not my fault that Sione rhymes with The One and Only."

A light on the back deck flickers, tempering our laughter. Then Greedy, Levi, and Spence file out through the sliding door and start their descent to the beach.

I sit up straight. Sione makes no move to keep me in place.

"You two look cozy," Spence remarks, approaching the fire pit and selecting a seat opposite us.

I rise up to greet him, but he raises both hands dismissively. "By all means. Don't get up on my account."

Spence typically means what he says and says what he means. He's the least of my concerns right now, though.

Greedy shuffles past me next, grasping and squeezing one hand as he passes me, heading for the chair on Spence's left side.

Levi moves to follow, his attention never flitting to me.

"Hey." I step in front of him, attempting to cut him off at the pass. "Sit with me?" I ask, nodding to the two available seats to Spence's right.

He veers right, brushing past me without actually making contact. "It looked like you already had a seat, Hunter."

Flovely.

As he settles beside Greedy, I close my eyes and take a steady breath.

Rather than rejoin Sione or claim a chair of my own, I stay on my feet.

Tension crackles between the five of us, punctuated by the audible snaps and pops from the roaring fire.

"I know Sione's arrival is unexpected," I start, looking from Spence to Greedy to Levi. "But I'd like to deal with this head-on. It's been a really intense few weeks, and it felt like we were finally making progress." I seek Levi's gaze, but his eyes are set on the fire.

If he won't look at me... if he's not even willing to try...

This can't be happening.

No. determination rushes through me, fortifying me. It can't happen. I won't allow it. Not now, when we've fought so hard and come so damn far.

"Duke."

His head snaps up at the callout, flames dancing in his dark blue eyes.

"You're my wild card. The one I'm worried about the most." I shoot Greedy an apologetic glance, then turn to Spence and offer him the same look.

Neither one of them reacts. They know what's at stake just as well as I do.

"I'm not giving up on us." I zero in on Levi again. "If you want out, you have to look me in the eye and say it. Otherwise, we're going to work through this and figure it out together."

Levi plants his feet wide, resting his elbows on his thighs with his head hung between his legs. He cracks the knuckles on both hands, although a few fingers on his right don't make a sound.

I hold my breath, waiting and willing him to speak. To say anything at all.

"What, exactly, are you asking of me?"

A modicum of relief works its way through me, making it easier to breathe. Skirting around the fire, I step up in front of him. When he doesn't immediately look up, I sink to my knees and force his gaze to meet mine.

Ignoring the jagged edges of beach rocks pressing into my skin, I take Levi's hands and make my case. "I'm asking you to give this, to give us, a chance. To be flexible as we figure out how to operate as a unit. To accept that Sione was a significant part of my life and that he still is now."

Levi shakes his head, his eyes falling closed. "I don't even know him, Hunter. You want me to what? Give it a go and see how it feels next time we all fall into bed together?"

"Whoa, whoa, whoa." Sione shoots to his feet.

He marches to my side and reaches one tatted hand down. With a long breath out, I take it and allow him to pull me to my feet.

"There's an important piece of the puzzle missing here," he says to Levi. He shifts back and crosses both arms over his chest, looking from man to man to man, then finally settling his gaze on me. "Hunter isn't telling you something about me that you need to know."

Swallowing past the emotion in my throat, I step up to him. "You don't have to do this," I say on a whisper, my words intended just for him. This wasn't the direction I wanted this to go. It shouldn't matter—Levi either wants this or he doesn't.

"They're too important to you, Mahina. I see it in your eyes. I feel it in the energy that surrounds them all. It's okay." He tucks my hair behind my ear once more. "I want them to know. It will make things easier."

Eyes closed, I exhale and squeeze Si's hand. Then, with an arm wrapped around his bicep, I hold him tight.

He takes his time assessing each man around the fire before finally speaking. "I have no sexual interest whatsoever in any of you."

"Is that so?" Spence teases, resting an ankle over one knee. "You're hetero, then?"

"No."

All eyes are on Sione.

It means so much to me, that he'd open up about such intimate details with people who are practically strangers, but I hate that he has to at the same time.

"I'm demisexual," he tells the group. "My heart, soul, body, and spirit belong to this woman. I want for no one else. I've only ever been intimately satisfied with her."

His words cause heat to flood my cheeks. It's the truth, though. Sione has only ever orgasmed by his own hand and while partnered with me.

"I'm not opposed to sharing her with you," he continues, glancing at me for confirmation.

I nod emphatically. He's on the right track.

"But I cannot and will not share the part of myself I reserve for her."

Sione goes quiet, the only sounds now the crackling of the fire and the lapping of the lake water as it hits the rocks on the shore.

The silence isn't awkward. Rather it feels as though we're all processing the information he's offered.

His truth can be difficult to understand. It took me a while to comprehend the distinctions between demisexuality and asexuality. Sione was patient with me and willing to answer my questions and redirect me when I wasn't quite grasping a facet of his explanation.

He's infinitely tolerant and so beautifully self-assured. He's truly one of a kind. *Sione: my one and only.*

The silence is interrupted when Spence emits a low whistle. "Thank you for sharing that with us."

Greedy nods, his lips pressed into a thoughtful line.

Levi clears his throat, looking from Greedy to Spence, then up to me. Finally, his gaze locks with Sione's.

"I'm sorry you felt like you had to out yourself to get your point across. I feel like shit that I put you in that position, man."

"It helped, though, yes?"

"Yeah. It did." Levi rises to his feet, strides forward, and offers Sione his hand. "Looking forward to getting to know you." Before Sione can respond, Levi is wrapping him up in a hug and thumping him on the back.

"Right. Well, then. This is starting to feel like an original episode of *All Creatures Great and Small*. Let's wrap up this part of the evening, shall we?" Spence, who's usually much more composed and patient, is clearly still on edge from the last few days.

Rightfully so. I make a mental note to carve out some time for just the two of us tomorrow.

"In summation," Spence continues, "Sione is with Hunter and only Hunter. Hunter is with Sione. And with me. And with Garrett. And with Levi."

I huff. "When you put it like that—"

"I'm with Hunter and with Levi," he continues, paying me no mind. "On occasion, Garrett isn't completely closed off to the idea of me giving him a hand—literally."

"Yikes," Greedy shakes his head and chuckles.

"Am I wrong?" Spence pushes.

Greedy looks at me, then Levi, before finally raising both brows at Spence. "Not entirely," he admits. "But only when we're all together."

"Noted," Spence states. "Levi is with Hunter and with Garrett and with me." He surveys each of us, deadpan. "Any objections, amendments, or corrections to what's just been shared?"

We're all silent for a breath. Then Levi snickers, and a moment later, Greedy loses it, doubling over with laughter.

I press my lips together to fight back my own smirk. Listing out our sexual dynamics like he's reading minutes from a board meeting is way too on-brand for Spence.

"Are you going to write that all down somewhere for future reference?" Sione asks.

I groan. I know he's teasing, but—

"Excellent idea." Spence pulls out his phone and makes a note, then stashes it back in his pocket. "I'll distribute a draft memo of our dynamic to each of you by tomorrow at noon for your review."

Chapter 32

Kabir

NOW

A light knock on the door startles me enough to pause my rage-typing, but only for an instant. Apparently the Formula 1 team I acquired partial ownership of in the Empire Forest deal is a ticking time bomb of egos, in-fighting, and overspending. I have no interest in attaching the Spencer Enterprises logo to a flailing company, so changes are being implemented immediately.

"Come in," I call out as I hit Send.

My gorgeous darling girl waltzes through the door and strides right up to the opposite side of the desk. She plants her hands on her wide hips and bites down on that pouty bottom lip I want to pull out from between her teeth and suck into my mouth.

I sense what she needs. I yearn to bend her over on this desk and give it to her. But not until I check in with her.

"Are you well, love?"

One perfectly arched brow lifts. Gods, I love the way she bounced back so quickly, sassy attitude and all.

Eyes narrowed now, she assesses me. My dick twitches with eagerness, waiting for her reply.

"No," she says flippantly. "I'm not well at all. I'm pissed you've gone soft on me."

The air evacuates my lungs in a huff. "Excuse me?"

I give her the out.

"You heard me," she sasses, tilting her head, still watching me in challenge. "You've gone soft. Your friend *Garrett* must be rubbing off on you."

This may be the first time I've ever heard her say his full name. The mocking in her tone has nothing to do with the other man. That I can guarantee. No, her ire is aimed directly at me.

I hold her gaze, calculating.

She stares right back with those wide green eyes, showing me exactly what she wants. Really letting me see her. Once I'm sure I'm reading her correctly, I smirk. Brat Mode has indeed been activated, and I fully intend to take care of that.

Steepling my fingers, I rest my elbows on the desk and regard her. "Safe words still red and pink?"

She bites back a smile and nods.

"I didn't hear you," I tell her flatly.

Her eyes sparkle with delight. "Yes, Sir," she coos.

Gods, I love this woman. "Undress and get on your fucking knees, whore. I'll show you how unsoft I've become."

She's naked and crawling under my desk in no time at all.

Quickly, I unfasten my belt and unzip my trousers to grant her easy access to my rapidly hardening cock. "I have to be on a call in three minutes," I inform her. "Take out my cock. Put it in your mouth."

Eagerly, she complies, and I have to bite my fist to fight back a groan as the first undulating wave of pleasure washes over me.

I reach down and pet her cheek, then slap it lightly for good measure.

"Oh, and Hunter? This meeting typically runs well past the scheduled ninety-minute mark. Settle in, love. You're going to be down there a while."

Her mouth. Her sassy, smart, cheeky, beautiful mouth. It's so warm. So fucking wet. The slightest swallow threatens to undo me completely.

She's barely moving. Such a perfect, obedient thing. The occasional swirl of her tongue around the crown coupled with the way she suckles on the tip each time she needs to swallow the saliva pooling in her mouth has my entire core spasming.

I'm moments from ending the meeting when movement below the desk catches my attention. It's subtle at first. A slight shift. A more noticeable moan.

When I glance down, I spy the source of the uptick in commotion.

She's touching herself.

She's touching herself, and by the looks of it, she's feral for release.

Eyes wild. Mouth full of my fat, weeping cock. She absolutely knows better, and yet there she is, with one hand woven between her bare thighs, frantically rubbing her cunt.

I clear my throat, and at the sound, her eyes grow wider. She freezes the instant she knows she's been caught.

Reaching over, I mute the call and turn off my camera. Then I place a sticky note over the lens for good measure. No one else gets her like this: so desperate and needy she was willing to defy me for the briefest moment of relief.

I roll the chair back a few inches, forcing her to shuffle frantically on her knees to keep my cock in her mouth.

"Did I instruct you to touch yourself?"

Her pupils blow out. She attempts to swallow.

"Answer me." I grip the back of her head and thrust into her mouth until my crown is momentarily lodged in her throat.

"No," she says, the single word garbled around a mouthful of hard, aching cock.

"And yet you chose to do it anyway. Such a needy little bitch, so hot and bothered from warming my cock under this desk for two hours. You're a slutty little thing, aren't you, love?"

"Yes, Sir." She nods fiercely, her eyes welling with tears. "I'm a slut. A needy, cum-thirsty slut."

Satisfied she's repentant, I reach down and squeeze her nipples, using the edges of my manicured thumbnails to pinch the raised buds until she moans. Then I graze her sides, smoothing my palms down her torso.

I can practically feel her holding her breath, desperate to see if I'm going to address the growing ache between her thighs.

I don't.

Instead, I bring my mouth to her ear and whisper, "I've just thought of several more questions for my admin team. Questions that must be asked and answered right now."

She whimpers in understanding.

"Hands on my thighs, love. Don't move a fucking inch. We're going to be here a while more."

When the call finally ends, I'm so desperate for release I nearly knock the laptop off the desk in my haste.

I pull back quickly, violently freeing my cock from her warm mouth, then grip myself hard to stave off my orgasm.

I'm right fucking there. So fucking close. But Hunter is my priority. Even if I don't plan to let her come until I do.

Her cheeks are flushed. She's panting. And her thighs are coated in a glossy slickness.

"Look at you, whore. Drenching yourself. Dribbling on the floor."

To her credit, she stays stock still and silent as I degrade her. Such a good fucking girl.

I shuck off my suit jacket and lay it out behind her.

"Lie on your back, Firecracker. *Now.*"

I squeeze the tip of my cock again. The sight of her splayed out under the desk is enough to tip my arousal into overdrive.

"Do you want my cum?"

"Yes. Please, Sir. Please," she begs.

"Such a cock slut. Desperate for this cum. Desperate to be filled."

I shove my pants lower, then drop to my knees so I'm hovering over her writhing, naked form.

"Spread your legs wider. Let me see that needy cunt."

She does as she's told, revealing the glistening pink perfection between her thighs.

She's a sight to behold.

"You're perfect," I praise. "Only one thing could make you prettier..."

I jerk myself in rapid motions. Eyes wide, she captures her bottom lip between her teeth.

"Good fucking girl. I see that look in your eyes. I see you holding back and resisting. You're doing so well for me, love." Through gritted teeth, I tell her, "I'm going to paint you with my cum. Spread my cream all over your pussy. Coat you from clit to taint."

The first warm jet of semen to escape me lands on her clit. She whimpers on contact.

"Take it, whore. Fucking take it."

She preens as I deliver on my promise. Several productive tugs later, her aching cunt and smooth, pale stomach are dripping with my seed.

She's a fucking sight: pussy lips bright and swollen; chest heaving with exertion and barely contained restraint.

Carefully, I retrieve my phone from the desktop. I move slowly and methodically, showing her the device so she's fully aware of what I intend to do.

"Spread wider for me, love." I meet her gaze and wait for her to nod her consent before taking the picture. "Such a pretty image, my needy whore spread out and covered in cum."

Smiling, I turn the screen so she can see how gorgeous she looks.

"I'm going to keep this picture forever," I tell her reverently. Then, an idea strikes. "Or perhaps I should send it to your brother. Your boyfriend, maybe? Your *other* European lover?"

Her face reddens as she fights the compulsion to sass back.

I tsk. "All these men in this house, eager and ready to please, yet my whore always comes back to me."

"Yes, Sir."

"You've been such a patient thing. I think you deserve a reward. Would you like that, Firecracker?"

"Please, Sir," she pants.

I smear my fresh cum around her clit—*around* being the operative word—taking my time, gliding the sticky seed up along her pubic bone. Then I use two fingers to gather most of it back up and trail it through her folds, bypassing her pussy entrance completely.

She whimpers.

I swat at her clit in warning.

"I know what you need, Firecracker. But you did attempt to take over without permission. You know better than to top from the bottom. Naughty girl."

Another quick swat above her clit has fresh tears rolling down her cheeks.

I pause, allowing her to take a breath and to utilize a safe word if needed. When she doesn't make a sound, I probe the tip of one finger between her folds.

"So as much as I'd love to push in here"—I give her half an inch and fill with pride when she stays perfectly still—"and press into your G-spot just the way you like—" One more inch. The slightest crook of a single finger. Then I pull out and leave her empty. "I'm afraid that's not an option today."

Her eyes widen, the pupils blown out so she's left with the wildest, most frantic expression.

"Hunter." I command her attention back to me. "You're still going to come, love. I assure you. Just not how you want."

She gulps past the objections I'm certain are clawing up her throat. Then she nods.

"I feel compelled to remind you who's in control when you give yourself to me. Do you understand?"

"Yes, Sir."

In an uncharacteristic move, I break from the scene. Bending low, I capture her lips and kiss her deeply. When we're both breathless, I pepper her neck and chest with kisses while simultaneously showering her with praise.

"You're doing beautifully, love. Such a good fucking girl. You know I'll take care of you, Hunter. I'll always make it feel good in the end."

She curls up, cups my face with both hands, and kisses me once more. "Thank you, Sir," she murmurs, the simple words filled with such assured trust and satisfaction, it's hard to fathom she's still on the brink of orgasm.

Pulling away, I snap back into character. "Play with your nipples while I finger your ass. It's your only option if you want to come."

With a grin, she lies back and does as I command.

I gather up my seed along with her own arousal, then coat my finger in the fluids. I watch, enraptured, at the way her rosebud stretches beautifully to accommodate my index finger as I enter her ass. She takes me all the way to my ring and whimpers in pleasure when the metal pushes past her puckered hole.

Another idea comes to me then. Removing two rings from my free hand with my teeth, I spit them into my palm. Then I slide them onto my other middle finger. I smirk down at my beloved, spit directly onto her arsehole for a little extra moisture, then work my ring-clad middle finger all the way into her ass.

Her body flexes and convulses with the intrusion.

"Do you feel that, love? My fingers and rings rubbing on your insides? Do you feel the intense stretch? The extreme fullness? Gods, you look beautiful. You're taking me so well."

She's tugging on her own nipples so fiercely it must be past the point of pain.

"Hold on," I tell her, once again reaching for my phone. "I need a picture of this pretty little sight."

I position the phone near my hand, then pull out enough to show the glistening of my gold metal rings at the base of the two digits I have fully encased in her ass. Her back door clenches—needy little thing—as her body stretches and fights to take me deeper.

I snap a picture, then hold it up to show her what I see.

"Fuck. Sir. Fuck..."

Oh. She loves the visual.

"Freeze," I command.

And freeze she does.

"Good fucking girl, Hunter. So responsive. So compliant."

I switch the device to video mode, push record, and film myself finger-blasting her ass. "Got it. Now you may ride my fingers."

Her hips rise and fall in rhythm with my ministrations. Her rosebud puckers and pulsates around my fingers as she takes me deeper.

Her pussy flutters, too. She's so fucking close. I can practically feel her channel spasming through the thin membrane that separates her ass from her cunt.

Twenty seconds later, I stop recording, pull up the fresh video, and hand her the phone.

"Play the video, Hunter. Watch me work you over while I finger fuck your tight little arse."

She does as I say, her body clenching around my fingers so tightly I swear I'm losing circulation.

"Look how well you take me, slut. Watch how desperately your hole slurps up my cum."

"I'm close. Please, Sir. Please, may I come?"

"Keep watching," I instruct.

With my free hand, I use the lightest of touches on her clit. In response, her whole body shudders and seizes with attempted restraint.

"Such a good little slut. So patient. So serene," I mock.

She is the anthesis of serenity as she quivers and clenches beneath me. But the trust she has in me—the power she grants me in this dynamic—satisfies every carnal urge that creates the makeup of my being.

I inhale sharply. Behold my beloved. Then press into her clit once more.

"Come for me. Now."

On command, she screams, then sobs, dropping the phone in the process. Head thrown back, she writhes in ecstasy and relief as her cunt gushes around my hand. "Well done, love," I praise. "That's it. Let it out. Give it all to me, Firecracker."

As the orgasm wanes, I gingerly remove my fingers and scoop her into my arms. She's shaking, her body sinking into sub drop from the intensity of the scene.

This was to be expected, especially because we haven't been alone together like this in a while. The primal need to comfort and care for her rips through me. It's my sole directive in this moment—in this life. I hold her close, rubbing a soothing hand up and down her back whilst I cradle her head to my chest.

"You did so well, Hunter. My perfect girl. You did beautifully for me. Such a perfect partner."

Praise flows out of me, and minutes pass, but despite the soothing words, her body shakes.

Gripping her chin firmly, I tilt her head back and look her in the eye.

"What do you need, love?"

Tears spill down her cheeks as she forces out her request. "Just hold me."

Chapter 33

Hunter

NOW

Spence's touch is tender; loving and soothing. He rubs my back and whispers words of praise as he holds me, providing me with the exact aftercare I crave after such an intense scene.

"You're incredible, love. You did so, so well."

I hear his words. I feel the sincerity of his affirmations. But I can't do anything but nod and curl tighter into his lap.

When that alone doesn't satiate my need for comfort, I nuzzle my face into his side.

Several minutes pass, but the heady haze of subspace lingers still. Typically, I love reaching this state. It's one of the things I crave most from our dynamic. Letting go completely is pure and utter bliss for me most days.

Tonight, though, I feel an awful lot like I did when I was drugged by my mother.

A sob racks through me at the reminder.

"You're all right, love. I've got you. You're safe, Hunter. I swear you're safe with me."

I know I'm safe. Even so, my heart and my soul are still reeling from the events of the last week.

Spence hugs me tighter, then checks the time on his phone. Not because he's preoccupied, but because, clearly, I'm not recovering the way I normally do.

Tentatively, he kisses my forehead, then bows lower to meet my gaze. "Should you have safe-worded, love?"

It's a fair question. With the low I'm riding now, I can understand his concern. He's not sure the crash is worth the pleasure.

Yet...

I refuse to let my mother change me. I refuse to become a victim of my trauma, especially in this case, when it's so closely tied to something I genuinely love.

Decidedly, I shake my head.

"I just need to let it out," I force out between hiccups.

Spence cups my head to his chest once more, then places his chin on the crown of my head.

"Let it out, then. I'm not going anywhere. I'll hold you like this forever if it's what you need. But remember: You're strong, Hunter. So magnificently determined. You can do anything you set your mind to, love. I believe that with the entirety of who I am."

I cry harder.

Spence holds me tighter.

We exist like that for what feels like hours—me, allowing my emotions to surge through me, knowing I'm safe in his arms. Him, holding me through it all, letting me process without judgment. He's my release and my safest harbor; the person I trust most in the whole wide world.

Eventually, I must drift off, because I'm softly jostled awake by the soft but persistent noise of his phone vibrating on the desk.

"Are you well, love?" he asks, his attention still singularly focused on me.

Yawning, I stretch my neck to one side, then the other. Then I take a deep, fortifying breath. "I am." It's the truth. Quickly, I turn and straddle his lap. "Thank you," I tell him, kissing him with the next breath.

"Always, love. Always."

"Spence?"

"Yes, Firecracker?"

"I love you."

They're words I've felt for years but have never been brave enough to say.

But that's what he does for me. Spence makes me brave. He builds me up and makes me feel like I'm invincible. He brings me back to life when I've hit my lowest low. He provides for me in ways I didn't even know I needed until our fate aligned and we established this deeply trusting dynamic.

I love him.

I love him with my whole heart, in all the ways one person can love another.

His face is even and stoic as he brushes my hair away from my forehead and cups my face in his hands.

"There isn't anything I wouldn't give you. There's nothing I value more in this life than your happiness and well-being. You're the sun and every other star in my sky, Hunter St. Clair. My life's purpose is to help you shine." He brings his lips to my ear, his scruff tickling my jaw, and whispers, "I love you, too."

And I melt into a puddle.

His phone vibrates on the desk again, bursting the intimate bubble we've hidden ourselves away in.

Chuckling, he reaches forward then shows me the screen.

"As much as I'd love to stay locked away with you in my arms tonight, I fear that's not an option. Garrett is quite concerned about our whereabouts. Dinner's been ready for nearly an hour."

Panic lances through me as I remember where we are, who else is here, and what Spence mentioned in the heat of the moment when he had the camera pulled up on his phone. "Wait—did you send him any of the pictures?"

He scowls as if I've insulted him. "No, love. I would never do that without explicit consent."

In my heart of hearts, I knew he wouldn't. Still, it helps to hear him say it. Spence always has a way of reminding me that I'm ultimately the one in control.

"Would you like me to delete the pictures and video?" he asks.

Smirking, I shake my head. "No. Save them. You have my consent to use them any time you need to jerk one out and I'm not around to lend a hand, mouth, or hole."

He swats playfully at my ass. "Naughty."

Hopping to my feet, I snag my clothes from the heap I left them in on the floor and start redressing.

"Where do you think you're going?" he teases.

My stomach grumbles, as if on cue. "I'm starving."

That inspires him to start shutting down his devices and fix his clothing, too.

"Well, then, let's go see what your brother has prepared for us this evening, shall we?"

Chapter 34

Hunter

NOW

"It doesn't have to be London, although I can assure you, the accommodations are top-tier, and you'll want for nothing. I'm committed to keeping us together and seeing this through."

Thoughtful silence falls over the group, punctuated by subtle chirps of insects and the ebb and flow of the lake hitting the shoreline.

We ate a delicious—although slightly cold—meal, prepared by Greedy and Sione, out on the upper deck. We're still gathered around the table now, dressed in layers and wrapped in blankets I found in the living room, discussing what's next.

It's more clear than ever that Magnolia has no boundaries when it comes to getting her way. We can't go back to the Ferguson house while she's there. I'm not sure we should even stay in North Carolina at this point.

So this is it. As a group, we need to work through a plan. Decide what comes next. Where we'll go, where we should live.

Guilt nags at my gut. All of this is only necessary because of my mother... because of *me*.

The guys have all agreed that they want to stick this out and see it through. For Greedy and Levi, that makes sense. They also have each other—a point that still thrills me when I think about our moment in the pantry. Or about what we'll share next.

Sione's desire to stay doesn't surprise me either. His plan was always to come to the States for chiropractic school. It was the fantasy we'd lie awake talking about. Once I left Italy, though, it felt like a forgotten dream. When I left, he remained, feeling compelled to stay to care for his grandparents and Villa Viola. A hopeful "someday" became a distant "someday" when we parted. But now that he's here, I don't see him leaving my side.

Kabir has the most to lose. Although he's an international mogul, his day-to-day business operations are based in London. He's already disrupted his life in significant ways since his arrival. It doesn't make sense for him to stay here.

It's not just him I worry about, though. It's the people who work for him, who depend on him for income and benefits. What happens to Gerald if Kabir remains in the States? What happens to the hundreds or maybe thousands of employees who work for his various ventures if he chooses to consolidate or change business operations?

"I'm not outright opposed to London," Greedy eventually replies, studying Kabir, then shifting his gaze to me. "I didn't apply to any international schools, though."

Greedy's life plan has always included medical school. He's been working toward this goal for as long as I've known him.

"Where did you apply?" Levi asks.

"Carolina Coastal. Northern State. A few Ivies up the East Coast. And a few schools in Northeast Ohio."

Sione rests his forearms on the table and angles forward. "You're waiting to hear back from those institutions?"

Greedy gives a quick shake of his head and a tight smile, as if he's embarrassed. "I already heard back. I got into all of them."

Tenderly, I squeeze his forearm. When he lifts his gaze to meet mine, I smile. I'm so proud of him for all he's accomplished, as well as all I know he's destined to achieve.

"Well done, you," Spence remarks. There's a softness and genuine sincerity to the praise.

"And you'll finish your undergrad this year?" Sione asks.

Greedy tips his head from side to side, then shrugs. "I could, but I wasn't planning on it." Sheepish now, he side-eyes me. "I was going to stick around here for another year."

For me.

He was going to stall his life for an entire year because of me.

My stomach twists in knots of devotion and guilt and shame. I'm startled from my spiraling thoughts when calloused fingertips caress my arm. When I glance up, Greedy takes my hand and squeezes. There's an unspoken confession in his touch, a truth I've known in my heart of hearts since the moment I returned to North Carolina.

He never gave up on us. More importantly, he never will.

I clear my throat. "What do you think, Si?"

Sione raises both hands behind his head, stretching back far enough that his T-shirt lifts to expose a peek of dark, taut, tatted abdomen.

"I have not even acclimated to this time zone yet, Mahina. I'll follow you anywhere."

Tears well in my eyes. Not because he's willing, but because there's an ease in which Sione cares. His love is effortless. It doesn't have to be earned, fought for, or cultivated. It just is.

I fight the sudden compulsion to rise from my seat and take up residence in his lap.

Leaning forward again, he taps out a rhythm on the tabletop with his knuckles. "If we head to Europe, we could use the villas until tourist season picks up. That would buy us a few months." The villas are his grandparents' main source of income. They rely on tourism season to support themselves all year long. I wouldn't want to be a hindrance to their ability to make a living, but this time of year, they're vacant. "You know Mamaie would love to have you back at the lake."

Pressure builds behind my eyes at the reminder. I love Sione's grandparents as if they are my own. I would be so happy to see them again, even if the circumstances aren't ideal.

Blowing out a long breath, I look to the only man who has yet to state his intent.

"Duke?"

With a pained sigh, Levi rests his forearms on the table. Lifting his backward ball cap off his head, he runs one hand through his blond tresses, then replaces it.

Wary resignation rolls off him as his brows pinch together in concern. "I can't really afford to go anywhere."

Kabir and Greedy instantly sound off their objections.

Despite knowing damn well money doesn't have to be an issue for any of us if we're together, Levi won't easily accept the idea of either man bank-rolling his life.

Slowly, I rise and circle the table. I hover beside Levi until he sits back in his chair. Once he's made room, I plop down into his lap, curling my legs underneath me and circling my arms around his broad shoulders.

"Hold up. Had I expressed hesitation, you would have straddled my lap?" Sione teases. "Perhaps now I want to change my original answer."

Snickering, I shoot him a mock glare. Then I turn back to Levi and cup his face in my hands. His denim-blue eyes meet mine, wary and uncertain.

He's not doubting us, but he is doubting his own worth. Judging himself against the others. Worrying about how he'll contribute.

"Wherever we go, you can find work. I'm not asking you to accept a handout indefinitely. Just long enough for us to make a clean break." I brush my lips against his, squeezing him tighter. "I don't want to do this without you, Duke."

Seconds tick by. The sound of the lake grows louder in my ears, water lapping at the shoreline in time with my heartbeat as I hold my breath and wait out his answer.

Eventually, he exhales, and the tension drains from his body.

"Yeah. Okay." He pecks my lips, sealing his promise with a kiss, then raises his gaze to the other men around the table. "I'm in. Up for whatever. I don't have much to contribute at this point, but I'll go wherever you go, if it's okay that I'm figuring my shit out along the way."

Quiet assurances and confirmation rise up around us.

I inhale a fortifying breath. "Okay. We're doing this."

"Apparently," Spence remarks. "Now, the only question remains is where we're going. I'd be remiss to not strongly advocate for going overseas. It just feels... safer... putting an entire ocean and several nations between you and Magnolia."

"I don't disagree," Greedy pipes up. "But I'm not sure I want to relocate permanently. I need to know if and when I'll be able to attend medical school. If we really think this needs to be a long-term arrangement, then I need to consider international options."

Ugh. The last thing we need is more dissonance in the group. If Spence and Greedy can't agree on a plan, I won't be able to take sides.

Groaning, I sit up, preparing myself to serve as mediator.

Levi tightens his grip on my hips, locking me in place. "Let's see how this plays out. I think Spence has got it," he whispers in my ear.

With a long exhale, I lean back and will myself to wait it out.

Spence regards Greedy thoughtfully, his lips pressed together. "If Europe is where we land, it wouldn't be forever. I doubt Magnolia will receive a partial transplant without Hunter's donation. I assume she has a year left, two at most?"

Greedy settles back in his seat, elbows on his armrests, considering Spence's assessment. "I could do a bit of digging. See if I could find her latest test results or medical records in my dad's office at home. That would give us a lot of insight into the situation, but given what we know about her prognosis, I believe you're correct."

"I usually am," Spence quips.

A snort escapes me. Spence is such an abrasive egomaniac when he wants to be. I'm really fucking lucky the guys warmed up to him the way they have.

"I hate this for us," I comment, the words intended for no one in particular.

Levi wraps me up in a hug from behind. Out of everyone, he's most likely to commiserate with the layers of anger, grief, and shame that come with having such a toxic parent.

"I know, Tem." Greedy reaches over and squeezes my arm. "But when people show you who they are, you have to believe them."

Spence chimes in next. "She's not human, love. Her mind is twisted. The hard reality is that you're not her daughter. You're a product of her own making, and by that strain of logic, you are a possession she is entitled to. That she'll always feel entitled to. Where would it end? How far would she go?"

Silence hangs between us as the weight of Spence's ominous questions linger in the air.

The world is quiet and still for a breath.

Then Greedy sits up straighter, looking out over the lake. Spence notes his reaction, then follows his gaze before hurriedly rising to his feet and rushing to the railing.

They say nothing. They offer no clues beyond the urgency of their reactions. Their movements are stiff, though. Concerned.

Though I can't see what's caught their attention, a deluge of dread washes over me, and tears well in my eyes out of habit.

Everything I love leaves.

I try to form a question. When that doesn't work, I try to muster up a plea.

Sit down.

Don't leave.

What's happening?

Please stay.

I open and close my mouth several times, but no sounds escape me.

When Greedy rises from the table and stalks over to join Spence along the handrail, that's when I know something isn't right.

"What's going on?" Levi asks, shifting me to his good leg so he can see more clearly where the guys are hovering. "What's out there?"

Sione stands, then silently walks over to our side of the table and places a hand on my shoulder.

We wait. I stare at Spence's and Greedy's backs, their bodies tense and guarded as they stand shoulder to shoulder.

Finally, Spence turns back to us, his face stone cold and somber.

"There's light on the water, love. A boat is approaching."

My stomach bottoms out, and trepidation washes over me like a wave.

Flovely.

Fucking. Lovely.

Chapter 35

Sione

NOW

Hunter stiffens on Levi's lap as the energy around us transforms into an angry, palpable force.

A boat is approaching.

Based on the reactions of the group, this is not an anticipated visit or a welcome surprise.

"I'll grab the radio," Greedy comments, sidestepping the Brit on his way to the house.

"Mahina," I murmur, aiming to soothe and comfort. Instead, Hunter's eyes grow even wider, her panic simmering right below the surface.

Hers isn't the only maniacal, desperate energy I sense among us.

"Let Levi up," I suggest, offering her both my hands.

She freezes in place as her baser instincts vie for dominance.

"Up," I repeat, my tone more assertive this time. She complies, and I take her hands and pull her gently to her feet.

A heartbeat later, Levi bolts up and rushes to stand by the Brit's side.

"Detain them. Don't allow them off the boat," Greedy says into a walkie-talkie-type device as he returns.

Crackles over the device make the "affirmative" barely audible, but it's there.

"The guard doesn't know who's approaching. They don't have any deliveries or other scheduled arrivals on the manifest. They're sending someone to check the marina for unregistered vehicles."

Hunter tries to pull away.

I tighten my hold on her hands, then guide her body until her back is pressed against my chest. Wrapping my arms around her shoulders, I dip my chin and find her ear, wanting to soothe her.

The erratic, frantic rhythm of her pulse distracts me instead.

"Your heart, Mahina. Your heart. You need to breathe," I tell her softly.

"It's not just my heart I'm worried about," she replies on a broken whisper. Tears cascade down her cheeks and land on the tatted skin of my hand.

Another call comes through the radio. From where we stand, it's difficult to make out each word, but from what I can piece together, there are two people on the boat: a man and a woman. Based on the direction they're traveling, they're clearly intent on docking here.

"She found me," Hunter whispers, her breaths ragged. "She found me." The words are louder, more panicked this time, garnering the attention of the three men standing at the railing.

They are strangers to me in so many ways. Yet we are united in this moment. For this woman. In this cause.

"What should we do?" Hunter attempts to pull away from me again, panicking, and this time, I let her go, but I remain close.

As she strides toward the others, her frenetic energy blooms like a mushroom cloud of dread.

"Should we hide? Go into the house and lock the doors? Decker has a security system, and Kylian has a secret room upstairs, but—" A sob escapes her.

Panic lances through me as I absorb the intensity of her despair.

"What should we do?" she cries once more.

Hunter's blond hair whips around her shoulders as she looks to Greedy, then Levi, and then back over to me.

"*What should we do?*" This time when she asks, her attention is singularly focused on the Brit.

Steely gray eyes meet mine over her head. Though I've only just met this man, the resolve on his face is crystal clear to me.

"Take her inside," Spencer commands. "All of you, go inside, secure the doors, set the security system, and wait for further instructions."

Levi and Greedy break into a litany of objections.

"Do as I say!" Spence barks. "You're still healing." He points to Levi. "And you cannot be complacent in what I am prepared to do, should it become necessary. I swear to gods, all of you go inside *now*."

Hunter rears back, but Levi and Greedy stay frozen on either side of Spencer.

He pulls out his phone and frantically types out a message while muttering under his breath. "I told her to stay away. I warned her she was done."

"She" could only be Hunter's mother.

Tugging my girl into my side, I hold her tight, sheltering her with my body. When she lets me support her weight without putting up a fight, I take her in and discover a blank expression. Fuck. She's shutting down.

"Let's go." I cock a brow and zero in on Greedy, then Levi. She needs to be inside, away from this threat and out of harm's way.

The two men look from me to Hunter to the lake, conflicted. Whether they're resisting Spencer's missive due to their egos or are driven by a true need to protect and defend, I don't know. What I do know is that the girl in my arms is liable to fall apart at any moment. The anxiety and stress of her mother's threatening surprise visit is too much to cope with in this moment.

"She needs you," I add simply.

That gets the attention of both men.

Levi locks eyes with me and nods. He takes two steps toward us, then reaches back, snatches Greedy's hand, and pulls him along behind.

Greedy's jaw drops, his expression sharp, as if he's about to object.

The radio squawks in his hand again, startling all of us.

"Identities have been confirmed. Mrs. Lansbury and an approved skipper are on the boat. He only intends to drop her off, then head back to the North Marina. Can we allow her up?"

Another sob racks through Hunter. This time, it's a strangled cry full of pure exhaustion.

Greedy radios back down, and Spence stays glued to his phone, locked in on its screen.

Levi comes to stand by my side and pulls Hunter into a hug, whispering quiet reassurances in her ear.

Despite the rapid turn of events for the better, a much-needed sense of relief alludes us. Anxiety remains high and energies are still off, even as an older woman ascends the stairs and joins us on the deck.

Her white hair is twisted up into a tight bun. The concern marring her face makes the natural wrinkles around her eyes appear even deeper than they are. She appears to be older than my Mamaie, but her kind smile and warm, maternal nature feel so beautifully familiar.

As she takes us all in, the tension in the air finally dissipates. Her energy is warm, soothing, motherly. She's a divine feminine spirit if I ever encountered one. The worry creasing her brow is apparent. But at her core, she is good and pure and deeply caring.

"The guard said I gave you lot a fright. My apologies, dears."

Hunter untangles herself from Levi, then cautiously approaches the older woman. "Hi, Mrs. Lansbury. It's okay. We just weren't expecting anyone tonight," she says, offering the older woman a hug in greeting.

"Josephine sent me to look after you. I'm thankful she and Decker called when they did. I've been awfully bored sitting at home waiting for them to return."

"You work for Crusade?" Greedy asks.

"Work for him? I practically raised that boy." Mrs. Lansbury laughs, the sound melodic and cheerful.

"You're British?" Spencer asks.

"Born and raised in East End she says, chin lifted with pride.

"You don't say." A lightness twinkles in Spencer's eyes for the first time in hours. "I look forward to introducing you to my valet, Gerald. He's from East of Aldgate Pump."

Spencer reaches for Mrs. Lansbury's belongings, then offers to escort her inside. Levi says something about hitting the gym and needing to blow off steam.

"Come on, let's get you settled," Greedy tells Hunter. With a look at me, he tips his chin toward the house.

I stand still, watching them all move around me. What just happened is something I hope to never experience again in this lifetime.

Hunter's fears are so palpable—so real and raw and valid.

Her mother is a menace, a threat much greater than I originally understood.

Despite not knowing where we go from here, one point is crystal clear: we cannot go on like this.

Chapter 36

Hunter

NOW

I took a bath. Meditated with Sione. Sent a request for a next-day telehealth appointment with my therapist from London.

I did everything I could think to do to settle my nervous system.

That's when it hit me.

This isn't the time for settling. For keeping my cool and staying calm.

This is a time for action.

We have decisions to make. We have an offensive strategy to plan.

I'm done sitting around waiting to see what happens next.

It's time to take my fate, along with my future with the men I love, back into my own hands.

As I step into the theater room, the mood of the group already gathered shifts. All four guys are here, and it wasn't until I texted Spence after I was done blow-drying my hair that I discovered where they'd gone.

Though this is a movie room, the big-screen is dark. The guys are sitting together in the first row, save for Sione, who's sitting in front of them on the floor. They're talking quietly, listening to each other intently. No one is cracking jokes or throwing jabs. Apparently, the arrival of the mystery boat and the chaos it created changed the dynamic between my men.

It makes sense. It rewired my brain, too.

It's necessary. This change. Something has to give. The idea of relying on old habits doesn't sit well with me. In the past, I ran from my problems as a means of survival. I don't want to live like that any longer.

A sudden, steadfast urge to shed all former versions of myself hits me. It's time to break free from the facets of myself that no longer serve me in order to protect this group. These amazing, sincere, dedicated men that I love on so many levels.

I stop before them, wait for the room to go quiet, and make my intention known.

"No more running."

Four sets of eyes land on me, their expressions a full spectrum of concern, admiration, and wonder.

"Tem—" Greedy chokes out, already rising to his feet.

I knew he'd be the first to object. Just like I know he'll be the hardest sell.

Arms out, I silently invite him to approach. His steps are cautious, as if he doesn't quite know what I want from him in this moment.

Although I'm aware of the three men watching us, I keep my gaze solely focused on my first love. "I need you."

He's by my side a second later, wrapping one large arm around my back and anchoring me to him. "You have me," he vows with a kiss on the crown of my head. "Always."

I close my eyes, sink into his hold, and revel in the deep-seated trust and care this man and I share. He has *always* been worth fighting for. Worth staying for. It was me who wasn't ready, who wasn't worthy or sure enough in my sense of self to know that I deserve his love.

I'm not giving this up for anything. Not now. Not ever again.

"I want to stay here. I want to fight. I want to build a life with all of you, where we're not constantly on alert or worried about what's next."

"No more running." I peer up at Greedy, finding fresh understanding in his gaze, then turn back to the others.

When I look to Levi, he's nodding earnestly, just like I knew he would be. "I'm in," he declares. "For all of it." He pauses and looks around at the other guys. "With all of you."

Greedy squeezes into my side, and I nuzzle even closer, willing him to feel the silent assurance I'm communicating. Assurance that this is real, that this is happening, and that this is how it's meant to be.

A love like ours? It's the rarest kind.

It endures and it waits. It galvanizes and it grows.

It's also delicate in the most fragile of ways. It needs nurturing. It needs the kind of devotion Greedy has poured into it, despite my past choices and my attempts to push him away.

What we have is special. It's that once-in-a-lifetime love people dream about. And I get to experience it four times over.

I want it. I trust it. I'm willing to do whatever it takes to fight for it now.

No more running.

This love is worth staying for.

"Sione?" I worry my bottom lip between my teeth. "What do you think?"

His smile is wide and his posture relaxed. When his warm brown eyes lift to meet mine, I already have my answer. "I'm here. I'm in. As long as my presence does not cause any turmoil, stress, or harm to anyone in the group."

The others instantly break out in reassurances, denying any concern about his presence.

A silent sigh of relief escapes me. God, it's incredible, how easily they've accepted my sweet Si. It just reaffirms for me that this is how it was always meant to be.

Sione nods, murmurs his thanks to each man, then fixes his attention on me. "Then where you lead, I will follow. Or, in this case, if you ask me to stay, I will bloom where we settle."

"Come on, man," Levi groans. "Why does everything you say sound like fucking poetry? I feel like I'm back in English lit trying to keep up with all your fancy declarations." With a teasing huff, he nudges Sione with his sneaker.

Si captures the other man's leg in defense, but his face falls a moment later. "Is your leg hurting right now?"

Levi's brows raise in surprise. "It doesn't feel great. I worked out earlier but didn't stretch much afterward—"

Sione hops to his feet. "May I work on it for you?"

Levi stammers something that sounds like "be my guest," but when Sione's massive, tatted hand clamps down around his upper thigh, he freezes, holding his breath.

We're all silent as Si closes his eyes and gently rubs up and down Levi's quad, assessing him over his pants.

"You're holding too much tension in this muscle. It's healing from an injury, yes?"

Levi's blue eyes are bright with shock and curiosity.

I haven't said a word to Si about the injury or surgery, but I'm not surprised he could sense and identify the root of Levi's pain. Sione is a Reiki master, yoga teacher, and energy healer. He triple majored in premed, biology, and philosophy. He was offered a full ride to three chiropractic schools because, clearly, he's enormously talented when it comes to helping and healing.

I press my lips together and watch the two of them, Sione intent on helping Levi, while Levi stares on in awe. After a few moments, I tilt my chin up to Greedy, then bump his hip with mine.

He reads me like an open book, freely offering up the assurance I crave.

"You don't have to ask, Tem. You have me. You've always had me."

Spence rises from his seat and saunters to my free side. He takes my hand, caressing my knuckles with the pad of his thumb. When we lock eyes, I know he's in as well.

"I am yours, Firecracker. I am theirs. I'm not going anywhere."

"It's settled, then." I tilt my head up to Greedy, desperate for him to see the sincerity in my eyes. "This is it. This is what I want."

His responding nod is solemn. Bending low, he places the tenderest of kisses on my lips.

Levi turns to us. "If we're staying—"

"We have to fight," Kabir finishes.

Greedy and I pull apart, and with a steadying exhale, I nod. Staying means putting an end to Magnolia's efforts once and for all. How we go about doing that? I have no idea.

Spencer squeezes my hand, then straightens his spine and addresses the room. "I have a plan of sorts. It will take a few days to coordinate and implement, and I may need to call on outside assistance."

"Who?" Greedy asks.

"Walsh and his cohort."

I fight back a snicker. I can't wait to tell Joey that Kabir called her relationship a cohort. Or that he thinks Kylian is their ringleader. Although, nowadays, I guess he kind of is. Also, I suppose I've technically got a cohort of my own, too.

My heart tugs when I think about Joey and her guys. I miss her fiercely. Being at the Crusade Mansion without her is way less fun.

"Hunter trusts them," Kabir continues. "Do you as well?"

Greedy rubs my low back, his touch reassuring. "I do."

Another flash of relief washes over me. For a short time, we may have been at odds about how to handle this situation, where to go, and how to proceed. But it's clear that the incident with the boat changed our perspectives and fundamentally set us on a new course.

One where we stand our ground. One where we stick together, no matter what.

"You'll need to follow my lead. Play along. There may be some... surprises, depending on how things unfold. Can I count on you in that way?"

Spence's question is directed at Greedy, but it's Levi who interjects. Rising to his feet, he turns and offers Sione a hand up.

"We can help."

"You can, and you will," Spence says. "We'll all need to play our parts. But you need to trust me to assign the roles."

"I trust you," I tell him wholeheartedly.

He pulls me away from Greedy, wraps one hand around the back of my neck, and brings his lips to my ear.

"I know, love. Endgame, forever and always." He places a kiss below my ear, then bites at my neck for good measure. "Now be a good girl and help me get our boys on board."

Turning me, he bands both arms over my chest, holding me in place.

With my hands cupped around his strong forearms, I take in my other guys one at a time. "I want to stay. I want to fight. And I want to try Spencer's plan. Is that okay?"

Three sets of eyes—mossy green, dark denim blue, and warm brown—all meet my gaze, and each man before me nods.

"Okay, then. We're doing this."

"First things first," Kabir says, still holding me tight. "I've coordinated with a private nurse. She will come here in the morning to draw Hunter's blood. We need to have it evaluated for traces of flunitrazepam or anything else that indicates she was drugged."

"Is that really necessary?" Levi asks.

I go to him and link my arm through his, curling into his side. His concern for me makes my heart melt. But I'm with Spence on this one. I want proof of what Magnolia did, by any means necessary.

"It is," Greedy offers before I can speak up. "If we're fighting this, we need proof. My dad is the smartest man I know. He's also the dumbest when it comes to Magnolia. Hard evidence and data will make a difference." Lowering his head, he gives it a shake, and his next words come out far more softly. "It has to."

"I have not met Magnolia, but I fear she is conniving and boundless in her limits," Si says. "How will you ensure results are not tampered with?"

Spence grins. "I have a friend to help in that arena. All bloodwork will be run through Crusade Labs. Kylian Walsh will supervise."

Based on Spence's expression and my knowledge of how he likes to operate, it's safe to assume that he's already set this up with Kylian. I don't know why the idea of him and Kylian plotting together makes me giggly. I can't wait to talk to Joey and gossip about our guys' budding bromance.

"Since the nurse is coming by the house tomorrow anyway," Spence continues. "I propose we all have blood drawn to evaluate for disease or infection."

Oh. That's an unexpected twist.

"Evaluated? For what? STIs?"

"Precisely. Seeing as how our group has grown"—he tips his chin toward Sione—"and certain dynamics have evolved"—this time, he looks to Greedy, then Levi—"I think it best we all get tested and treated if needed. A clear bill of health for everyone now that the gang's all here."

Greedy's the first to consent. "That's a good idea. I'm in."

"Yeah, me, too," Levi says softly.

I squeeze his arm once more, then turn to the fifth member of this group. "Si?" He doesn't love conventional western medicine. I'm also certain he hasn't been physically intimate with anyone but me for the last few years. I don't need to see his results, but I'm not the only one who should be considered here anymore.

Sione shoots me a sly grin. "A bit of blood never stopped us before," he declares, his voice as melodic as ever. "I'm in."

Chapter 37

Sione

THEN: WINTER, YEAR TWO
MENSTRUATION PHASE

"My period started."

Hunter shuffles toward the bed, her soft features marred by a pained grimace. I sensed the discomfort when we were working in the kitchen, then again as we got ready for bed.

Her aura is drawn suffocatingly tight around her subtle body, brushing right up against her tan, freckled skin. Her energy shield is so weak it's nearly transparent in some places.

She pulled the Nine of Wands when we worked with my deck earlier this week. In retrospect, the impending battle and need to pause makes perfect sense.

We're in my room now, both freshly showered and ready for bed after a long evening deboning chicken and cooking matzo balls for Mamaia. Tourism season is over, but the group of three couples who rent out the entire compound for a few months each winter will be here soon. Most guests who come to Villa Viola want authentic Italian cuisine. These guests have come for decades, staying so long and so often that they've sampled every meal Mamaia knows how to make. Apparently, her matzo ball soup is their favorite, so we've been making huge batches of it ahead of their arrival.

"How do you feel?" I sit on the edge of the bed and open my arms.

She comes to me with ease and sinks into my embrace.

Some of Hunter's cycles are physically harder on her body, while other months, the emotional turmoil and intrusive thoughts are what wreak the most havoc.

I want to help. I want to *heal*.

What ails the beautiful being in my arms, though, cannot be completely relieved by a single methodology or treatment plan.

I've spent hours upon hours researching PMDD and alternative methods to alleviate the symptoms. Ultimately, I've concluded that the poison is the antidote; the chemical reactions affecting her brain and body aren't just ailments: they're clues. Universal nudges.

If she's more tired than usual, she needs sleep.

If she's more irritable than usual, she needs space and permission to go inward.

If her uterus is cramping and her body aches, she needs heat and comfort, massage and orgasms—anything that will alleviate the intensity of her body's contracting, spasming physiological response to the onset of her period.

The poison is the antidote.

Whatever she needs, I will give it to her. However I can support her, I intend to.

I can fetch her a hot water bottle from the main house if the physical ache is her main complaint. We can meditate together, or I can just hold her if her emotions feel out of control.

"Mahina," I urge, desperate to help but needing her feedback and consent. "How do you feel?"

"I'm okay," she sniffles.

I balk at the blatant lie, reeling back and pinning her with a frown.

"Well, not okay," she amends. "But this feels... the same way it usually feels. I'll be fine," she says hollowly. Then, directly into my bare chest, she murmurs, "I just didn't want you to be disappointed tonight."

I still, waiting for her to expand on that statement.

When she doesn't, I clear my throat. "What do you mean?"

She pulls back, her uncomfortable grimace clueing me in to the heart of the issue.

Our physical relationship may have started as the slowest of burns, but over the last few weeks, it has erupted into a blazing inferno.

She's insatiable. I'm voracious.

We seek each other out each night. We make love before bed, in the early hours before the sun rises, sometimes even during our afternoon break.

Now that my sexuality has been fully awakened and I've experienced the limitless bliss derived from connecting my body with hers, there's no place else I want to be. When I'm not buried inside her, I'm thinking about being buried inside her. It's an honor and a privilege to pleasure the physical container of her soul.

"You don't want to make love tonight?" I keep my words even, despite the way my chest constricts at the very thought of not physically being connected to my soul match.

With the cutest wrinkle of her nose, Hunter says, "It's not possible."

Possible? Of course it's possible.

"Anything is possible, but we don't have to if it makes you uncomfortable or you think it could exacerbate your pain. But if staying in here would be a comfort to you, I would prefer it."

I can't imagine sending her back to her own room down the hall, knowing she's hurting like this. If she wants or needs the space, I'll grant her that illusion of privacy. But that doesn't mean I won't stay up all night and sit outside her door.

She's quiet as she contemplates. Too quiet, and for too long.

Throat tightening, I run a hand down her back. "Mahina..."

Her voice is small and shaky when she speaks. "You would... have sex with me tonight? When I'm on my period?"

I scoff at the doubt she harbors. "You speak as if it would be a hardship. I can assure you—it wouldn't be."

She smiles up at me then, and I cannot resist pressing a kiss to the tip of her nose. "There's not a day, night, time, or place where I don't want to be buried inside you."

She cringes. "It'll be messy."

Grinning slyly, I run my nose against her jawline, then leave a little path of kisses from her ear to her collarbone. "I'll be sure to help the housekeeper change and wash the sheets tomorrow."

She smiles against my neck. "You're the housekeeper this week," she says, the lightness in her voice restored. Then, a little less certain, she asks, "You're sure?"

I seek her lips with mine and kiss her with all the tenderness I possess, then press harder, silently asking to be let in.

When she opens for me, I caress her tongue with mine. She releases the softest sigh into my mouth. Before we can get too carried away, though, I pull back and answer her question.

"As sure as I am of the moon's permanent presence in the night sky, I want to make love to you tonight. I want to slide between your blood-slicked thighs. I want to move inside you, stroking your core and connecting with your soul, until your walls quiver with a pleasure so intense, it wipes out all the pain."

Situating back on the bed, I beckon for her to join.

"Undress, Mahina. Reveal yourself to me, and I promise to reveal the very best secrets of the universe to you."

She rolls her eyes at the corniness of the line, but she scrambles to disrobe quickly anyway. I, too, remove my clothing. Then I gather my hair into an elastic and relax against the headboard.

She crawls to me, the sight causing my body to hum in recognition.

My cock throbs with an ache that can only be sated by her.

Her breasts swing beneath her, heavy and pink from her shower. When she positions herself between my legs, I home in on the apex of her thighs.

She is my first and final resting place. My home. The sanctuary where we both find our salvation.

"See?" She inhales a sharp breath.

I follow her gaze to where four or five drops of blood have already dripped onto the sheets below her.

"It's gross," she panics, worrying her bottom lip and searching my face.

I offer her the kindest, calmest smile. "It's not gross," I assure her. "It's you. Your essence. One part of yourself that you only share with me."

Guiding her body toward mine, I help her spread her legs wide and straddle my lap.

My abs clench with anticipation. My legs tense with eagerness.

"Let me care for you," I whisper, guiding my shaft to her entrance and coating myself with the blood escaping between her folds. "Let me fuck you and hold you and make it all feel better, from the inside out, from now until eternity."

Her delicate throat bobs as she swallows. Finally, she nods and rests her forehead on mine, then lowers herself onto my length.

Slickness and heat encase me. Comfort and wholeness surround me.

This sensation is unlike anything I've ever experienced. It isn't just physical. It isn't even just spiritual. We connect on a cosmological level. Her soul matches mine, the two of us fusing together in a bond I swear will sustain through this lifetime and all still to come.

"Spread yourself wide and give it all to me," I choke out as pleasure radiates up my spine.

She widens her legs, piercing herself on my throbbing tattooed cock.

"Now look down, Mahina. Watch us together. Watch how you paint me. Watch how I claim you. It was always supposed to be like this. You were always destined to own me, mind, body, and soul."

Her head bows, and together, we focus on the sacred place where we're joined.

When she rises to her knees, she exposes the blood-drenched rod I wield for her and only her. I hold my breath, waiting for her to reconnect us. I would wait forever for her. One lifetime will not be long enough to express the love and affection I harbor for this woman.

Placing my hands on her back, I guide her down until her thighs connect with my pelvis. Her body opens for me completely, and when she bottoms out, we moan in unison.

"Claim me, Mahina. Soak me with your blood the way you've steeped me in your soul. I was made for your pleasure. Use me and banish all the pain."

Desperately, as if she finally is giving herself permission to relish in the moment, she grips my hair and tips my head back. She kisses me frantically, as if she can't wait another second to take all I'm willing to give.

When she bites down on my bottom lip, I groan in pleasure, secretly hoping she'll puncture the skin and draw blood. I want to bleed for her, to give her everything she's giving me. I want to offer her the world and stay by her side through every experience.

As my desperation mounts and my arousal rises to unimageable heights, I take over. I need to deliver on my promise. I want her to feel so good she forgets all about the blood and the cramps, the fogginess and the backaches.

I hold her hips steady, reverently.

I thrust up inside her with slow, measured strokes.

Blood coats my cock, my thighs, her pubic hair, and low belly.

In all my travels around the sun, I've never witnessed a more beautiful sight.

"I can't wait to see you gush for me," I tell her, panting and thrusting with every ounce of strength I possess. "You're so slick and warm already. Just wait until all our essence combines and drips out of your needy, pulsating pussy."

"Close," she cries, her head thrown back in pleasure.

I capture one nipple in my mouth, then move over and ravish the other. "Look at me," I command.

She drops her chin, her eyes locking with mine. As her mouth forms into the most perfect O, I know she's got to be right there.

Her inner walls tighten, choking my length so hard I can barely move inside her. As the first ripple of pleasure takes hold, I yank her down so we're chest to chest and grind my pelvis against her clit.

"Coming. Coming. Coming," she chants. As if I can't feel her most sacred vessel pulsating around me like a vise.

I hold back and let her use me, clenching my abs and thighs, desperate to bring her every ounce of pleasure she deserves.

Once the spasms slow and her thighs melt against mine, I lift her up my body, holding her close and rubbing the length of my cock through her blood-soaked folds. My orgasm catapults through me, shooting off hot ribbons of cum that fall to the sheets below us.

Groaning, I settle back and resituate Hunter until she's draped over me. Her body is soft and lax, warm and still.

"How do you feel now?" I drag my fingers up and down her spine, then circle back to trace her rib cage.

As I brush against her invisible tattoo, tingles course up my arm. I was with her when she got it. I held her hand as she endured the chair. The rib cage was a bold choice for a tattoo virgin, but my girl was sure and fiercely determined.

The UV ink makes the piece of art invisible, and there within lies the true magic of the permanent design etched into her skin. The tattoo is always there, yet remains hidden. Five moons in a row, in various stages of cycle, ever-present, despite not always being visible to the naked eye.

Her tattoo is identical to the moons inked along my rib cage, though my piece was created with bold black ink. It's a physical reminder of the soul match we share.

Hunter yawns. "I feel amazing. Lighter. Spineless. Satisfied and hopeful."

"As you should." With a kiss to the crown of her head, I hold her tighter.

I want to make her feel just like this forever. I want to be the one who guides her through the darkest night and reminds her to chase the light. I want it to be me and her, in this lifetime and all the rest.

Chapter 38

Hunter

NOW

I'm brushing my teeth when a commotion down the hall catches my attention. This is it. The nurse who's going to take our blood has arrived.

Quickly, I finish and rinse out my mouth, then stare somberly at my reflection in the mirror.

My eyes still look tired, their usual sparkle dulled by the dark bags that have been ever-present since my mother returned to North Carolina. I've been without my usual skincare and makeup products for days. Thankfully, I've made liberal use of Joey's stash during our time at the Crusade mansion.

"Tem?" Greedy calls.

"Coming." I splash my face with cold water and pinch my cheeks to bring a bit of color back to my face and call it good, then I make my way down the hall, following the cacophony of voices and chatter in the kitchen.

I haven't had any matcha yet today, so my brain is a bit slow on the uptake. It's only after the familiar, husky laugh of a man I've known most of my life rises above the chatter that realization slams into me.

I jog past the pantry and weight room, desperate to confirm that I'm not imagining it.

My heartbeat is racing double-time as I dash into the kitchen.

"*Joey?*"

My best friend turns around and grins, and I nearly bowl her over as I wrap her in the biggest hug. I fight back tears of relief and joy, my chest trembling with emotion as she returns my embrace.

"What are you doing here?" I ask.

She pulls back enough to meet my gaze, her bright blue eyes filled with concern. "You needed me." Her words are succinct, as if it's a no-brainer. As if ending her honeymoon early to check in on me is perfectly reasonable.

In her arms, as she hugs me back fiercely, I close my eyes and soak in the comfort of her nearness. Just being in her proximity eases the stress weighing on me.

When I was younger, no one ever showed up for me simply because I needed them. My dad traveled for work nearly every week. My mom only wanted my company when she needed something from me. My old habits of running when things got tough robbed me of the opportunity to ever rely on anyone. The way I saw it, if I didn't count on anyone but myself, I could never be disappointed.

I didn't realize how much joy, hope, and love I was shutting out by living my life that way. Between my men and my best friend, I know I'll never be alone in a time of need again. They show up. Not because they have to, but because they want to.

"I really did need you. Thank you." The words are whispered into her hair as I give her another squeeze.

"Uh, Hunter?" Joey asks.

"Hmm?"

"Who's your new friend?"

My cheeks heat at the call out. Scrunching my nose, I fight back a grimace, then put on my big girl panties and introduce my bestie to man number four.

"Joey, guys, this is Sione. We met in Italy a few years ago and, well, he's going to be sticking around for a while."

To their credit, Joey's guys don't crack any jokes or make things awkward. They gather around Sione and take turns greeting him and offering him handshakes and back smacks.

Smirking, Joey leans in close. "Girl, please tell me this is the last of them. I'm not sure Greedy can handle anyone else."

I snort. She's not wrong.

"There's no one else," I assure her, looking on as the guys all make introductions.

Locke breaks away from the pack first. He strides to us, mischief dancing behind his eyes. "Damn, Hunter," he teases, pulling me into his massive, tatted arms for a hug. He's so solid and warm. Joey is so lucky to have him in her life.

"You claiming a spot in the Shittiest Parents Club with Cap and me wasn't on my bingo card."

Sighing, I pull away and give him an unamused eye roll. "Believe me, Nicky. I had no desire to join the club. We don't get a say in the hand we're dealt or the family we're born into."

His eyes flash with sadness, then soften. "Don't I know it." Cupping the back of my head, he angles in and places a quick kiss to my forehead. "We're all glad you're okay."

"We are," Kendrick confirms, splaying one enormous hand over Joey's abdomen and holding her tenderly. "You're not alone in this, St. Clair. We'll do anything in our power to help protect you from your ma."

Emotion clogs my throat. I know he would. They all would.

Decker and Kylian come over next, forming a loose circle that my guys end up joining as well.

"You're physically okay?" Decker asks, inspecting me like he has to check me over himself to believe it. It's very on-brand for Joey's control-loving husband.

"Physically, yes."

I leave it at that, and he doesn't dig deeper.

I've got a lot of emotions to sort through and a lot of trauma to heal from. That'll be the real work of recovering from this ordeal. But I know in my heart of hearts I can't even think about any of that until Magnolia is no longer an imminent threat.

"What can we do to help?" Decker asks.

"This helps." I hug Joey again, still blown away that they'd come home early for this.

"I'm serious. What else can we do for you?" His question is laced with desperation, and his eyes fill with determination as he surveys each of my guys.

Resting my head on Joey's shoulder, I play-punch him in the arm in an attempt to lighten the mood. "Don't you think cutting your honeymoon short for me was enough, Cap?"

His obsidian eyes darken as he hits me with a disapproving scowl.

Before I even realize what he's doing, he's wrapping Joey and me up in a hug. His hold on us is intense, as if he's still trying to convince himself that I'm here.

"I'm so sorry," he whispers as he holds me. "Back then? In high school? I had no idea what your mom was like or what you were going through at home. I wish you would have told me. I don't know if—"

I shake my head. There's no reason for him to blame himself for something neither of us could have fixed, let alone begun to understand when we were just kids.

"I wasn't even fully aware of what was happening back then," I tell him. "Between my parents' divorce and all that happened the summer after graduation..." I look to Greedy and Levi. "I downplayed her behavior to everyone, including myself. I don't know if I was secretly trying to protect her, or—"

"It was survival," Kylian chimes in, the statement flat and logical.

Survival.

The innate desire to stay alive.

My instinctive need to endure... then, eventually, to run.

It was always a means of survival.

"Yeah," I finally reply. "It was survival." Images of the lonely nights I spent holed up in my room assault me. All the times I snuck down to the kitchen in the middle of the night, starving, because I'd locked myself away all day to avoid my mom's unpredictable mood.

Joey slinks out of her husband's hold and shuffles over to Kylian.

Decker wraps both arms around me, hugging me even tighter. "I'm still sorry. If I had any idea, I would have done everything in my power to help."

I know he would have, because that's the kind of man he is to his core. He's always been a leader, but more importantly, he's always been a protector. Decker Crusade takes care of his people, full stop.

"Right. Well, then." Spence clears his throat. "I've witnessed just about as much physical affection between my girl and this group of men I've literally just met as I can tolerate. I think we can wrap this up now."

Levi tucks his chin and snickers.

"They're *fine*. Relax, your royal highness," Greedy teases.

"I will not *relax*, Garrett. He has his hands all over her. I don't even know these blokes, save for Walsh."

Decker's chest shakes with laughter. I keep my arms wrapped around his waist and hold on tight. Riling up Spence has become a beloved pastime for our group. May as well let Joey's "cohort" in on the fun, too.

"He's fine." Greedy strides over to Joey, snags her hand, and pulls her into a hug. "Now we're even, okay?"

He smirks at Spence, who's looking less and less amused and more like he wants to spank Greedy for his defiance.

Now that is a visual I wasn't expecting. I bite my bottom lip at the thought and the sudden flicker of heat in my belly.

"I can assure you that Crusade's heart belongs to one person only." Greedy playfully ruffles Joey's hair.

With a shriek, she tries to spin out of his arms. But rather than let her go, he guides her over to where Decker and I stand and plants a kiss on my shoulder.

He pulls back, his gaze fixed on mine but his words intended for my best friend. "Thanks for coming back, Joze. She really did need you."

Joey's eyes well with tears, making mine do the same. I'm so damn grateful she's here and that she so willingly and openly loves me, messy parts and all.

"You're welcome," she whispers to Greedy. "She needs you, too, ya know."

Eyes softening, Greedy zeroes in on me. "Yeah," he chokes out. "I know that now."

Chapter 39

Hunter

NOW

The day disappeared too quickly for my liking. Between the nurse's visit and helping Mrs. Lansbury prepare a huge meal for all ten of us, and then laughing until our stomachs hurt at Decker and Kendrick's stories about playing Little Dukes U-12 football with Greedy and Levi on their rival team, it was the kind of night I wish would never end.

Joey, Kylian, and Locke excused themselves after dessert with murmurs about being occupied for the rest of the night. As if we didn't know they were running off to have a sex marathon in Kylian's small room on the third floor affectionately dubbed the Nest.

Kendrick left soon after their departure. He hasn't seen his little sisters since Christmas, so he plans to spend the night with them at his dad's house. He has a training session in the morning anyway, so he has to be on campus early. From the sounds of it, he has a real shot at being drafted. He's working harder than ever to prepare for the scouting combine.

Decker excused himself last. He plans to sleep in Joey's room, that way no one in our group has to deal with moving belongings tonight.

That's all well and good, though I'd be thrilled if a few of my men would relocate after all.

Once Decker has disappeared up the stairs, I rise from my seat, stretch my arms overhead, and yawn.

"What's on your mind, Mahina?"

Sione's always been able to read me. Whether it's my mood, energy level, or attitude, he's perceptive as hell, and he's expertly tuned in to me still, even after being apart for so long.

Looking at each of my men one at a time, I just come out with it.

"Can we all sleep together tonight? In Decker's room?"

Spence smirks and raises both eyebrows. "You want to have a four and/or five way in your best friend's marital bed, Firecracker?"

"I'm in if we can go somewhere *besides* Decker's room," Levi pipes up before I can explain.

Wrapping my arms around my torso, I shrink in on myself. Maybe it was a silly idea.

"I'm anxious about tomorrow," I murmur. "Saying we're going to face this is one thing. Having to see Magnolia in person feels like a whole other level of scary."

Because that's the plan. Tomorrow, we'll head to the Ferguson household, all five of us, and we'll face Magnolia and Dr. Ferguson head-on.

Spence shoves back his seat and strides over to me. "I feel like a right arse." He strokes his knuckles over my cheek. When the cool metal of his rings brushes against my skin, I shiver.

"As you should," Greedy scolds from where he's tipped back on two legs, arms up behind his head.

Levi's sitting straight, face lit up. "I'm still in."

I can't help but roll my eyes.

"I think it's a good idea, Tem," Greedy agrees.

Chin tipped up, I search Spence's expression.

Thoughtful eyes assess me as he continues to stroke my face affectionately. "I shouldn't have said what I did. I'm sorry."

"It's okay." Pressing up on tiptoes, I kiss his lips and cover his hand with mine. "Will you join us?"

Spence removes my hand from his, bringing my fingers to his lips and kissing the tips. I stroke his cheek the way he just stroked mine, loving the way his short, bristling stubble feels under my palm.

"I have a few meetings scheduled tonight. I won't be done until about four, but I'll join you as soon as I'm able."

I kiss him again, more reverently this time. I'm so damn grateful to him for so willingly upending his entire life to stay here with me. I feel honored and truly treasured because of the sacrifices he's making to be by my side.

"Are you okay with this plan, Si?"

"Of course, Mahina." Sione yawns. "Although I'd like to go to bed sooner rather than later. The time change is still not registering for me, and I could use a good night's sleep."

When we exit the dining room, we find Mrs. Lansbury in the kitchen, hand-washing a serving dish. Interestingly, Gerald is also stationed near the sink, drying towel in hand.

Greedy nudges me in the side, jutting his chin toward the pair. When I meet his gaze, he waggles his brows. I have to cover my mouth to keep from laughing. He's such a hopeless romantic.

"Do you need any help?" I ask the older couple.

Mrs. Lansbury drops the dish into the sink with a clatter and sucks in a startled breath. "No, no. Not at all. We're—I mean, I'm fine here, dears. Just going to finish up, then set the coffee and kettle for the morning."

"I'll be up a while longer, but I plan to be in the study," Spence tells them.

We all say our good-nights, then head down the hall that leads to the primary wing.

Greedy turns and walks backward, his voice a mock-whisper. "So if Mrs. Lansbury gets with your butler, does that mean you and Decker will be related?"

With ridiculously fast reflexes, Spence playfully knocks Greedy upside the head.

"*Boys.*" I admonish them before Greedy can retaliate and they start wrestling right here in the hallway. I refuse to disturb anyone in the house with their rowdy antics. Thank goodness the Nest is completely soundproof.

Levi catches my drift and slyly comes between them to prevent any potential escalation.

"His name is Gerald," Spence corrects, rolling up his shirtsleeves as he struts ahead of us now, head high. "Which you already know. And he's my valet. Which you *also* know. What he gets up to on his own time is of no mind to me." Then, with a smirk over his shoulder, he adds, "Why do you think I warned them I'd be up a while? Wouldn't want to catch *them* snogging in the pantry now, would we?"

Levi's eyes double in size. Greedy barks out a laugh. Sione just shakes his head, meeting my gaze with a curious tilt of his head.

Without another word, Spence makes a ninety-degree turn into the study.

The rest of us take our time winding down before bed. Sione stretches, which is standard for him. Though I'm surprised when Levi and then Greedy join him and follow his lead. Sione strays from his usual flow, the ritual I know by heart, and instead shows the guys a few seated stretches focused on the upper thighs.

When they're finished, we all take turns using the bathroom. Greedy walks in on me brushing my teeth and sidles up beside me to do the same.

We stand shoulder to shoulder, scrubbing away. I giggle every time I meet his gaze in the mirror. It feels so normal, so domestic, going through a bedtime routine with him by my side. This was exactly what I needed tonight. A few hours of calm in order to shut out the world and all of tomorrow's problems. They'll keep. Tonight, I just want to snuggle my guys and be thankful that we're together.

Levi's already in bed when Greedy and I emerge from the bathroom.

Sione passes us, giving me arm a light squeeze. "I'm going to shower, but you don't need to keep the light on if you're ready to sleep."

As he lets go, I grasp his hand, then let my fingertips brush along his palm and fingers as the distance breaks us apart.

At the foot of the bed, I inspect the room and my guys. "Do we have a plan here?" I ask, worrying my bottom lip.

"Just get in, Daisy." Levi's eyes are closed against the overhead light. "Don't overthink it." But then, on the next breath, he adds, "G, save the spot beside her for Sione."

And that's how I find myself in a dim room, on one side of a Levi sandwich, snuggled against his chest as Greedy takes his other side.

I burrow closer to my guy, then link hands with Greedy and let them rest on Levi's bare chest.

"Taking me right back to that night at the Moon Mist," Levi teases.

Squinting, I search his face. "The *what*?"

"The Moon Mist Motel. This awful place we stayed the night before we found you."

"Oh. Wait. Let me guess!" I giggle. "Was there only one bed?"

"How'd you know?"

"It's a classic romance trope, Duke. And one of my personal faves," I add, snuggling closer.

He sighs. "We tried a million places."

"Three," Greedy deadpans.

"Then, when we finally stumbled upon the Moon Mist Motel, they had one room left—the Mystical Misty Suite."

The bed shakes beneath us as Greedy chuckles. "It was the Mystical *Master* Suite."

Levi fake-shudders. "I must have repressed the name. Although I'm not sure I'll ever be able to scrub that room from my mind completely."

Intrigued, I peek up at my boyfriend. "So what happened at the Moon Mist?"

"Everything," Levi declares at the same time that Greedy says, "Nothing."

"G!" Levi scoffs. "You wound me."

Greedy snorts at his dramatics. "*Wound* you? Seriously, dude? Is Sione already rubbing off on you?"

With a snicker, Levi settles back against the pillow again and lazily traces his fingertips over both our hands. "I guess we have very different interpretations of the experience."

An uncomfortable silence settles over us. Greedy must feel it, too, because eventually he sighs, turns onto his side to face me, and props his head on one hand.

"Levi helped me out that night. He... comforted me, when I couldn't sleep."

"Comforted how?" I ask salaciously, desperate for more details.

"Not like that, dirty girl."

"Yeah. *That* didn't happen until the next day in the showers," Levi taunts.

A thrill shoots through me, followed by a tingle of anticipation that takes root deep in my belly. "The pantry wasn't a one-time thing, was it?" I hedge. Because as hot and fun as our little tryst in the dark was yesterday, I'm anxious for more. To experiment. To play. To figure out how we fit and just how intense it can be when it's the three of us together.

"No, Tem. That wasn't a one-time thing. At least not for me." Greedy's tone is low, reassuring.

"Me neither," Levi says. "You craving a Hunter sandwich, Daisy?" His fingers trace up my arm, catching my chin and tipping it toward his mouth for a kiss.

"Or a Greedy sandwich. Or a Levi sandwich," I mewl, straining forward, desperate for more of his kisses. "Who goes where doesn't matter to me."

Greedy angles closer. "Does it matter to you, Leev?"

Levi swallows audibly, but he's silent for a moment. Finally, he meets Greedy's gaze. "I want to feel you everywhere."

A cocksure grin erupts on Greedy's face. Levi meets it with a timid smile of his own.

Before I know what's happening, Greedy rolls on top of Levi, their hard chests hovering inches apart and a few strands of Greedy's dark hair tickling Levi's forehead.

He rolls his hips, and Levi moans on contact. Sinking his teeth into his bottom lip, Greedy turns and winks at me, then brings his mouth just an inch above his best friend's.

"Everywhere, huh? Does that mean you're gonna let me claim this ass and make you mine?"

Levi whimpers, like maybe Greedy has ground into him. "Yes." The one-word answer is both sure and shaky.

"Fuck, Leev. I can't wait to feel you like that." Greedy kisses him quickly, then props himself up again. Running his nose along his best friend's jaw, he murmurs, "Think about it. You filling Hunter while I fill you."

I whimper this time, biting down hard on my bottom lip to temper the lust warming me from the inside.

Greedy kisses Levi's throat, worshipping him with his lips and his words. "It's going to be so fucking hot to see you stretched out around my cock as you ram into our girl."

"I want you, G," Levi confesses, the words disjointed and breathy, like he's trying his hardest to keep it together. "Not tonight," he quickly adds. "But soon."

In response to his declaration, Greedy makes a feast of Levi's mouth, throat, and chest.

"I'm never going to be able to sleep now," I bemoan, snaking one hand down between my legs and pressing it into my center through my panties.

Greedy chuckles. "And why's that, Tem?"

Why? Is he serious right now?

"You know exactly why," I shoot back, heat that has nothing to do with my current state of arousal rising in my chest. "You're making out and dirty talking with my boyfriend right beside me in bed. My blood is so hot I might spontaneously combust."

With a laugh, Levi shakes his head.

Greedy silences him with a bruising kiss. Then he lowers his body in a slow, sensual thrust that makes Levi moan into his mouth. Breaking apart, he turns to me. "Do you need to get off, Tem?"

"Yes," I practically beg.

"What about you?" he asks Levi, biting his shoulder before kissing the spot to soothe the ache.

Surprisingly, Levi shakes his head. "I told you earlier; my dick is *not* interested in getting off in Decker Crusade's bed."

Greedy snickers. "Mine is."

"Hornball," Levi shoots back.

"I can't help it," he laments. "I'm in bed with the two people I—"

He cuts himself off, but I still catch his drift. I wonder if Levi caught it, too.

"With the two people I care about most in this whole damn world. After the last few weeks, I didn't dare dream we'd get a chance to be together like this. You can't blame me for wanting to feel as close as possible to both of you tonight."

We all fall quiet, the reminder of the weight of the last few days quelling the playfulness that came so naturally moments ago.

As if sensing exactly what I need, Greedy nudges Levi's body, indicating he should move over. "Switch and let me in."

Situating himself between us, Greedy cups my head and kisses me. Deeply. Tenderly. As if I'm his whole world and there's nothing he wouldn't do—nothing he wouldn't give—to keep me forever.

When I'm breathless, he breaks away, turns his head, and kisses Levi with the same passion.

That's when the bathroom door opens and Sione walks in.

"Am I interrupting?" he asks, pausing in the doorway as he takes us all in. He's illuminated from behind, with steam from his shower curling around his massive frame. In a pair of shorts and a cut-off shirt that put his muscles and intricate tattoos on full display, he looks fucking delicious.

And now I'm even hornier.

Flovely.

Greedy is the one to respond. "No. It wasn't going much farther than this."

Outraged, I slam a hand against the mattress. "Like hell it wasn't."

Levi chuckles to himself and Greedy turns his head toward a curious-looking Sione to give him more context.

"Hunter's horny."

Sione cocks one brow, then gives my body a knowing perusal that makes it feel like rays of sunshine are lighting up my insides. "Hunter's insatiable," he counters, smirking.

"You need me to get you off, Tem?"

It's a ridiculous question. Greedy knows what I need. Nevertheless, I answer him with a shaky "please."

Sitting back on his knees, Greedy turns to the newest member of our group. "Si."

My heart hammers in my chest a little harder at the sound of Greedy using his nickname.

"Is this okay to do with you in the room? I don't want to make you uncomfortable. We can go elsewhere. We won't do anything in front of you without your consent."

Sione saunters forward, closing the distance between us with long, assured strides. When he reaches the side of the bed, he tenderly strokes my cheek.

"Absolutely. Hunter in the throes of passion is my personal version of a masterpiece. I love watching her come undone." His dark brown eyes heat, lust simmering between us as he cups my face. With a blink, he steps back and clears his throat. "Although I've never witnessed her pleasure at the hand of another. Thank you for asking. By all means, carry on."

He strides away and situates himself in a wing-backed armchair in the corner of the room. Close enough to give him an excellent vantage point, but not so close that he's involved in the mix.

"Hear that, Tem?" Greedy teases. "Sione wants to watch. He wants me to make a masterpiece out of you. So how should we do it? Should I suck on your tits until you come?"

Levi perks up from Greedy's other side. "Is that physically possible?"

"We've done it before," Greedy brags, looming over me.

We have. It was so fucking hot. I pinch my own nipples through the thin fabric of my silky tank top, wanting more than anything for Greedy to be the one doing it instead. Right now, I want him any way I can have him. I want to get off, sure, but more than anything, I want the intimacy with him.

"Or should I fuck you with my tongue? Put on a show for your boyfriend and your other European lover?"

He's egging me on. Working me up. I should be agitated, but I don't have enough blood in my brain to formulate a sassy response. It's all in my vagina. And my clit. And my nipples.

I'm so flustered and hot and ready that it doesn't even register when Greedy rolls to his back and scoots up the bed.

"Crawl up here, Tem. Ride my fucking face."

I scramble to pull my clothes off and situate myself. The second I sink down, lining myself up so Greedy has complete access to my most private parts, I groan.

He starts off hard, fast. Licking and sucking on my clit in a way that has me clawing at his hair, and then the headboard, in desperation.

In a few short minutes, though, we find our rhythm.

Greedy fucks me with his tongue, going so deep I can't help but swivel my hips forward. Every few passes, he brushes my G-spot with just the tip. Each time he hits home, more arousal leaks out of me and coats his face.

"You're dripping all over, baby, but it'll never be enough for me. I'm fucking starving for you, Tem," he tells me when he comes up for breath. "Tweak those perfect nipples and keep riding my face. Let's give the boys a show they deserve."

I peer over my shoulder at Sione and find his heavy gaze fixed on me. His chest heaves with deep breaths. His fingers flex into the firm armrests of the chair. As if it's taking a concerted effort to keep his hands to himself. As if he feels as desperate and needy as I do.

Greedy sucks my clit back into his mouth and nibbles on the bundle of nerves, his fingers gripping the flesh of my hips. He uses his hold on me there to drag my body back and forth while pressing down. The pressure alone is enough to send me soaring into the next universe. But then he nips at my clit and releases a string of desperate, needy curses.

"Fuck. Fuck, fuck, fuck... yes," he groans as he hoists me up. With a smack to my ass cheek, he says, "Turn around, baby. We're not the only ones putting on a show anymore."

On shaky knees, I awkwardly turn, repositioning my body so Greedy can bury his face in my pussy once more. When I look up, I'm met with the most incredible sight.

Levi is situated between Greedy's legs, savoring his cock, his attention locked on me, his dark denim baby blues searing into my soul as his best friend eats me out from behind.

With his tongue, Greedy finds my sweet spot once more.

Whimpering, I give in to the heady, primal urges inspired by the tension gathering in my core and buck against Greedy's face, letting his tongue fuck me as his stubbled chin grinds into my clit. I stretch forward, desperate, licking at the base of his shaft while Levi keeps his lips stretched around him.

Then I shatter, effortlessly, so completely enraptured by the moment that all I can do is grind and suck and scream and *feel*.

I feel it all. I feel them everywhere.

And in that moment, I've never felt more alive.

Chapter 40

Greedy

NOW

Levi and Hunter are both out by the time Sione approaches the bed. He pauses, despite the space clearly reserved for him on Hunter's other side.

It's dark in the room, but not so dark I can't make out the sharp lines of his face or the shadowy ink decorating one side of his body. With his brow furrowed, he analyzes the space, then scans the bed until his eyes connect with mine.

"Okay?" I ask quietly, tilting my head in question.

"Once I join you, there won't be any space for the Brit."

Damn. It's impossible not to like the guy. He's the epitome of a team player.

"It's fine," I assure him. "Spence will take my place. I'm usually ready to get up by the time he comes to bed."

With a nod, Sione slips under the covers, and once he's settled, he turns onto his side and cocoons his enormous body around Hunter. Or at least the parts of Hunter I haven't already claimed, seeing as how I'm snuggled up just as close on her other side.

As he situates himself, Sione's hand brushes against mine. I don't withdraw or even concern myself with the random touch. What he shared with us around the bonfire that night went a long way in explaining how he fits into Hunter's world.

His authenticity makes him easy to like. His clear boundaries and distinct sense of self have made his introduction into our dynamic smooth. If anything, it's helped define facets that, until now, had been left unnamed and undiscovered. Sione knows who he is. What he wants. How he operates. There's a pureness that comes with that sort of self-awareness. I respect it. Hell, I might even envy it.

"Are you a lousy sleeper?" he asks, pulling my attention from my rambling thoughts.

I snicker. The guy really is perceptive as hell. "Not usually. Just have a lot on my mind these days."

Understatement of the fucking year.

"Hunter always amazes me with her ability to sleep after pleasure. If I orgasm, I'm awake for hours. Perhaps you're wired in a similar manner."

I grunt a noncommittal reply.

"Is Levi your first male partner?"

The question seemingly comes out of nowhere. Yet it's aligned with one of the many errant thoughts plaguing my too-busy brain and making sleep elusive. This is not where I was expecting the conversation to continue.

I glance over my shoulder at my best friend. He's been out for a while. I swear he can sleep through anything. When I turn back, I study the smooth, rhythmic rise and fall of Hunter's chest, concluding she's deeply asleep, too.

"Yeah," I finally answer, seeking Sione's gaze in the dark. "My first and only."

"You haven't experimented?"

I shake my head. "I had only ever been with Hunter until recently."

For a moment, Sione is quiet. Considering. Then, he asks, "May I ask when you knew you were bisexual?"

A choked cough catches me completely by surprise, but I muffle it to keep from waking Hunter and Levi.

"I—shit..." Exhaling, I force my jaw to relax, along with my hold on Hunter. "That's not something I've thought about before," I admit. "I'm not sure I even am. Bisexual, that is."

Brows raised, Sione breaks into a knowing smirk. "I'm sorry for assuming. I should not have even commented on your sexuality unless you broached the subject first. Please forgive me. I did, however, just watch you get sucked off in record time by a man while our girl rode your face. My mind filled in the blanks based on what I witnessed."

Yeah. Okay. Fair assumption on his part.

"No worries," I mumble, despite my own mind swirling with a vortex of fresh concerns.

I've never thought of myself as bisexual. Not once. As ridiculous as it might sound, considering I'm currently sandwiched between a man and a woman post-coitus, I've never given any real consideration to my sexuality.

I just *am*.

Levi's bisexual, and he's always seemed so sure of it. Me? I'm not sure of my sexual identity in the least. I've never been outright attracted to a random man. Hell, I've never experienced true attraction to anyone other than Hunter, and more recently, Levi.

"I just... I just like that it's Levi, I think." I say the sentiment out loud, sharing my inner thoughts with a man I only met days ago.

"How long have you known him?" he asks.

"Over a decade." Levi's been my best friend since middle school.

"And how long have you been in love with him?"

It's another outlandish assumption. One that stuns me into silence. When I find my voice, I prepare to tell Sione as much, but the denial is sour on my tongue. A deep-rooted sense of knowing stops me from rebuffing the idea.

"I... I don't know how to answer that," I finally admit.

Hunter stirs but settles without waking. I adjust my hold on her, then check over my shoulder, confirming Levi is still asleep as well. Once I know they're okay, I let my gaze drift back to Sione's.

"Would you like to stop talking about this?" he asks.

"No." My answer is fast and definitive.

I don't want to stop. Hell, I want him to keep going, to keep pushing, to keep unlocking truths inside me I wasn't aware existed.

"Very well. You said you don't know how to answer the question about loving Levi. Is that because you're unsure, or because it's not true?"

I don't even have to consider the question. Maybe it should surprise me, but it doesn't. "It's because I'm unsure," I confirm. "I don't know when things changed, but now, I can't imagine not being with him or with Hunter."

Silence blankets us once more. My mind doesn't war against itself like it did earlier, though. If anything, I feel more settled, more calm and secure, having shared the revelation about my love for my best friend.

Sione shifts, sitting up a bit so he can see me over Hunter's sleeping form.

"May I share about my journey?"

I nod my consent.

Stroking Hunter's side affectionately, he keeps his attention fixed on her. "I didn't know the truth of my sexuality until I experienced all the things that did not work for me. I spent several years thinking I was broken or that something was fundamentally wrong. Sex with women felt like a chore, so I tried to be with men. I couldn't top. But I didn't enjoy bottoming, either. I had an embarrassing number of misfires before I gave up on sex altogether."

My chest constricts as I process his story. It feels like an honor, to hear his truth.

"By the time I graduated from high school, I assumed I was asexual. It was the best label I could find at the time." He glances up at me, then quickly back at Hunter. "Then I met her."

Clearing my throat quietly, I, too, keep my gaze fixed on Hunter. "How did you figure it out?"

"It started as a low simmer. I can appreciate a beautiful person, both physically and spiritually. I noticed Hunter's beauty the moment I laid eyes on her. From there, we became friends. Secret-sharers and keepers. Partners in nearly every sense of the word. I'd known her for almost a year when the first inklings of my sexual attraction made themselves known.

We were doing hot yoga. Have you ever watched her stretch? Or heard her moan during a massage?" His words are hushed but reverent. "One time I was so hard watching her work her body over a foam roller, I came in my pants."

"Been there," I chuckle quietly. The number of times I felt so viscerally charged by Hunter that I couldn't control the arousal is embarrassing. "She's magnificent, isn't she?" I tuck a piece of hair behind her ear as I admire her sleeping form.

"She really is," Sione confirms. I don't have to look up to know he's gazing lovingly upon her as well.

After a few breaths, I find the courage to ask the question niggling in the back of my mind. "So... you're demisexual. That means you just want to have sex with one person?"

With a thoughtful hum, he stretches his neck from side to side. "For me, yes, that's mostly what it means. But there's no hard and fast rules that apply to all humans who identify as demi. For me, being demisexual means I have to foster a deep, passionate, emotional connection to my partner before I can indulge in a sexually gratifying experience. I'm lucky to have found that in her."

A pregnant pause fills the space between us.

A minute, maybe two passes before he murmurs, "Just like you're lucky to have found that in both of them?"

It's not a statement, but a question.

It's not a limit, but an invitation to finally adopt a label that works for me.

Sione's question percolates in my mind as I close my eyes, intent on drifting off to sleep. The question doesn't stay a question for long, though. My mind grapples with the idea for a short time, then eventually calms, granting me a sense of inner peace that allows me to truly rest.

I'm demisexual.

I'm also really fucking lucky.

Chapter 41

Levi

NOW

The kitchen is chaos—laughter and chatter, with music playing in the background as well. Everyone has gathered in the space, and although there's plenty of room around the long granite island, it feels crowded, but in the best way.

There are twelve of us here—the five of us, Joey, all her guys, and Mrs. Lansbury and Gerald.

I make a mental note to ask Spence if he caught the older two getting up to anything last night. Partly because I'm nosy. But also because I like the idea of it never being too late to find love.

Fucking hell. I sound like a lovesick puppy. G and all his romantic tendencies must be rubbing off on me.

I'm seated on a barstool, taking it all in and nursing a mug of coffee that's more flavored creamer than sludge. Joey makes that shit strong, and apparently, there's no room for compromise between her and her coffee.

Kylian is seated two stools down, tapping away on a device with another sitting on the counter in front of him. He has these low-profile earplugs in his ears that, from what I can tell, drown out the noise and chaos that surrounds us.

Locke comes over and wordlessly places an enormous plate of bacon in front of Kylian. The man with glasses tips his chin in acknowledgment but doesn't take his eyes off the screen he's concentrating on.

A second later, Decker appears and places a glass of water and a cup of juice in front of him, then snatches a piece of bacon off his plate.

There's an assuredness to the way they operate. Like they all know their roles, and they're willing to fill in the gaps for one another when needed. As I survey Joey and the men attached to her, I see it. How it could work. How there's so much love between them. How they respect each other's boundaries, too.

I'm not sure whether their dynamic is as involved as our is and is growing to be, but I want what they have. Desperately. I want to be with all of them: Hunter. Greedy. Kabir. Sione, too. Even if what we share is strictly platonic, I want him in the mix as well.

I was an asshole when Si arrived, but it didn't take long for me to see how he slots in perfectly with the rest of us and makes us even better as a unit. He's calm and nurturing. He has this wisdom about him that I admire; he's the antithesis of toxic masculinity. He's clearly comfortable with himself, but also great at making others feel comfortable, too.

Plus, he's wise. And he helped my best friend figure out something he may have grappled with unnecessarily for years to come.

I heard the two of them talking last night.

I don't think I caught all of their conversation, but I definitely caught the part that matters. When I woke, I kept quiet, which I feel a little ashamed of. I wasn't sure if it counted as eavesdropping, or if it would have been ruder to interrupt.

My chest constricts with emotion when I remember their words. Greedy's revelation. The sensations only compound when I think about the implications of that revelation for us.

My best friend is bisexual. He's also demisexual. And he picked *me*. He wants me. Greedy loves me.

"This is something, isn't it?" G says, coming to stand next to my barstool.

Under the lip of the counter, I reach for his hand. He lets me take it, his smile timid but warm as I interlace our fingers and use my grip to pull him closer.

Once he's standing between my open thighs, I grin back, then survey the kitchen and assess the scene.

Sione is sitting on the opposite side of the island with one arm pulled out of his T-shirt, showing off his ink to a fascinated Locke. Kylian appears to be paying attention to them now as well. My suspicion is confirmed a few seconds later when he removes the noise-reducing earplugs from his ears, hops off the barstool, and makes his way over to them. I didn't know Kylian was into ink, but maybe he's more than meets the eye. Hell, maybe he even has a tattoo himself.

Hunter is stationed near the stove, holding a cup of tea in both hands. She's talking with Kabir and Decker, and judging by their serious expressions, they're deep in conversation.

Joey and Kendrick are in their own little world, with his arms wrapped around her from behind as they lean against the fridge and he whispers in her ear. He walked in a few minutes ago, fresh from conditioning on campus. When he arrived, she ran into his arms with so much fervor I was afraid she was going to knock him on his ass. I love how they love each other. It's loud, unapologetic, and without limits.

The chaos, commotion, and genuine love that fills this room is more beautiful and complex than anything I've ever dreamed of having for myself.

Admittedly, I never thought I'd get to have anything close to this. Being an only child born to shitty parents, I had no sense of place or belonging when I was a kid. Nothing ever felt like this.

"Yeah. This is something," I say, my throat clogged with emotion. This is love personified. This is unconditional commitment. This is something I get to call mine. This is *family*.

"Whatever happens today, we're solid." Greedy squeezes my hand for emphasis, holding my gaze until some of his conviction washes over me as well.

We're solid. And we're only going to get stronger from here on out.

Chapter 42

Hunter

NOW

"We have arrived," Gerald announces dutifully as he puts the vehicle in park. He exits the car but doesn't open any doors. He won't until we give him the signal.

This is it.

No more running.

Even though every cell in my body is screaming at me to move, to leave, to flee.

I can't. I won't.

This isn't just about me anymore.

It's not just about Magnolia.

This is about the four men in this car. This is about our future and all the what-ifs I so desperately want to turn into happily ever afters.

I made a promise.

No more running. We're going to stay. We're going to fight. We're going to *win*.

Spence insisted Gerald drive us to Dr. F's house, and I'm grateful for it. It allowed all four of my men and me the ability to focus, which is critical to the success of this plan.

I'm situated in the third row of the large SUV, between Greedy and Sione. They're both touching me, the contact keeping me grounded as my heart threatens to riot out of my chest.

Spence turns around from his place in one of the captain's seats, and Levi matches his posture. The heaviness of the moment is suffocating.

Forcing air into my lungs, I unbuckle my seat belt. I don't plan on moving until I have to, but I need a distraction.

Spence rests his ring-adorned hand on my knee and halts my movements. "Wait."

At his command, I freeze.

"Look at me, love."

Obediently, I lift my head and home in on him.

"Look at me, all of you."

Not a single argument goes up, not even one in jest. The guys give him their undivided attention.

"We're going in there together. We are walking out together. Whatever happens in between, I can assure you with everything I am that it *will* be okay. Have faith that it's all coming together exactly as intended."

Greedy attempts to interject now, no doubt desperate to know what, exactly, Spence has planned.

Before he can get more than a single unintelligible syllable out, Spence silences him with one raised finger.

"Please. I'm asking—no, I'm begging—you all to trust me. There are a few ways this could play out, but I swear, each path I have plotted is uniquely designed to rid us of Magnolia's hold on Hunter once and for all."

His words are ominous, the hints of action a threat as much as they are a promise.

When Greedy silently, reluctantly nods, I squeeze his hand in appreciation. This is hard for all of us, but for him, it's even more of a challenge. We aren't just facing my mother today. We're facing his father, too.

"Whatever transpires inside those doors, know this: I'm aware of all possible scenarios and outcomes. We are prepared. We are in control here. We will get through this. Together."

Anticipation wells inside me so violently I start to tremble.

Sione senses the shift and instantly wraps his arms around my shoulders protectively, kissing the crown of my head.

"Let's go," Levi, whose leg is bouncing so vigorously it makes the entire SUV move.

We're all more than ready to get this over with.

Spence raps his knuckles on the glass twice, and a heartbeat later, Gerald opens his door, then moves around to the other side of the vehicle.

With a hand held out, Spence guides me out next. Once I'm steady, I reach behind me for Greedy's hand.

"You okay?" I whisper, turning to face my first love and trying like hell to reabsorb the tears welling in my eyes.

"*We're* okay," he assures me, the two words full of a hope I don't dare allow myself to feel. He cups my face and kisses my forehead, then releases me into Levi's waiting arms.

Spence and Greedy lead us up the circular driveway. Levi keeps me tucked under one arm, holding me close. Sione hums softly as he brings up the rear.

As he approaches the door, Spence steps aside so Greedy can enter first. Once inside the mudroom, he calls out to announce our arrival.

Our parents know we're coming. They're expecting us, based on the text Greedy sent to his dad last night at Spence's instruction.

What I wasn't expecting?

The joyful, childlike jubilation that greets us when we find Dr. Ferguson and my mother waiting for us in the kitchen.

"We're a match!" Magnolia cries. "We're a match! We're a match! We're a match!"

Chapter 43

Greedy

NOW

Tension crackles through the kitchen as I brace myself for the destruction of the illusion my father has been living in.

This is my role. Spence and I discussed it ad nauseam. I loathe the idea of having to pull the rug out from under my dad's feet, but it has to be done. It's time to destroy the misconception of happiness he holds dear.

Hell, I should have done it three and a half years ago. I should have told him everything I knew about Magnolia the night he introduced me to her.

I should have fought harder. Been braver.

I owe it to him, to Hunter, and most importantly, to myself, to do that now.

Magnolia tried to hug Hunter when we first arrived, but Levi and Sione physically blocked her and prevented any sort of access. She was jilted, but not deterred. She and my father are seated at the kitchen table now, both smiling and looking at me expectantly.

"Dad. Hunter didn't know she was going to the spa." The words are thick, my voice almost unrecognizable, but I get them out. "Magnolia drugged her and took her from her bed."

"What?"

The sincere shock in his reaction guts me.

Bracing my arms on the table across from where he's seated, I nod. "We have proof. Hunter's memories and firsthand experience can be corroborated by the trace amounts of Rohypnol still in her system yesterday."

"Bloodwork? What bloodwork?" Magnolia's nostrils flare, and her eyes widen with panic.

"The bloodwork recently processed through Crusade Labs. Hang on…" Spence pulls out his phone and scrolls for what I can only assume is a longer-than-necessary amount of time. "Ah. There it is. Hunter St. Clair. Detection of metabolites of flunitrazepam: positive."

"This can't be right…" My dad looks from me to Hunter, his face screwed up in confusion. Rather than ask us to elaborate, though, he turns to his wife, who's seated by his side. "Magnolia?" he questions. As if she holds the answers instead of being solely responsible for all this chaos.

A few seconds too late to be considered genuine, she emits a shocked gasp. "*Hunter*. Have you been dabbling in *drugs*?"

To her credit, Hunter stares at her mom, deadpan, for a solid five seconds before she lets out an exasperated sigh. "No, Mother. I've never willingly taken drugs. Stop *lying*. Stop trying to manipulate me. I didn't consent to going with you to that spa—if you can even call it that. You drugged me, and all day, you continued by making me take little sips of whatever you had in that water bottle."

Magnolia's eyes widen in terror. "Something's wrong with her," she accuses, her voice pitchy and loud. "What did you give her?" she demands, looking first to Spence, then Levi, then Sione, and finally me.

Whatever she sees in my gaze has her recoiling as if she's been hit.

I stand to my full height, prepared to go off on Magnolia St. Clair-Ferguson once and for all. Though before I can, Hunter steps up to my side and strokes my arm, soothing me into submission.

Eyes narrowed, Magnolia homes in on the place where her daughter is touching me.

"Stop, Mother. You're not going to turn the tables on Greedy. Or Levi. Or anyone else here. It's time for you to come clean."

Magnolia's skin reddens, although her forehead and facial muscles barely budge, then the waterworks begin.

Sobbing—genuinely sobbing with her full chest—she gasps for breath and flops into my father's arms.

"I don't know where any of this is coming from," she manages to say through chest-racking cries. "I wanted to treat my daughter to a special weekend. Just the two of us. Before... before..." Magnolia buries her head in my father's chest.

His face is etched with torment as he tries to soothe her. With one hand on her back and the other cupping her head, he murmurs placating words that only she can hear.

"Dad."

His gaze lifts to meet mine, dissonance warring in his expression.

"You're really buying this?"

His eyes widen in surprise at my clear lack of concern for his wife's theatrics.

That's exactly what they are—theatrics. How I wish we would have taken pictures or even a video when we found Hunter in New York. Our only priorities were her health and well-being at the time, though. I never imagined we'd need to prove the insanity of the narcissist who continually makes my worst nightmares a reality.

"Garrett, this isn't like you," my father calmly says. "You're being unkind. Your stepmother is clearly distressed."

Fuck kindness.

"She's clearly *delusional*." I pound my fist into the tabletop, desperate to get through to him. "She kidnapped her own daughter. *Drugged her*. Drew her blood—"

"I know she drew her blood."

The confession cuts me off and takes my breath away, and the kitchen falls eerily silent.

He knew? He fucking knew?

My gut twists so painfully I have to fight the urge to double over.

"It was my idea." My father continues to run a hand over Magnolia's hair as she hides her face in the crook of her arm.

"When Magnolia mentioned they were at a med spa, I assumed they had the staff available to complete a simple blood draw. We got the results this morning. It's why we thought you wanted to meet."

Hunter's breath is audible in my ears. So is an incessant ringing, like the toll of a bell chiming to warn me of what's about to happen.

In my periphery, Sione appears behind Hunter. Touching her. Murmuring in her ear.

Thank fuck. Because not only am I confused as hell, I'm also fucking useless and lost as to how to process this information or move forward. My throat clogs with so much anxiety I can't get my mouth to form words.

Thankfully, Spence steps in and takes over.

"This blood draw. What sorts of information did it reveal?"

The question seems odd, especially the way Spence worded it.

Thankfully my father is too caught up in Magnolia's despair to ask for clarification. "It was a liver function test and a blood type confirmation. Both are standard for potential living transplant donors."

Then, before any of us can ask any follow-up questions, my father rises to his feet. He helps Magnolia up, too, but keeps a tight grip on her upper body. Thankfully, he keeps the kitchen table between us and them.

"Hunter," he says, his focus set solely on our girl. "You're a match. You can save your mother's life. I know it's scary and inconvenient, but knowing that you're able—"

"She's not," Spence declares.

"Pardon?" my father asks, blinking in confusion.

"Hunter is not able to be a partial transplant donor, despite the promising bloodwork." Kabir steps forward, taking up residence between Hunter and me. With his head bowed low, he whispers, "Trust, Firecracker. Trust me to handle this." Then he turns his back to my dad and Magnolia, squeezes my bicep, and just as quietly says, "React. But do not overreact."

I nod, desperate to ask what the hell is happening, but knowing I can't do that right now. Then I search Hunter's face, seeking answers. Hell, even the slightest hint, that she has any clue. With a quick shake of her head, she confirms that she's just as in the dark as I am. Inhaling deeply, the breath shaky, she reaches for my hand. I shuffle closer, using Spence's body as a shield, and grasp her fingers in my own hand.

"It's not possible for Hunter to undergo any sort of invasive medical procedure. It won't be for the next several months." Spence's words are blasé, his posture relaxed. He scrolls on his phone without looking at any of us. The instant he looks up, multiple devices in the room chime and vibrate with notifications.

"I just AirDropped the bloodwork to everyone in this room. It shows the drugs we mentioned—certified by Crusade Labs. If you'll pull it up on your phones…"

Spence pauses, giving everyone, including my father, time to open their devices and download the results he just sent.

"You'll see a full panel workup for Hunter St. Clair. If I can encourage you to look past the roofie results and down at line sixteen, I believe everything will make more sense."

Frantically, I search the small screen in my hand.

Thirteen…

Fourteen…

Fifteen…

Sixteen.

Line 16, hcG: 4,102 mIU/ml.

I curse. Close my eyes. Hold my breath. Then squeeze Hunter's hand tighter in mine.

I brace myself, but it's no use.

The blow is still swift and disorienting when Spence announces, "Hunter will not be donating any part of herself to anyone, because she's pregnant."

The Boys of South Chapel series concludes with the fourth and final book: So Right.

Afterword

Thank you so much for reading So Rare. This is officially the last cliffie of the series... we're almost there! Hunter and her cohort's story concludes in So Right, Boys of South Chapel Book Four.

Want to see the gorgeous character art from this series and read excerpts from future releases? Check out my Patreon for even more South Chapel and Lake Chapel content!

Also By Abby Millsaps

The Hampton Hearts series:
interconnected standalone small town romance novels

Golden Boy
Mr. Brightside
Fourth Wheel
Full Out Fiend

The Boys of Lake Chapel:
a why choose sports romance series

Too Safe: Boys of Lake Chapel Book One
Too Fast: Boys of Lake Chapel Book Two
Too Far: Boys of Lake Chapel Book Three

The Boys of South Chapel:
a why choose second chance romance series

So Wrong: Boys of South Chapel Book One
So Real: Boys of South Chapel Book Two

So Rare: Boys of South Chapel Book Three
So Right: Boys of South Chapel Book Four

About The Author

Abby Millsaps is an author and storyteller who's been obsessed with writing romance since middle school. In eighth grade, she failed to qualify for the Power of the Pen State Championships because "all her submissions contained the same theme: young people falling in love." #LookAtHerNow

She's best known for writing unapologetically angsty romance that causes emotional damage for her readers. Creative spicy scenes and consent as foreplay are two hallmarks of her books. Abby prides herself in writing authentic characters while weaving mental health, chronic illness, and neurodiverse representation into the fabric of her stories.

Connect with Abby
Website: www.authorabbymillsaps.com
Patreon: https://www.patreon.com/AbbyMillsaps
Instagram: @abbymillsaps
TikTok: @authorabbymillsaps
Email: authorabbymillsaps@gmail.com
Newsletter: https://geni.us/AuthorAbbyNewsletter
Facebook Reader Group: Abby's Full Out Fiends

www.ingramcontent.com/pod-product-compliance
Lightning Source LLC
LaVergne TN
LVHW030320070526
838199LV00069B/6510